BRANDON TWENTY-FIVE

A note on the editor

Born in Dublin, he set up an international literary magazine in England and published his first book (by Octavio Paz) when still in his teens. A former chairperson of the Irish Writers Co-operative, he co-founded Brandon in Dingle in 1982 and set up Mount Eagle Publications in 1997; he served as President of CLÉ, the Irish Book Publishers' Association in the late '80s. His books include a memoir, *Open Book: One Publisher's War* (1999), a local history, *The Dingle Peninsula* (1994 and 2000), three volumes of poetry and a book of photographs, *Dingle in Pictures* (2001). Amongst books he has edited are *The Rushdie Letters* (1993), *The Brandon Book of Irish Short Stories* (1998), and Walter Macken's posthumous collection, *City of the Tribes*.

BRANDON
TWENTY-FIVE

Edited by Steve MacDonogh

A Brandon Original Paperback

First published in 2007 by Brandon
an imprint of Mount Eagle Publications
Dingle, Co. Kerry, Ireland, and
Unit 3, Olympia Trading Estate, Coburg Road, London N22 6TZ, England

www.brandonbooks.com

ISBN 978-086322-371-6

2 4 6 8 10 9 7 5 3 1

Mount Eagle Publications/Sliabh an Fhiolair Teoranta receives support from
the Arts Council/An Chomhairle Ealaíon.

Cover design: Anú Design
Typesetting by Red Barn Publishing, Skeagh, Skibbereen
Printed in the UK

CONTENTS

INTRODUCTION

Brandon has offered readers a wide variety of quality fiction over its first twenty-five years. It goes with my role as editorial director that I am always most interested in what's most recent and what's coming up next, and I look with great pleasure and some pride at the fiction we published in 2006/7, while also looking forward to what we are planning for 2008/9. There were novels by Irish writers Emer Martin, Sam Millar, Jack Barry, Mary Rose Callaghan, Paul Charles, PJ Curtis and John Maher; by American writer Douglas A. Martin, and by Nenad Veličković from Sarajevo; short story collections by the Slovenian author Drago Jančar and by Cork's William Wall; an anthology of international crime writers from the USA, Britain and Ireland, and an anthology of twenty-five writers from eighteen east European countries. So in this selection, *Brandon Twenty-Five*, I have been keen to include plenty of pieces from our most recent books.

Since 1982 we have published the first novels of writers as varied as Dermot Bolger, John B. Keane, Dermot Healy, Alice Taylor, Brian Leyden and many others. We have published fiction by Irish writers as diverse as Aidan Higgins, Evelyn Conlon, William Wall, Neil Jordan, J.M. O'Neill, Kitty Fitzgerald, Leland Bardwell, Ken Bruen, Philip Davison, Anthony Cronin, Vincent McDonnell, Robert Welch, Ronan Sheehan, Pádraig Standún and Tony Cafferky. We have also republished some writers whose work had gone out of print: most notably Patrick McGill and Walter Macken.

Although most people probably associate us with certain of our Irish writers, our international focus did not begin with our recent east European series. Our list has included South African novelist Sylvester Stein; Australian David Foster; American writers Jennifer Cornell, Chet

Raymo and Kate McCafferty; English writers Jennifer Chapman, Barbara Rees, Marie McGann and Michael Dickinson. In 1994 *The Alphabet Garden*, featuring short stories from twelve western European countries, was published simultaneously in twelve countries – in Ireland by Brandon.

We would have published more international fiction if we had felt we could. After all, I started out as a publisher in 1968 of an international literary magazine, *Cosmos*, and the first book I published was by Mexican poet Octavio Paz. But we have found amongst both the media and the book trade a definite coolness towards fiction from Brandon that is by non-Irish authors.

"What are you doing publishing a South African/ Slovenian/ American/ Australian writer?" is a question I have been asked by Irish writers, booksellers and literary editors. No one, I think, would ask a similar question of a British, French, Italian, German or Slovenian publisher.

In many countries quite large percentages of published books have been translated out of other languages, but in the English-language world remarkably few are. About 40% of all books bought in Holland and Spain are titles in translation; in Italy, the figure is just over 22%; in France, 14%. But the number of titles published in translation in the UK is only 1.4%; no figures are available for Ireland, but the percentage is probably no higher than in the UK.

Of course, internationalism is not just about writers from other countries. The last anthology I edited was *The Brandon Book of Irish Short Stories*, in a review of which the *Observer* drew attention to "the confident internationalism of these mostly young writers". From the short stories of William Wall to the novels of Emer Martin, John Maher, Ken Bruen and Evelyn Conlon, an international scope and perspective is characteristic of many of the writers of the new Ireland.

Recent years have seen a massive decline in the sales of new fiction across the English-speaking world, and this has posed enormous problems for publishers such as Brandon who wish to maintain a commitment to contemporary fiction. Through most of our twenty-five years we have enjoyed the support of the Arts Council in Ireland for our literary programme, without which so much less would have been possible. Given the dramatic decline in the market for serious fiction, both Brandon and the Arts Council face considerable challenges in elaborating and adopting new approaches to the publication and promotion of new writing.

Finally, Ireland has an unfortunate history of censorship, and one of the stories included in this book was the subject in 1993 of High Court censorship proceedings. The state and independent broadcast media considered it too threatening to the stability of the state for it to be permitted to be advertised on radio, and the High Court upheld their view. The story was "A Good Confession" by Gerry Adams. Conor Cruise O'Brien, a principal witness in favour of the ban, said about this story:

> There is a bad priest, who tells the penitent that he can't get confession until he renounces IRA membership. And there is a good priest who says forget it.

Readers can decide for themselves if O'Brien represented the story accurately, and if the broadcasters and High Court were right in their view that it constituted propaganda so dangerous as to require the suppression of any advertisement for the book. (A fuller account of the controversy may be found in my memoir, *Open Book: One Publisher's War* and at www.brandonbooks.com.)

I have fought against censorship, sometimes successfully, sometimes unsuccessfully, and I have fought to keep alive a literary fiction list that has, I think, offered much to readers over the years. As a result of changes in the market for books we face difficult new circumstances; but new problems invite new solutions. The liberating power of literature is a vital humanising element, and in a society that has become more and more dominated by commercial imperatives the importance of literature is greater than ever.

Steve MacDonogh,
Publisher and Editorial Director
Brandon/Mount Eagle

For further information about new fiction and about authors
featured in this book, please go to

www.brandonbooks.com

New titles are first announced here, as are details of readings,
discussions and signing sessions by Brandon authors.

William Wall

"What Slim Boy, O Pyrrha"
from *No Paradiso*

I GIVE YOU the image of a man running naked into battle. Not quite naked, because he wears his helmet. Why do we feel he is peculiarly vulnerable? As if his uniform of coarse cloth could protect him against a high-velocity rifle-round or a stream of bullets from a Maxim gun. The period, of course, is 1914–1918—the Maxim gun is the key. Is he an officer or a private soldier? And why is he naked?

Say, his trench has been surprised during the night, and now that the initial raid has been repulsed, he leads his men in a counter-attack. "*Carpe diem!*" he shouts to them, although they do not understand the language. "*Carpe diem.*" He has a battered copy of Horace's *Odes* (Everyman Library Edition) in his kit. He waves his revolver above his head, and they grin and say the old man has finally gone bats.

The image has certain engaging qualities: a naked man (under the mushroom cap of his helmet) stands on the lip of a trench and urges his men to attack, in Latin. But they follow him because he is the old man, because he talks to them in some foreign lingo, because he's starkers and he doesn't give a tuppenny damn. They pour over the trench, chuckling affectionately, and into the brilliant artificial day of no man's land, and the bullets fly and the star-shells pop and hiss. The men hear the bullets that do not have their names on them whispering suddenly in the air, but nobody hears the bullet that has his name. It nips the jugular, holes the aorta, or slips in above the ear and exits into the helmet set at a jaunty angle, filling it with brain.

At some time in the half-hour of this particular battle, the naked officer stands above the corpse of a German soldier who has been shot through the eye. Another distressing image. A bullet in the eye is a barbarous wound. The naked man looks down at the one-eyed un-seer.

Now that his sexual organs have come into our field of view, the issue of his sleeping naked arises. It is well known that officers in the frontline trenches slept in their uniforms. We are familiar with descriptions of the damp dugouts, lit by a single candle, full of the thunder of the cannonade, in which sensitive and insensitive men of various ages sit about or doze, in uniforms of various ranks, the highest usually being a major. The officer who packs Horace's *Odes* before leaving Blighty is also a familiar figure. He may well have started the war with *Odi pro-fanum vulgus,* but will end it, if he survives, with *occidit occidit spes omnis.* The *vulgus* will become closer to him than the people of his own class, and he will emerge into Civvy Street a hopeless misfit or a revolutionary. He inspires fierce loyalty among his men, who refer to him by various insulting names which are, in fact, terms of endearment, such as "The Old Man" or "Mad Harry".

But this beats all. Even his batman is shocked by his appearance on the lips of the trench. They are all looking up at him, and from that angle he is an impressive figure, almost sculpted in the heroic mode. He might have graced a pedestal in Rome or Athens. Various comments about his genitalia (Are they large or small? Something to come back to later if we have time) that pass along the sap in the few moments before they realise the mad bugger wants them to counter-attack are silenced by the non-commissioned officers.

But now to explain his nakedness necessitates a deliberate switch in time. We consider the possibility of a nostalgic passage encapsulating the memory of an incident which led him into this aberration and realise immediately (or after a few hundred words) that the effect will be to slow the narrative without adding in any way to the suspense. Nor can he reasonably be expected to begin telling someone a sub-narrative at the height of an attack. This is a story, and devices available to novelists—interleaving chapters in a complex time-frame, for example—are not appropriate here. In the end, because I want to get on with it, I type three asterisks and go straight into his memory of the day he said goodbye to a certain woman in Beaulieu (it is pronounced *Bewley,* and, surprisingly, is in the south of England, not France) on a languid summer afternoon in 1914.

* * *

The sun is low on the evening of a perfect day. The cypress trees cast long irregular shadows on the manicured lawn. In the distance, the pock of mallet and ball can be heard. (Or perhaps the pock of bat and ball? The villagers have come to the house of the rich man—the lord?—for their annual cricket match against the tenants. They linger in the edge of memory, in white, doing very little for long periods and then rushing about in inexplicable patterns. The whirling arm, the swing of the bat—pock.) Down the cypress walk you go, from shadow to shadow, following the woman and the man. You hear their tender conversation. He wears the uniform of the Hampshire Regiment, and with a gasp you realise that this is the first time in the story that you have seen him with his clothes on. It creates a peculiar kind of intimacy which you find contradictory. At first you see them at a distance, moving elegantly among the trees. Then you approach more closely, and finally you are a secret third party to their conversation, the ghost of the future standing with them, shoulder to shoulder.

It comes as a shock to discover that their conversation is salty and sexual. They are reliving an actual sexual encounter in detail. The language they use is pure D.H. Lawrence. Because you are a ghost, you are privy also to the man's actual thoughts, and I have given him certain phrases from Catullus and Ovid (we have already established that he is a classicist) which confirm the universality of the terms. But her thoughts are out of bounds because it suits the direction of the narrative to have an inscrutable heroine. She is always other in the story, an object of his thoughts, his memories, his fantasies. And yours. After a time the subtle interplay of the still, warm evening, the gentle sound of the cricket game, the sex and the Latin, create an extraordinary sensuality, a Mediterranean languor set against the battlefield images with which the story opened. Now the felicity of that switch (indicated merely by three asterisks) becomes clear. And because we have really moved in time—rather than merely moving into memory—the detail can be piled up to add to the overall effect. What do they look like? She is tall and slim and moves with a fluid grace. He is taller, thin because he is a scholar, with the stiff back of the stoic (or the officer). He thinks poetically, seamlessly, in several languages, but he speaks haltingly. His words are clipped, uncertain, hesitant. His accent is Anglo-Irish, hers is Swiss finishing school via Chesterfield Ladies' College. When he is required to utter complete sentences, he stutters as though he is aware that he is a foreigner in several tongues. He loves her madly, of course. At least this is the way he thinks of it, the precise phrase in fact. When he is away from her, he dreams constantly of her body and certain parts of it in particular. Now, as he walks, he moves his hand to his face and smells her on it, and she laughs because this is a shared joke. She knows where his hand has been. Even at the dinner table, or at stilted gatherings in her father's drawing room, or in a railway carriage, he only has to make the shadow of the same gesture and she smiles. We know she likes to use the most vulgar terms for parts of his body and hers, the coarseness itself exciting her—her face is a little flushed now—and all of this is somehow related, in an extraordinary way, to her elegance and refinement.

They walk side by side but not arm in arm, because there is something that prevents them from being seen as a couple. In fact, there are two things. Firstly, of course, she is the daughter of a lord, a millionaire who has made his money in the shipping business and now sails a yacht in the same races as King George and the Kaiser. On the other hand, he comes from a middle-class family of university teachers, clergymen and scholars. His family may construct the way England thinks (a hundred years before, Ireland too), but England, or at least its rich, use the construction to ignore or despise anybody who thinks at all. Her father has envisioned a marriage of alliance for her, with the son of a man who owns, among other things, a commercial insurance company.

The second impediment is a more subtle one: they are cousins. The term *scion* is appropriate but vastly overused in relation to the English nobility, a metaphor drawn from the practice of grafting plants and redolent of a certain vegetable quality in that class. Equally, the term *distaff side*, a metaphor drawn from the manufacture of clothing at cottage industry level, is not entirely appropriate. I leave the construction of the relationship for the rewrite. Suffice it to say that he is from the Irish branch of the family which labours under some disgrace incurred during the eighteenth century and which the stern and dour behaviour of six or seven generations has not been sufficient to erase.

They are cousins and therefore the odour of incest permeates their bed. This is an inappropriate and an illegitimate relationship and is therefore doomed.

At this point you realise that the young man will die.

He can never return to find his lover married to a boring fart who drives a Bugatti or a private aeroplane. She would be miserable, and he would feel futile. A tragic as opposed to a depressing ending has become a necessity. When we last saw him in the battlefield, he was standing (naked still) with his revolver by his side, looking down on a German soldier who had been shot through the eye. We return now. No asterisks are necessary. Perhaps they were not necessary in the first place.

A momentary silence has fallen over the battlefield. His men have seized the enemy trench and so, as usual, the silence indicates that the enemy is regrouping. In a few moments they will return. In this silence, he gazes down at the dead man and various allusions are placed in his mind. He thinks, in fact, about one-eyed monsters and the ill omens that attend them. He shivers and is suddenly acutely aware that he has no clothes. He looks down at his genitals and wonders did he lose his trousers in the course of the fighting. He has seen a man, stripped bare by the force of an explosion, walk away from a near direct hit by a trench mortar. Then he notices that the physical activity of killing has caused a tumescence, not quite a full erection, but a happy state of engorgement such as exists immediately after coitus. He thinks of the woman he has left behind in Beaulieu and laughs softly.

The counter-attack must be now or never. The very first round fired will strike him in the chest, just slightly to the left of the heart, but close enough for the bone splinters to rip it open. He spins and falls. The very simplicity of his nakedness, the apparent savagery of it, the barbarian disregard for the niceties of twentieth-century warfare, made him the number one target for German sharpshooters. There is irony in the iron inevitability of it. His revolver and his disregard for his own safety marked him out as an officer. Later he would get a posthumous award for leading the charge and survivors would chuckle over their pints in 1925 and say, "If the brass only knew," or, "They wouldn't have known where to hang it."

Where to next?

A brother officer, a scholar of the same college at Oxford, arrives to gather his effects. The chaps in the dugout (a major is the highest ranking officer) point them out. "He was mad," they say. "He always slept naked." Of course, the CO never mentioned that when he wrote to break the bad news. The major says that he hardly thinks it necessary to bother the poor family with the fact that he was ballocks naked when the Hun got him. Nobody laughs. They all loved him.

In a small notebook, in a pocket of the tunic he never put on, the brother officer finds the following words from Horace's fifth ode of the first book: *quis multa gracilis te puer in rosa/perfusus liquidis urget odoribus/gratto pyrrha sub antro.* And in an often-worked translation underneath: *What slim boy, O Pyrrha, perfumed and drenched in rose-water, have you pressed into service in your privacy now?* From the crossings-out, it is clear that he has already translated and rejected certain words in certain ways: "smells" for *odoribus,* for example. *Urget* was rendered as "forcing" at one point and "ravishing" at another. In particular *perfusus liquidis* was given, in one version, as "drenched by your juices". The brother officer understands nothing of the background that we have given his friend, but he understands the pain well enough. And when he finds her letter, his understanding is complete. It is, of course, both unnecessary and unworkmanlike to reproduce the contents of the letter in our story, but we can be certain that they would explain why the officer slept naked, went into battle naked and died naked. And so we return to that initial image.

Why is it that the idea of a man going into battle without underwear or a serge jacket seems so abhorrent?

EMER MARTIN

BABY ZERO

MY MOTHER OPENED the door and pulled me inside. We had not seen each other in months, but the talk was not of homecoming.

"Did you come alone? You must play by the rules here, or they will have you flogged. Did you speak to immigration before you left? They've taken my passport. How can I get out without it? How will I get in anywhere without it?"

After a meal of plain rice, she told me, "I have nothing else. I'm too afraid to go to the market by myself. I have no money. They won't allow us work." The sack of rice was almost empty. I had always been afraid of my mother. More than my father. He was a dreamer. My mother Farah was a midwife and had done all the practical stuff: getting us out of the country, organising schools abroad. Now she hid in a one-bedroom apartment in a crumbling block, her hair grey and thin.

And she had shrunk. Her flesh was loose on her bones as if a strong wind could whip off her skin and leave her insides facing out. I tried to look out the window on to the narrow street. She had painted the windows black. "If you cannot afford dark glass and you live on the ground floor, that is what you have to do. Another new law." As my mother dozed off on the chair, I stared at the black and thought of the home the family once owned. Not far from here. Across the city edge. We once had a three-storey house by the river.

My father said that the river had another river inside it. A separate flowing. A contrary current. I never understood. I put my hands flat on the black window and felt the heat from the outside.

If I could not go outside by myself, why was I here? If my mother and I were stuck here without a man to escort us, what would we do in this dark, hot place with only a bit of rice left? I had made it from the airport in a taxi alone. Maybe I could call the taxi man and get back out of the country before she woke up.

I called the taxi driver and begged him to come over and take us shopping for food. He was not a relative, but he felt it would be a problem only if we were stopped. "How likely is that?" I asked. And he laughed nervously and bitterly. I waited for him in the kitchen away from her. Roaches roamed like cattle across the counters. I put my little finger out to stroke one of them. It scurried away and waited under a plate. There was nothing to eat here. Poor starving cockroaches. There were cups and jugs and chipped bowls stacked up in three precarious towers. They looked like figures, individuals leaning aggressively toward one another. I decided that they were female, stuck like this in the kitchen. Crockery battling bitches. Every surface was glistening with grease. The old woman must be depressed not to clean up. Our house had always been immaculate, my mother the very picture of efficiency.

"Who were you calling?" Her eyes had red veins like blood-soaked tree branches.

"A taxi. He's going to pose as a brother and take us to the market."

"They stoned a woman to death because she was with a man not her relative."

"I'm an American citizen. They'll leave me alone. I'll just plead ignorance."

She shrugged. Too worn out to fight. She was as hungry as her roaches.

"Your aunt still has a job. We can't go any more to the hospital, but they set up a separate one outside the town for us."

"But she's a dentist."

"She's everything now."

"Maybe you could work there."

My mother jumped in fright at the sound of the doorbell. The taxi man was reluctant to come in. As if it were a trap. Like a spider, I coaxed him into the hall. I told him I had dollars from America. He came inside. I struggled to get the voluminous black clothes over my head. My sneakers were white.

"You can't wear those," my mother hissed.

"What? But I bought them specially. You told me to bring only quiet shoes." I hadn't understood her at first. My shoes would hardly start singing in public. Sneakers were noiseless shoes. They did look so high-tech, with their air bubbles and fancy cushioning. My mother took some black paint from under the window and painted my very expensive shoes. I let her because she seemed to enjoy it so much. Glancing triumphantly at me as she did so. As if to say: "Here are the rules I live by while you are driving your jeep under the palms on Sunset Boulevard."

We were now alike, my mother and I—ageless, shapeless phantoms. The taxi man had a long nose with a bump on the bridge; he had an uneven moustache over a wide mouth. His eyebrows joined in the middle, and they were alive as caterpillars—moving up and down when he talked. It turned out that my mother had delivered three of his children. We told him that all the men in the family had left during the revolution. He shook his head and said they had abandoned my mother.

"But my father and brother can't come back. They would be shot or enlisted into the army. We were all in America at one stage, even my mother."

"Why come back?" he asked.

"The new regime said the refugees could come back and get their property. She wanted to sell the house . . . that sort of stuff."

"It was a lovely big house by the river," my mother said. "Many families live there now. They just took it over when we were away. I never got it back."

All through the conversation, I was watching his face in the rear-view mirror. It struck me that he could not see ours. We were stripped of expression. I turned to my mother, and she was facing me. I squeezed her hand and she stroked my palms. There was no air conditioning in the cab. My scalp was sweating under the veil, and my eyelashes kept scraping off the gauze rectangle in front of my eyes. Every time I blinked, I could feel an irritating scrape. This was new to me. Only poor people wore the veil when my family lived here.

The streets looked almost normal. A little bombed out, perhaps, but still bustling with people and lined with vendor stalls, and slogans written all over the walls. But the preponderance of black cloth in the heat was startling, as if these lives were angry paint strokes gashing through a bright canvas.

We were dark holes on the street. If you touched us, you would fall inside and disappear. We had eyes, but you could only imagine them. Our silence had the whole country tied up and despised. Then there was the fact that we had disappeared but were everywhere.

When we got home, we stacked the freezer with meat. Fruit in the bowl. A new bag bursting with rice. I dismantled the three crockery towers that had tottered aggressively on the counter since my arrival. There was something useless about the idea of rebelling crockery. When I took them apart, I couldn't help feeling that I was dismantling three totems. Then I washed up, scrubbed all the surfaces, and sprinkled poisonous powder for the roaches.

My mother sat on the couch with the TV blaring. She complained about everyone and everything in a tone and rhythm reminiscent of a prayer. First it was the government, the war, the revolution, US Immigration. Then, when she had exhausted the general, she moved on to specifics. My father the waster; the time they had been stuck in a refugee camp with a newborn baby and he had walked around boasting how he knew the king and queen, who he still referred as "Your Majesty", even though they were a jumped-up military family with no aristocratic blood. My brother for running off to Silicon Valley, marrying a Chinese, and never calling; my uncle Mo for being Mo; my aunt for not helping her out, how she got to keep her job and be sent to the women's hospital while all the other women were forced to quit work; me for becoming too Americanised, forgetting my culture and roots.

"What culture is this?" I said as I lit the gas stove under a pan full of tomatoes and aubergines. But I was used to my parents' ability to hold two opposing viewpoints in their mind at once: loving America but not wanting to become American. Liking the stuff but looking down on the people. I cooked a big meal, but later I heard her get sick, and she was too embarrassed to catch my eye. "Are you okay? Was it too much at one time? Too rich?" I asked. She looked at the black windows and rapped her knuckles off them. "It's hard to tell if it's day or night," she told me, as if in answer to my queries, "but you can always check by the heat of the glass."

That first night, I dreamt of the crockery wars. Womanly figures as stacked empty vessels, precariously lurching toward one another. Dark holes where their eyes should have been. I awoke sweating and sat bolt upright and naked. My mother was sitting in a chair at the end of the bed.

"Have you been watching me sleep?" I pulled the sheet up to cover my breasts.

"I've been alone a long time," she told me in the darkness, and her face was so devoid of expression, she might still have been wearing a veil.

TWO: THE DEAL

While I stood in the hall in the hot air of morning, I looked at all the photos my mother had put up of the family. None of us had ever been to this cramped, dreadful apartment, but she had our history pinned to the wall. Rows of faces pressed against small rectangles of glass. I gazed through my veil at the postage-stamp-sized faces of my grandparents.

"I must get some of these copied before I go back. I'd like to have them in the apartment in Los Angeles."

"Copied?" my mother said. "Where are you going to get them copied?"

She was also fully veiled, so I could not see her reaction. It struck me that it was going to be very hard to leave her here. She opened the front door and marched out. We met the taxi driver on the corner and got in quickly. Somebody might see us and report us.

My aunt embraced me at the hospital. At first, the building looked abandoned. Most of the windows were broken and painted black. There was electricity but no running water. There was no operating room. My aunt led me through the peeling corridors. There were a few beds with veiled figures lying inert under tattered blankets. I was afraid to go close and find their eyes through the cloth mesh. The wards were overflowing with women. Some were crouched on the ground with their hands over their heads. Leaning against walls. Rocking silently. My aunt informed me that many had gone mad. "The suicide rate has skyrocketed. Most were widows because of the war and had no menfolk. They had been supporting children and elderly parents, so when they lost their jobs, they all starved. We have almost no medical supplies. There's no running water. Male doctors aren't allowed to see women patients, but there are no women surgeons. So they just come here to die while their children roam the streets hungry." She waved her hand towards the beds with the women stretched out on them. "They don't even move. They just lie there. We can't treat them."

"The men's hospital is probably not much better," my mother said.

"Yes, the West has imposed sanctions on the new regime because they've nationalised the oil. They punish us for having leaders who torture us."

"Can I see your face?" I asked. We went into her office with my mother, and the three of us unveiled. My aunt and I smiled at each other and kissed. She was younger than my mother and always had been prettier. She did not appear so defeated and was even wearing light make-up.

"If we don't get some medicine and supplies soon, the staff have threatened to take all the women down to the government buildings and leave them there as a protest."

I shrugged. "Why not? They're dying here anyway."

My mother looked worried. "Don't risk yourself. You could be killed for that."

"What can I do?"

"Did you ask about getting me a job here?"

"They say you are politically suspect because of your husband's ties with the royal family."

Outside my aunt's office, two women waited. One had a two-year-old girl on her knee. The child's head was wrapped in an elasticised bonnet covering all her hair. She sat very still on her mother's knee. Glaring at us.

On Friday, we drove with my aunt and her family to the river. The sun roared and opened up the sky. Mountains folded back on to the horizon, cutting a clear line where the seamless blue sky met the rumpled fabric of land. The ground shimmered with heat as if the road and tree trunks were made of liquid. We were so sticky when we got out of the car that all the women ran shouting towards the riverbank. I wanted to strip off and dive into the crystal-clear water. But we halted like a herd reaching a precipice, and then someone pointed to the trees. We galloped under the trees into the shade and lay there, panting like dogs. The men were carrying picnic hampers, which the women took to prepare lunch. Then the men went to a section hidden by a canopy and stripped down to their shorts. We could hear them splash in the water. For every splash, my throat ached. We festered like black slugs under the trees and no one talked because the heat was roaring like a furnace. I felt like we had been buried.

"It is beautiful here in the mountains," my aunt said, as we all lay side by side and murmured in acquiescence.

"Remember Baba used to say no one could swim to the middle of the river because there is another river inside this river with a different current?"

"Your father never knew what he was talking about. He couldn't even swim himself."

"No, he was right," my aunt said. "I forget what it's called. They're dangerous because plumes can form. Polluting parts of the river if it's too close to the factory or a pollution source. I can't remember now, but there used to be a lot of stuff in the newspapers."

"Why don't you try to get out of here?" I asked my aunt.

"This is my country. I'm not abandoning it now in its darkest time. What would all the women at the hospital do? The poor can't leave."

"The poor!" My mother spat. "The poor are always starting revolutions with their childish bias. It's all right for you. You have male relatives who live with you and can take you out. You have been allowed to work. You are living in your own home."

"Why are we so passive?" I asked my aunt and mother. "Like the Jews going to the ghettos, then getting on the trains still hoping the authorities would let them live. It isn't as if we were always like this. Women used to have relative freedom in this country."

"Ask your aunt. She's the activist. She has all the answers."

My aunt stood up. I could tell by her curt movements that she was angry. I shushed my mother. "Be nice. No wonder she doesn't come to visit you."

"She lets me starve to death in that slum while she plays saviour to the poor. The poor, ha! You should see the house she lives in. She didn't have to lose her home."

I fell asleep and dreamt that my mother, aunt and I were down by the river and stripping off layer after layer like small onions. As I was about to plunge into the delicious cool water, I woke up, frightened that I was naked.

I walked down to the river by myself. I had always been two different people in so many ways. East and West. Good daughter, bad daughter. I could not touch the water without falling in. I realised now that this had always been inside me—a river within a river. There was always the danger I might drift into the wrong river, the wrong part of me.

The men were crawling out of the river. Tiptoeing in bare feet across the stony ground. A strange, punctuated dance. Their bare arms flailing and dripping water. While they ate lunch, the women went behind the trees. My mother sighed and spoke to us. "I don't see the point in this at all. All these retreats. Better to stay at home and socialise privately where we can eat and mix with the men."

"But it's so beautiful here," my aunt said. "We can't let them take this country from us."

"And what do you think, Miss America?" My mother turned to me.

"I was just thinking that it would be really easy to be a drag queen here."

My mother laughed loudly. It was the first time I had heard her laugh since I had arrived. I wished I could have seen her smile. My aunt was puzzled. "What's a drag queen?"

My mother sniffed. "Abnormal people. Only in America would men want to be women."

My mother and I sat side by side, day after day, sunk in silence.

I told her that I was leaving in a few days, and her face creased with fear. I told her I'd check on getting her a new green card, though that wasn't something I could do.

"But they took my passport, all my papers."

"I'll leave you with all my money."

"I can't leave the house to spend it."

The phone rang, and I was glad to run and pick it up. My aunt needed me; she urged me to leave my mother at home and bring my US passport. She sent my cousin to pick me up. My mother cried when I left. When I was young, I never saw her cry.

In the dim light of the hospital, my aunt and two other women were standing in a circle, leaning toward each other. "We need you. There's a truck outside. You're an American citizen, so you can pretend that you didn't know you were forbidden to drive. They won't touch you."

"What do I have to do?" I could feel many eyes in the corridor on my back.

"We're taking the patients to the government building and leaving them there to die under the feet of their executioners. In full view of the city. They can no longer pretend that this is a hospital. This is a death camp."

"I'm leaving in a day or two. I don't want to screw that up."

"How can you walk away and leave us?" one of the women said. "Look at your countrywomen."

"This is not the country I grew up in. My countrywomen are not these black spectres, dying and mad in this filthy, shit-smelling place. I've been in America most of my life. My countrywomen are currently sipping cosmopolitans in bars and showing their belly buttons."

"We had three suicides this morning." Another woman grabbed me and came face to face so that I could see her eyes behind the mesh. "Every day there are more and more. This is the end of the road. As you're an American, they'll let you be."

"If I'm deported, I can't ever come back. Who will deal with my mother if anything happens?"

"I promise you I will." My aunt sensed a bargain. "We need to fight back for once. You said so yourself."

"Will you let her live with you and your family?"

"Yes. If you do this, I will."

"Okay, we'll make a deal. You take care of her, and I'll do this before I leave. I'll just drive."

"So you'll do it." The women were excited.

"I'll do it the day I'm flying back West. Then I'll drive straight to the airport."

My mother was terrified I was going back home to America, but she knew I couldn't stay here.

"I will die here. I can't believe I will die alone."

I wanted to let her know that she would be taken care of by my aunt's family now, that I had taken care of things, but I didn't dare let on that I was going to do something risky. The taxi driver drove me to the hospital.

Like giddy thieves, we loaded the patients on to stretchers and carried them to a waiting truck. Nurses stood on the truck and roughly dragged the very sick to the far corner. The patients expressed no surprise. None struggled. Most were catatonic. Wide open to fate. I had never imagined a human cargo so listless and passive. I raced around the ward like a demented sheepdog, herding the stragglers on to the truck. The women who were hunched by the walls I pulled by the arms and loaded on top of their sisters. I mashed them in together like livestock. I hurt some of them. Their discomfort and confusion was palpable, but any protest was paralysed by their fear.

Driving to the city, my aunt and I were the only ones in charge. She had sent her staff home to hide. The truck was huge. A man's truck. I'd never driven anything like it. At home, I had a jeep and thought I was tough. We had a patient beside us with stomach cancer. Her breath emanated from her clothes like something vile seeping from a rotten inner core. I would never see any of those women's faces. Never catch their eyes. They were objects to me.

They put my aunt in a sack and buried her up to her waist. Then they publicly stoned her. I sat on a chair in the interrogation room and watched them burn my passport. They told me I had no understanding of tradition.

I asked them why when they persecuted men for religion or colour, it was viewed by the world as oppression, and when they persecuted women, it was dismissed as tradition. I lay on the floor in a cell, bloody and bruised. The tiny cell was round and empty, but there was a window, a tiny slit in the wall, so high I could not reach it or look out.

Often I hear screaming behind the walls. Some nights, they come into my cell and hurt me. They always come in a group. I feel them exploring, tiny figures in a vast landscape. Fingers probe my crags to pull themselves up higher. I have to make sure they never stumble on the source of my second river.

I worry about my mother. I have not seen or heard from anyone. I'm not sure if they have even told her where I am. She must know my aunt is dead.

There are three layers of prison around me: the walls, my veil, and then the fact that I cannot see myself for the first time in my life. I have no mirror and I miss my face. It is the realisation that I might never see myself again that shocks me.

How far inside yourself do you have to go to be safe?

Imagination becomes my soul, and the past is my soul dreaming.

I recall one image from the cradle. My mother's face looming like a huge harvest moon above me, and when she smiles, her smile is a dark hole in her face.

Drago Jančar

"A Sunday in Oberheim"
from *Joyce's Pupil*

Not even a Sunday, just a Sunday morning. Three scenes, a thousand words. And the necessary backdrop of the melancholy central European provinces. The square by the Danube: the river has risen a bit in the last few days, and the long hulled boats, either on their own or with the aid of tugboats, struggle against the current, but they slide quickly and almost soundlessly in the other direction as the brown water foams. The wind stirs the tops of the poplars, clumps of white acacias toss in the breeze, somewhere up river it is raining, while here a dull and foggy light can be seen through the clouds. Organ music emanating from the church of St Egidio rolls over the cobblestones, and it bounces off the houses whose empty façades look like inside out city walls; the powerful sounds chase each other and swirl around the Gothic building. It is deserted. Everyone is at mass.

Several cars park in front of the abandoned brewery on the other side of the tiny street on which I am living. I don't know why I've never noticed before. They park here, and some men carrying elegant gun cases in their hands get out and disappear through the broad door which must lead into a cellar or warehouse. Once upon a time, they rolled beer barrels here and loaded them on to carts. The brewery tower looks over the roof at the Danube. I'd like to be up on it, right on top. I'd be able to see where the misty rain from the low clouds meets the river in its upper reaches. Beneath the tower is a smaller, pretty well abandoned building.

"It was an ice shed," Fastl explains.

Fastl isn't at mass, ever. He doesn't want me to use the formal forms of address, just "you, Fastl". He once worked for the railway. Now he keeps a hot dog stand in the small train station. Jadranka from Bosnia cooks and sells the hot dogs. Every Sunday, when the stand is closed, Fastl goes to drink beer at the Black Eagle. You can find some others who don't go to mass there.

"They loaded ice with the bee," he explains.

"And what's in the brewery now?"

"Nothing." In 1945, just here near the entrance, three people were killed by a grenade an American tank.

Another car parks in front of the brewery. A broad shouldered man rings the bell e door, waits and disappears inside.

"And where are those people going?"

"To the cellar."

"But you, Fastl, say there's nothing in the old brewery."

"Only in the cellar."

The small brown eyes in his big head shine puckishly.

He asks whether I'd like to see what is in the cellar.

"Yeah."

"Let's go," he says.

We cross the street. Fastl rings, and a man's voice can be heard through the intercom. They speak in a dialect I don't understand. The door opens and we find ourselves on a long stone staircase which leads down into the depths. It smells like sulphur and as if something is burning. I seem to hear a vigorous crackling, as if someone was smashing a heavy tree branch. Fastl walks cautiously, he is retired, and we are illuminated by the yellow rays of the cellar light. Down below is another door. My guide rings again and it opens as well. Now we're in a small room where a tall, close cropped man sits at a table reading a newspaper. He nods, which means we can proceed, and we suddenly find ourselves in a bigger, better lit room. It is full of close cropped, broad shouldered men, most of them wearing vests over shirts with rolled up sleeves. Those same elegant gun cases are lying open on the table, and inside them are neatly arranged revolvers of various calibres, together with gun cleaning supplies.

"Shchutzverein, says Fastl, a gun club. Some bigger pieces are leaning against the wall—shotguns, Winchesters, some automatics. The crackling is now louder, the smell of sulphur sharper than it was upstairs. A grayish-blue cloud floats above our heads, and it hugs the high vaults of the cellar. There are no windows. The men walk out through heavy, metal framed doors and come back in with serious faces. They handle their weapons like small animals, carefully and lightly, with practised motions. Fastl speaks with the broad shouldered guy who just arrived. He nods. From underneath a bar covered with a forest of beer mugs, someone pulls out a kind of earphones and presses them into our hands. We go through the same doors, which emit a cloud of bluish smoke every time they open.

As soon as we walk through the door, we hear an explosion. A young man is holding something like a pistol, a Browning, a Luger, a kind of bazooka in his hands. Fastl and I put on the earphones, his eyes shine. Two people are shooting at a target with small-bore pistols, a young man with a bazooka is shooting at panels covered with human outlines. Some are closer, some farther away. They rise and fall, run as if scared, hide and rush out the other side of the hall. But the bullets from the spluttering gun catch up to them there as well. The walls are covered with thick foam rubber. The shooter is satisfied, though he doesn't say anything, wordlessly giving way to the next in line. He has a long barrel which he balances on his left elbow, aims and shoots. Fastl points out to me that the shooter is hitting the target right on the head, in the forehead.

When we return to the first underground room, the broad shouldered hippopotamus offers me a beer, and a close cropped guy asks Fastl to ask me whether I'd like to try. I say no. The close cropped hippo says that I'm no Hemingway, and I say that I'm not. The broad shouldered guy asks whether I want a beer and I say no thanks. Fastl says that he will have a beer at the Black Eagle, just like he does every Sunday morning. Then the broad shouldered guy and his close cropped friend devote themselves to a discussion about the apparatus in fitness clubs, while Fastl and I climb through the yellow light up the stone steps. The grayish blue smoke clings to us, and the crackling, as if someone is breaking up tree branches down below, gets farther away. It still smells of sulphur.

Outside it is Sunday morning. It is completely quiet in front of the scorched and empty bakery. The wind stirs the tops of the poplars; somewhere up river it is raining, while here a dull and foggy light can be seen through the clouds. The brewery tower looks over the roofs at the Danube. I'd like to be up on it, right on top. I'd be able to see where the drizzly rain from the low clouds meets the river in its upper reaches. I ask what is in the brewery tower. Fastl says, nothing, but if I'd like we can go see. I say no. The street is completely quiet. "Nothing would indicate that people are shooting around here," I say. Lentia. The gun club is called Lentia. Fastl shrugs and cuts across the courtyard and the little garden plots on his way to the Black Eagle for a beer.

The main square is still deserted, and the organ in St Egidio has been joined by a powerful choir, whose slow *te deum*, as broad as the Danube, floats across the square and around the church. Around and around it swirls until it finds an outlet across the ground, across the cobblestones of the square, through the streets and over the roofs of Oberheim down to the brown water. I head down there together with the current of sound, to where a tour boat called the *Theodor Fontane* struggles against the river's current. Someone is standing by the railing and looking through binoculars at the town's façades, the poplars and the acacias from which clumps of white flowers hang.

A girl in blue jeans is sitting on a bench in the park by the river. Her shoulders tremble. She is crying. It is spring, the girls of Oberheim are crying. A boy stands next to her with his hands in his leather jacket. He is saying something to her, towards the current and then over it. They don't see me, though I pass close by.

Then I sit in my room and glance out at the brown waves that head toward the Black Sea. It is getting dark, the clouds have drawn nearer, beneath the windows someone is whistling, the light is no longer diffuse and translucent, it is almost opaque, then it disappears.

The radio announces that all the roads are blocked by Whitsuntide traffic. No one should travel unless absolutely necessary. I will write those thousand words, one or two more.

Translated by Andrew Wachtel

Bryan MacMahon

"November" from *Hero Town*

T A—Ra—Ra—Boom—De—Aye!
Here comes the ectoplasmic dead! Booo!

This is their month of course, the alleged gibberers. But as the country people remark with a wink behind the priest's back, we know where we are but we don't know where we're going. The month of the dead is a dangerous time for the inhabitants of Hero Town. The reaction to summer has set in; there are no diversions—there are no visitors, no hikers, no US kinsfolk, there is suddenly seen the need to gnaw at each others' vitals. Booo!

In the sky, intimidators, thunder clouds, gather up rear and threaten to browbeat the heavens above the streets of Hero Town. The crows perform their mock terrified antics in the sky. Peddah is filled with remorse born of an opportunity missed. Remorse!

"Oh yes, we shall make love. Stroke me and I shall respond. Denied, I shall scream."

The voice enticing Peter was a distant echo, indicating that she was truly woman, yet she flounced away and slammed the kitchen door. The terror in the heart—the terror of refusal. Boo! Terrified, Peter walked on as thunder roars in a leaden, livid sky.

But hold softly, we observe, all are observed. The function of the brain and the nervous system is to protect us from being overwhelmed by our ability to recall all that has ever happened to us. The brain is a sieve or screen, which eliminates the irrelevant and allows through to consciousness all that is useful to us as individuals. In Peter's case there's a bloody big hole in the net and every thing swims through. In the local paper there is an advertisement for the sale of three thousand headless mackerel. *Has a mackerel a soul? Presumably they are smoked. Hurrah for the headless mackerel!*

Peter drifts through this incipient cold death time seeking solace, release, even diversion welcoming the intrusion, the wild eyes, uncontrolled gestures and mouth-cornered foam of Darkie who confronted Peter out in the cold air of the Diamond. Darkie, intelligent, high with excitement, is troubled.

"Pardon your presence, Peter, can I curse? Amn't I shagged to death by a double negative and ignorance of punctuation?" The red gold flame of the plane trees has been brushed together in a heap outside the doctor's door. Rain. Spluttering. The wet, cold, whinging wind enclosing the shins, thighs, genitals, warns that it will refrigerate the bladder and turn the urine yellow. Darkie in Cowardly Custard Town.

"Give your attention, Sir. Pay me heed! Isn't it a pure cobweb to have me asking you for attention? For years now as you know well, I'm drawing money for VD—Valvular Disease of the heart, not the other thing. So I got this proclamation from Queen Granuaile to present myself at the Clinic a Tuesday last and place myself before a doctor to see if I'm fit to work. Up with me. Monty the Janitor beckoned me, when my turn came, to walk into a room where there was a clean nurse writing behind a desk. I don't know the geography of the Clinic very well so I kept looking at a white door wondering when I'd be told to go into the doctor. This nurse I took for one of the Gleeson girls from the Crosses so I whispers to her, is it the drunkard from Mitchelstown or the Total Abstainer from Glin is on duty inside? If it's the drunkard I'm frigged for he'll put me working. 'Strip off,' says the nurse without looking up. 'Is it out of your mind you are girl,' I says. 'Strip off,' says she raising her voice. 'I'm the doctor.' 'The curse of Christ on you, Monty,' I said, 'that never warned me.' I bared bollocks naked and I shivering. She put the tackle on my chest. I gave a convincing kind of a gurgle and I answering her. 'Is that brandy I smell?' she asked.

"'A spoonful for courage,' I said.

"I'll cut it short, Peter. I'm outside the door and home to my bothán and I still mystified. Two days later the letter came. 'I certify that he is not incapable of working!' 'Hurray, Ma,' says I, 'I'm past the post.' Back down to my own doctor. Down for my cert. 'You're shit out of luck,' he says. 'It's a double negative.' I'd write my life story only I don't understand punctuation."

Ha, ha said the wind to Peter. I'll scald your bloody bladder. Peter drifted home through Cowardly Custard Town—hurt.

* * *

Glug, glug, glug. Gurgle, gurgle!! O Fons Bandusiae, will it never stop spitting rain? The river roars by under the spindle shins of the race bridge. Is that the Chaser knocking at a fanlight, a born trier, the same man? Peter wishes he had his neck. A fine looking lad. Athletic, barely thirty, but let him talk to a woman for two minutes and he eagerly beaverly overwhelms her. He gets down to bedrock, to rock bed right away. No finesse. No sense of protocol. No terror. The women all respond. But who under God is Peter to judge? Should not their two natures be fused, mixed, shuffled like playing cards or the ingredients of a barmbrack, baked and halved—then the overhunter and the underhunter would average out in proper proportions. There he is, hunting in sight, tapping out the coded knock for the lady visitor at the Castle Guesthouse. Tally Ho!

Noontime Saturday. It was raining heavily again, the down

delving rain shot lit with sunlight when it hit the roadway had transformed the black road surface to a lawn that sprouted erratically in fleeting clusters of silver grass. A trick of configuration had ensured this, Peter told himself as he walked downtown on the quest of a living day in the tied-to-one another houses of dark Hero Town, that once had seventy-eight pubs for three thousand residents. Imperial intrigue in action, keep the Paddies blotto and faction fighting, all good cannon food when they sober up and memorise their regimental number in Chatham Barracks. Since the great truck was stopped and impounded by the Head Water Keeper with boxes upon boxes of Undersized Oysters, a new character was recruited to see Peter the Pedagogue to the year's end.

Fáilte, O Undersized Oyster!

The new girl at Madden's looks . . . feminine. Very feminine. Peter is not sure what feminine means, but thinks that she is just that. The Undersized Oysters certainly had a colourful story to tell their prosaic stick-in-the-mud mates when they got home after the buggy ride and the legitimate hijack. The problem is that Peter realises that women like men have desires but in a situation of reality he simply cannot imagine their translating these desires into deed. A mystery.

As the mind of women is said to oscillate between boudoir and altar, like every man Peter's oscillates between thoughts of blasphemy, lust and pious obscenity to thoughts of sanctity and bright white chastity. At the most sublime moments of the colourful, wonderful, ceremony of Ordination of a curly polled local in the thronged expectant church the voice of the mother of the candidate is recalled.

"The night before John was ordained he asked me to speak to him alone in his room. I sat on the bed. He put his head on my lap and cried bitterly, his head battering between my thighs. Few words passed between us. "The woman,' I said in a low voice whispering in his ear. He sobbed in a final convulsion. He sat up and dried his eyes. "Yes,' he said, seemingly satisfied that I had recognised the source of his trouble and his grief. He smiled and was an extrovert."

In the church the wonderful spectacle went on, the chanting of the choir, nostril titillating smell of incense, red and gold, colours reminiscent of John Duffy's Circus and before Christ no disrespect is meant or innuendo. The sunlight of the winter day strikes crazy-wise and the colours of the assembled prelates and clergy danced against the limestone grey in the crowded church.

The woman at Peter's elbow in the church, the beautiful girl with no wedding ring on her finger, when I went to shake hands with her, she trembled visibly. She did not understand. Was she too in the boudoir?

Peter is perplexed, yet later he breaks into laughter when he considers the verdict of a gabby old parishioner on the truly ennobling ceremonies. The old woman emerging in the wet crush of people turns back to the now lighted Gothic doorway saying, "Wan thing anyway, they needn't be a bit ashamed of the carry out." Peter, pondering this statement over, realised that this was the highest praise she could give. In effect she was praising to the full while propitiating evil spirits who lurked everywhere unseen on the alert, to wreak the havoc as a result of rapid overpraise. The child, or young priest, overpraised should by the protocol of dead religions be gently spat upon, in the old days, or at second remove in their moment of overpraise the acrid tobacco spit is cast on the flag of the hearthstone, the old bootsole drawn across it as if to say such beauty should not be greeted with unqualified praise. Hush! Demons are in the wings. Or perhaps it is the legacy of God's judgement ever since the fall of Lucifer.

Outside the rain had ceased and the bright sky from the south-west hastened to rush up the sky. With the trees now in rod, Peter glanced at the hill on the far side of the river and thought how the goldfinch would show up against the winter landscape.

* * *

The clock in its clock case ticks out Peter's life as he sits and watches the scene in Hero Town. From a rooftop a jackdaw swoops to the asphalt of mid-road and delicately and hurriedly places its beak under the almost flattened but almost completely clean pleated circle of a drenched paper bun case.

He smiled when the new chemist girl at Madden's passed him by. Would her body ever emerge from the white coat even if she were to burn all her clothing and don new clothes, as the old people say, from the skin out? After the vacuum left by her passing had gone he sniffled the wind that beat upon his face. He couldn't smell the woman in her, it was all overlaid with the thousand smells of the chemist shop.

A world of thoughts from Peter as he closes the door and arm pregnant goes to the scullery with an offering of vegetable marrow and a cluster of celery the whole harvest festival in miniature in his outstretched hands. "These are for Margo," the kindly neighbour had whispered, but the flecked marrow causes havoc, as it bounces and thuds to the polished tiles of the hall. "Awkward," Margo shouts, and dropping his load Peter thumps back out into the street in a hasty retreat telling himself, you can't win! Beaten to the ropes he returns later for lunch. Margo was generous. She acted as if nothing had happened. Woman is at her best when she acts as if nothing has happened. Her return to workaday world of routine, her calm acceptance and recovery after she has been man-ruffled is admirable. It is as if she accepts her role of being the sort of creature against whose body, mind and spirit it is wholesome and healing for man to be mad against.

Dark, dear dark dread, dreary, dismal, depressing month of the uncountable hosts of the dead. Their ambitions, their urgent desires, their cries, their virtues—puff, a lump of sweet shit all. Booh-ghost and booh to all other familiars of a semi crazy schoolmaster. Our Lady of Perpetual Extension, look down with favour on the recumbent form of thy obedient servant, Peter Mulrooney. NT in Hero Town, south-west Ireland. Voluntary Health number 100085 629 18. Amen. P.S. And aborted scribbler.

Knock. Knock. "Will you buy holly? The finest of red knobs, Sir?" "No, son. Too early."

* * *

Later in the week Peddah awoke to find the sky high, wide, blue and flawless and a winter sun breaking through with all the bravery of a summer's warm smile at the unexpected and as a consequence exhilarating change of battle fortune. The whole effect on him was that of an explosion. Margo too found the unusual day exhilarating. Our bodies or our metabolism must be on trial, Peter explained to himself, when he found she was arranging small variegated holly mixed with rosemary, its awkward lovely ungainly attractive sprigs evoking a sense of winsomeness. Interesting, but no more interesting than Restless Wife en route to encounter God.

As the traffic swished past, she gently manoeuvred Peter into standing with his back to a sun-warmed painted wall, for such walls can really exist even in the bland month of Booh-Ghost, to observe the life flow of her most beautiful town. "Do you ever raise your eyes, Peter, to watch the skies this time of the year? You should. And the sunsets, a pure delirium of delight." Restless Wife, her face is turned to the sky, as she began a delectable treble layered conversation with Peddah.

Watch out, she smells continence from you, Peter, and she's out to crack that continence in you and having cracked she'll run off leaving you with an emotional problem to tell other hecklers about. She tried all her tricks; she introduced words calculated to inflame the passion, bed, spread, fed, ejection, reflection, erection, trick, wick, click, and still he refused to see. "Your big empty bed, Peter, what a waste of talent! Aren't you ashamed? Admit it now." Restless Wife who knows he won't repeat what she tells him but will certainly if he is unguarded repeat what he tells her if in any way whatsoever it can be considered salacious or risqué. Restless Wife laughed lasciviously and walked off to encounter God in his silent but incense aromatic church. But perhaps words satisfy the restless ache she endures, and deeds not at all. Walking home to his tea Peter thought what it would be like to tell one's sins to a woman priest. Would a youngish newly ordained woman priest prove embarrassed on hearing from a man tales of rich concupiscence? Ah but when women get a set on a young priest, May God help him!

"Hey, Peter, watch yourself, chatting to that one. Gossip travels and she has a husband even if he is tormented. I'm only for your good, that's why I'm telling you."

The cordaline tree dark green was grumpy against the winter sky in the neat trimmed lawn while the witch's cap of Halloween with the book of spells dispirited lay soggy on the pavement. Near by the winter cherry tree in the Diamond, her garment blossoms spread about her feet, stood stark naked against the northern sky tempting the sunlight of spring that is yet in the remote future.

Oh well, fall back on the familiars, touch them lovingly, allow the sense of touch to become a protocol of obscure reference. Good old Undersized Oyster. Good old Headless Mackerel.

In the schoolroom Peter now became aware of a coiled spring of intensity within him, a powerhouse of intensity, when the word images and rhythm and cadence could be almost seen penetrating and fertilising and fructifying the minds of the children. It was a process akin to heterosexual coupling he dared to tell himself. What had terrified him before he realised could be translated into terms of penetrative power. Could Castle Cutjacks be included in the monthly list of totem words and phrases? Cry havoc! The Undersized Oysters would yet grow to maturity if returned to their beds. Only the thoroughbred shivers.

The day smells with sunshine. Downstreet close by the delicatessen the JCB snorts and bucks and farts like the offstage stallion in the house of Alba. The stallion roaring for mares designed to counterpoise the man roaring for the unnaturally cooped up woman in the house of the Spanish nobleman. The ground too in its own mute way cries out since the beginning of time to be broken. The digging head of the JCB like the head of a prehistoric monster dwarfed the donkey tied to a rusted black railing in the shadow of the Bank. A gleam of November sunshine is reflected in the chrome of the old motor parked with its rear against the kerb. Framed in the rear window is a small plastic skull which of its conformation can do little else but grin with a black mantilla flowing from the poll of the skull. Power begins to flow in him as again he strides home.

The new girl at Madden's is heading for the Post Office. Does he get a distinct vibratory feedback there? Her clicking heels echoing in the tappety-tap of a tinker's spring cart driven swiftly upstreet. Tappety-tap, into my life, out of my life. Peter grew in self-confidence and considered the ebb and flow of desire and sublimation at the other end of the keyboard in the convent outside the town. For Peter without his beliefs and the celebratory church ceremonies of the year, those accompanying birth, mating, death, the fabric of his life in Hero Town was reduced to ashes. The liberals with their promises of life free from flaw or sanction or poverty or injustice— he would wait and see before he chose. Given time they would evolve feast days and rituals of their own and sanctions and jealousy, poverty and injustices.

He'd stick by what he had . . . *but wait, the card in a shop window gave notice of a lecture on the life of the mystic Padre Pio in a singing pub by a singing river. The final line caught Pedagogue's attention— "Relics present to bless the assembly!" Relics, and the man not even a Blessed. But Hero Town did not mind such niceties of papal protocol. Skull and mantilla present to frighten the shit out of the assembly. Tappety-tap. All tied together. Salubrious, bran-begotten stools are to be saluted. The equals of women in the house of Bernardo Alba.*

While these sad, mad, glad and bad events were in train the trees peeping over the roofs of the townhouses mimicked and imitated the colours of the final fashioned winter garments in the mock mullioned white windows of Widow Holmes' Boutique which stood two doors from the urine saturated archway that led by a lane to the market. A splendid show outstanding against the backdrop of the ageing castle.

"Will you want holly?" the voice intruded.

"I will want."

"Well you won't want now as all mine is gone!"

* * *

Did all this make a single scrap of difference to Hero Town, to an intimate community with their yellow chrysanthemums, to the corner houses behind which the shared backyards were like rabbit warrens? It was all a game like Ludo or Snakes and Ladders.

The way forward was to find women when they were already emotionally aroused and to cash in on it. What did the widow woman mean by saying, "You should speak to Violet. She's tense and nervous." The lock on the front door clicked indicating that the widow had left them alone in the house. Peter found himself wholly inadequate to meet the situation and the whole dismal failure became appallingly Gothic.

The winter came, and mild. No strangers in the town. People said, "This mild weather will kill the winter." A wise listener replied, "If you kill the winter you kill time, and time is how precious life is measured."

* * *

"Hey, John, you're the very man I wanted to meet. I'm sorry to say that I was laid up when I heard of Francey's death. I'm sorry," Peter-he went on, this conversation was held beside a wet church at a bridge in the moorland hills, "that I wasn't present in person to pay my respects at the funeral. You and he were the best bodhran players in this barony. They found it hard to separate the pair of you at the Drumming Final in Oldcastle. By the way—did you drum over his grave?"

"No."

"Why not?"

"I didn't like the priest's eye. I thought that if I produced the tambourine at the graveside he'd rear up on me. And maybe bullrag me off the altar the following Sunday."

"Still and all—you should have drummed over your brother's grave. Yourself and himself were the last great drummers of our time. Ó Riada gave it up to ye."

"It troubled me, I can tell you, Sir. Listen . . . I have the bodhran above at Connolly's pub. If you hang on there a few minutes I'll run up and get it and then I'll hop over the stile and drum over his grave."

"But . . . But . . ."

Hang on there now one minute—no buts, Peter . . . I'll be right back."

Led with my jaw. This'll be in town before me. Is the Schoolmaster going off his nut? Up there is Slieva Nossil in a dripping churchyard and himself and the Drummer floggin' the goats skin. Over a grave. No one but the two of them. What harm but the local Peepee is a touchy boyo.

"I wasn't long, Peter. I gave the skin a small heat to the fire to tighten it up. Watch the flagstone at the other side of the stile— 'tis damn slippery. That's it."

The grave. Unfolded plastic flowers. Grass struggling through clay, drip, drip. Make the best of it. Take off your cap, Drummer. Hang it on the cross. Stand here by the grave. Face the east. The knuckles only. Don't work the rim. The naked skin is your man. Imagine there are 500 mourners around you. Now. Make it deep. Ornament first. Then deep, deep! Burrum, burrum. Deep. Skittle across the face of the skin. Knuckles bare. Barrumtitty, bumtitty bum. Good bloody man.

Close the eyes, Pedagogue. Are the people at the doors of the cottages? *I think so.* In the pub doorway? *Yes—yes!* Burrumditty dum. Dum, dum, dum—*Go on, Drummer, let 'em have it, send the rev-er-ber-ations far and wide.*

In a dripping churchyacd. Up in the hills in dark November. Voodooland. Crazy Billygoat for sure. The Master. No! Yes—yes— yes!

That I may be dead it was Peter Mulrooney!

* * *

Time passed—time galloped for Peter on the ten streets of Hero Town. The ten in time had become sixteen. Pining for the aristocracy they called the new clusters of buildings estates, the roads drives, and the bothareens avenues. There he waited among the people, his eye most remotely hoping that he would come face to face with the new chemist assistant at Madden's who seemed to spend the day running from one chemist to another in the town so as to fill prescriptions of drugs they did not keep in stock.

"You're doing the rounds, Peter. Shove in here off the street and witness my application to be exempt from Rates. Didn't I tell you, friend, that my eldest son married a common whore? I don't believe half of what she calls my grandchildren are any blood relations of mine at all. Amn't I out of my mind with that upstart!"

Stories. Queries. Questions. Is there no end to it, the Pedagogue asks himself? Have I nothing to show for my time? This is a query that stabs home. Peter is lost in thought as the loud voice of the grimy Mucking Man, who halts his tractor with its full load of steaming manure in the bottleneck that siphons off the main traffic, booms at Peter. He opens the cab door.

"Hey, you seen me coming up last night from behind the castle?"

"I did."

"I had my torch with me, the powerful beam with the red blinker on top."

"Corr-ect."

"Well, she calved. A bull calf. A white head. Twenty past five this morning. Already sold for seventy pounds."

"Well done, Joe."

Peep, peep. Hoot, hoot.

"What the hell hooting have those blasted cars? Let them go to hell. Can't a man salute his neighbour? The calf . . . you won't take offence if I name him N.T. Will you, Peter? 'Twas the young tinker fellah suggested it. He thinks it's dynamite."

"Have I any choice?"

"None." The reply was drowned in the engine's roar as the tractor shunted upstreet and passed the cemetery, where in the nearby field the whine of the newly purchased chainsaw was audible. The double first cousin of the vice chairman of the Town Commissioners had purchased the saw and arranged on the q.t. that he was sold the five oak trees that were standing at the demesne corner which the Council had taken over, moryah, as if to widen a dangerous corner.

The chainsaw slavered for the municipal timber, and it was likely that the fine trees would be disposed of as suggested unanimously and quietly.

Dear small town, miserly bitching intriguing small town Ireland at the ghost time of year. When the sky presses down on the barometric eardrums of the inhabitants you can be the lousiest, meanest, shabbiest most unpleasant minded hoarder of camel crap, rat crap, muesli crap, thrush crap that ever existed. Peter made up his mind not to have familiars unless they forced themselves upon him and already a quotation from the mouth of Oliver Cromwell intruded. "I beseech thee by the bowels of Christ to think that thou mayst sometimes be mistaken" kept offering the Bowels of Christ as a final familiar. If Holy Heart in Rome, then why not bowels—it was Satan whispering. No mistaking his soft, succulent, sibilant, saccharine suggestion.

Dear Sister Norina. You are engaged in trying to house tinkers, and you are encountering opposition from those already housed by the Corporation. Well. Society's fear of the outcast outweighs the outcast's fear of society. And now they threaten you . . .

Wouldn't doubt you, Hero Town, you never miss a trick. It's visceral.

New games for children appeared in the windows of the shops. Retrace, Ulcers and Blackmail, developments of the Monopoly and Snap syndromes. The chainsaw whined in the woods.

This time of year the pulse of life beats faintly.

Soon, soon Christ will come and blow his clarion over the dreaming earth, over rotten bitching Hero Town with snorting JCB and haunting skulls, over destructive saws and grasping paws as the dropped calf is sold the moment it hits the hay.

The pulse of life beating low, low and slow, slow, slow.

JUDITA ŠALGO

"THE MAN WHO SOLD SAUERKRAUT AND HAD A LIONESS-DAUGHTER" from *THE THIRD SHORE*

"WHAT SHALL I write about?"

I had already asked the same thing a little while ago. I've been trying to write for years. I've got the words all ready. I've got something to say, but I don't know what to write about. Whenever I ask my husband he says something nonsensical. I'd like to write something that makes him happy, based on an idea of his. Maybe it would mean something to him.

We left the car at the edge of the village and headed down a dusty dirt road that skirted a beech-covered hill. Around the first bend we were assailed by the acrid odor of decay. In the middle of the road lay a large, moldy, pickled cabbage. My husband kicked it and it rolled heavily, soddenly to the side. We left the road and took a shortcut along the ravines cut into the steep slope.

"I saw an amazing woman yesterday. Tall, lean, and powerful, dark-skinned. Her movements were rapid, controlled. She walked as if she were dancing. A cat."

We were standing on a plateau, in pasture. The grass was short, tough, steppe-like, so the sheep, accompanied by conscientious but indifferent dogs, made their way quite quickly, at the same speed and in the same direction, like a small woolly cloud. The sky was clear, there was no sign of the weatherman's "late afternoon thunderstorm," and everything was clean, clear on the evenly trampled ground. Anything anyone said or did there was important, worthy, and in its place.

But I can't write about a woman he has seen.

"What shall I write about?"

I took my husband's arm and leaned my head against his shoulder. He stopped, turned toward me, and drew me close. He was straight, with a flat stomach, solid as an oak. He squeezed my shoulders, patted them lightly, then let me go with a gentle shove.

"Write about a man who sells sauerkraut and has a lioness-daughter."

We headed down the southern slope of the plateau along a path through orchards divided into small plots. The slanted rays of the afternoon sun fell on his face. His right cheek was still warm, his left one already cold.

This was not such a pointless task. Or difficult. It would be quite easy, even, to describe an ordinary girl, the daughter of a man who sells sauerkraut, a few words about her life, begin the plot, and then, in passing, add: by the way, she's not a girl, but a lioness. Or: describe a beautiful powerful lioness, her silent, springy footfall as she paces nervously back and forth in her narrow cage, rubbing against the iron bars, slapping them with her flank, and then at one point, when the sentence has almost ended, mention in passing (once again, only in passing!) that, incidentally, she's not a lioness, but a girl, the daughter of a man who sells sauerkraut, and therefore quite an ordinary, run-of-the-mill lioness-girl.

The two of them, father and daughter, live alone in a garden apartment on Futoška Street (her mother died of septicemia after giving birth, without saying a word about her unusual child); between opening the door in the morning and closing it in the evening they live like everyone else in the neighborhood, and only her heavy, half-closed eyelids and her sleepy look indicate that the girl is a lioness. On the other hand, only her bewildered, sad expression indicates that the lioness is actually a girl. Her nature is almost completely without bestial traits. She never seems to long for the company of real beasts (like other young people, she likes dogs and cats); it has never occurred to her to attack a goat, a sheep, or a child: she is nothing like those notorious panther-women in the fables that the homosexual Molina tells to the revolutionary Valentin in their prison cell in Puig's novel *The Kiss of the Spider Woman*.

Her father, who makes and sells sauerkraut, does not bemoan his fate. He has never reproached his daughter for having been born a lioness unlike all the other womenfolk in his family, unlike the dozens of new little girls who come crawling out of the neighbors' apartments year after year. Father and daughter talk about business: how things are going at the market, how much has been sold. During the summer, the daughter helps her father bring the cabbage (from Futog, of course, that's the cheapest); she cleans it, cuts it, salts it, and packs it in plastic barrels (this causes a lot of friction with the neighbors, as they take up half the shared basement); she brings water and pours it over the cabbage. From mid-October, with her father's help, she takes the barrels out of the basement and loads them into his three-wheeled cart, only one each market day. She rarely goes to the market, however. They don't talk much about anything else, least of all themselves. Her father silently strokes the back of her head, pats her on the back, and mumbles to himself. Only sometimes does he rouse himself and says more clearly, "Don't worry, my girl, things will get better. . . ."

It would be simple to say that she was a lioness in her sleep and when awake a girl. Or vice versa. Because, awake or asleep, she was both: a lioness-girl. In fact, the girl would sometimes wake up as a lioness, and the lioness, particularly after a long afternoon nap, toward dusk, would sometimes wake up as a girl. The girl would come face-to-face with herself as a lioness, and the lioness, seeing her reflection from time to time in a bucket of water or in the puddle in the middle of the courtyard on a rainy day, would face herself as a girl. She was both human and beast, and therefore self-sufficient.

There was a time when I really liked Rousseau's painting *The Sleeping Gypsy*. The dark-skinned girl (her face, hands, and feet seemed to be made of sooty baked clay) sleeps on the bare ground of the wasteland. The light, multicolored dress she is wearing seems to be made of porcelain, next to her on the ground lies her guitar, a little further away is a jug, and above her, opposite the clear sky, which grows darker and darker toward the top, stands a lion, already touched by the gathering twilight, dark, but with his luxurious mane lit by moonlight. His bright, round eye is fixed sternly on her; he sniffs her, but does not touch. In the distance (which does not exist, as everything here is without perspective), parallel with the girl lies a narrow strip of water, separated from the sky by just a whitish wreath of sandy or misty mountains. The landscape is dreamlike, but the girl belongs to reality. She is real because of her heavy, deep, earthy sleep. The moment she wakes and tries to get up she will simply disappear. She will become (remain) the lion.

And now I really wanted the lioness-girl to be credible, authentic, real in my description. The request that I speak about her must have been made with some purpose. I had to make something out of nothing, create something compelling, essential, out of something purely random. Only if she were real would the rest of it be real: her deep devotion to her father, her simultaneous fear of and longing for the neighborhood children, the kind of children that—she has suspected for some time—she will never have; only then will her father's harsh life as a market trader be real, for whatever he puts on the counter to sell, fresh or pickled cabbage, onions, carrots, leeks, or potatoes, he always has trouble with the market inspectors or with the other vendors, and most of all with the fat women, red-cheeked in their youth and bluish in their old age, who, at the first sign of autumn, stuff their large breasts and stomachs into sheepskin coats over which they put white aprons, wet in front from the brine; it is only then that it will be real: the girl's heartache over her father's misfortune and humiliation, her deeply hidden yearning for revenge, her desire to let out a tremendous roar as she chases and tears apart those wretched market people who buzz like flies around rotting leaves and roots, touching, nibbling, tearing to pieces, and devouring like rats those tasteless, miserable substitutes for life, for raw meat.

It is only then that we will be real, my husband and I and this latest futile conversation of ours.

"I have to tell you something," he said.

Both of them, the man who sells sauerkraut and his lioness-daughter, live in a world apart, squeezed between the house and the market stall, each dependent on the other. It is not very likely that anything new could happen, such as the lioness-girl falling in love (and if that did happen, her love would have to be unrequited, unhappy from the beginning, and unalloyed misfortune does not make a plot); it is not very likely that some day, after all kinds of problems, she could get married, have children, be happy, worry, suffer, that she could meet and leave various people, welcome people she cares for and wave them good-bye, mourn for anyone, cry over anyone. Neither could the old man's life consist of anything but the daily, painful but calm progress toward death. So a story with two such characters can have no plot. It is only the shortest path between the beginning and end; it separates the narrator from his audience by only the briefest possible moment. While the girl was waking up and confronting herself as a lioness, my husband simply wandered off. When she opened her eyes, he was gone.

Having walked in a large circle, we were now on a path lined with blackberries, already bare, climbing once again to the open plateau. My husband was walking lightly, with pleasure. I was dragging my feet, dead tired. It was just getting dark. The sky was still light, but the moon was already up in its place, round, magnificent, in all its glory.

If I sit down, I thought, I'll lie down. If I lie down, I'll fall asleep. If I fall asleep, my husband will pass, give me a stern, astonished look, and leave. He won't even hurt me. But I didn't want Rousseau's picture to be repeated right now. I didn't want anything to be repeated. Bad things always look like art. Off-the-hook art. When I weep, I have the feeling that it has already happened somewhere. Suffering should not be exhibited.

My husband was twenty steps ahead. Then, in the middle of the plateau, he stopped, dropped the canvas bag from his shoulder, and as though suddenly overcome by fatigue, sat down and stretched out on the ground. I thought he would close his eyes and I would be able, unobserved, to lie down next to him.

But he watched me approach with wakeful eyes. I stopped, closed my eyes. I breathed in his smell. I wanted more than anything to lick his hard, tight mouth.

"But I don't even know how cabbage is pickled," he said.

"What cabbage?"

I didn't have the courage to touch him, or even leave. His damp look slid down my cheek. That's all I need, I thought. But the salty drops I tasted on my tongue didn't come from my eyes; they came from somewhere above. The sky was clear, only a damp film covered the moon. The wind was getting stronger and stronger. Who knows where it was bringing those drops from?

"Brine?" I said, wiping my cheek.

The moon had already been dipped in cloudy white juice. Wrinkled, with a sour expression, it was draining like a pickled cabbage.

Brine! Brine from a clear sky!

It was a miracle. I knelt and buried my face in my hands. The brine fell harder and harder.

"This is real," he said. "Real."

My husband looked at me calmly, seriously, from a great distance. He was absent, unreal.

But wet.

Translated from the Serbo-Croatian by
Alice Copple-Tošić

KATE McCAFFERTY

TESTIMONY OF AN IRISH SLAVE GIRL

HE LIES PRESSED face first into the pillow, aware of spittle pooled beneath the corner of his mouth as Lucy wakes him. "Suh," she says as neutrally as if she spoke the words "floor" or "dish," then waits, hands cupping each elbow folded across her waist as he settles his focus on her. How many times has she spoken before he woke? How many minutes stood there in the darkened doorway looking at the thin balding hair without its powdered demi-wig, his nightshirt ruched and twisted over thin thighs bitten red by the mosquitoes whining all around? In his cups he has forgotten to lower the fine netting over his couch. He can smell himself. "Suh," she speaks again, "suh," as flat and regular as the ticking of the clock on the mantle in his mother's small reception room on rainy afternoons when . . .

"What it it?" he asks, growling the phlegm away and clutching at the oversheet.

"The pris'nuh in her chair."

"What? I did not call her . . ."

"Cot Quashey waitin'."

"The damnable cheek . . . !"

But he enters the interrogation room dressed to the surcoat. The silver buttons on his waistcoat gleam as in a painting of Dutch burghers. The old slavewoman polished them most carefully before his dinner with the Governor. He will have them cut off and transferred to a new waistcoat, perhaps a ruby brocade lined with silver sateen. His mood brinks between peevish and mildly harassed. What does the old cow want with him? There is no point to further questioning. Colonel Stede has spoken: "Dispose of her" upon the morrow. During their excellent luncheon in the garden it was as if she never had existed; or had been a low mist pierced and burned entirely away by the ruling of the sun. Nothing. She is nothing. Not even worth discussing.

The Governor had been delightful, chatting about this episode from his past, that ball, a fine tailor about to come out from England, an opportunity to invest in an import operation shipping barreled herring from the northern colonies. When Peter expressed a tentative enthusiasm on behalf of his merchant group in Bristol, the Governor, who was dabbing at his lip with a fine lawn lace-edged handkerchief, moved the handkerchief to Peter's frowsy cuff. Continuing the daubing motion, he smiled. "Well yes, but you're here and they're there, and what they do not know . . ." A warm glow had suffused Peter Coote's chest at this camaraderie.

There had been a fine torte made with island oranges, and the Governor's gift of butter kegged in Ulster had still been sweet as the grass the Irish cows munched up with blunt patient teeth. The old slave Daniel had come forward time and time again with a pitcher of punch made of cool well water, fresh mint leaves crushed to paste with sugar, and the finest amber rum. But now . . . now his tongue lies thick, his feet squeeze swollen into cracked black leather pumps . . .

"What do you want with me?" he demands.

Before him sits the perspiring prisoner, Cot Daley, Cot Quashey, the disposable one, the waste/the wasted. The shutters are closed as they were left when the morning interrogation was dismissed. Only a thin lip of light plays from the ceiling to the windowsill, for they have not been latched. In the dark, then, the shape of the Irishwoman. Behind him he can feel Lucy standing. He himself stands impatiently beside his desk. "What?"

There comes no spoken reply. Lucy, who sometimes sings and hums, is silent as well. He feels wrapped, smothered, caught inside their silence.

"Biddy," he coaxes. "You are not well. You have been given the afternoon to rest, rest is often the only cure for an infection once washes and tinctures have failed."

From the sepia lump that is the prisoner a wavery voice begins to speak. "I am Cot Quashey, born Cot Daley in the city of Galway in the nation of Erin around the year 16 and 40; and my tale must be full told."

"What is the point . . ."

"It was in '75 when my husband, Quaco Quashey, led, with his brother and sister Coromantees of the island umma, plus many stragglers from nations like mine and your own, sir, a great uprising."

"A failed uprising!"

". . . Failed," she seems to echo. At the end of her completed testimony he fills in the words he misses now, before he concedes and sits, in weary desperation, curiosity, pique, ambition, to record her tale one final time.

"They failed only at the moment. But first the sun had to fail to rise another day. An imposter, that is what mounted in the sky. I stayed there in the corn shed with my child, the workmen calling and thumping in their thatching work above. I hid inside their noise, then when they too ran with torches to the overseers' houses I hid behind the piled sacks with Betty to my heart. I came out only when the militia galloped into the yard, swords slashing. When, at the end, they had rounded those of us remaining into the drive that circled the portico of the big house and reviewed us, they counted us the loyal ones. The ones not to be punished, but to be rewarded like pet dogs with a dry corner, no kick, a bone. But oh, the torment in my head. For Quashey, Jiba, Cudjoe, Mama Chiva, many others . . . they were gone. Before us the militia dragged, in chains, a dozen beaten men whom they would march to Bridgetown. And the pale ratty Lieutenant, wielding his musket like a scourge, shouted how Afebwa and others they had passed down the line were waiting to be tied onto Glebe's criminal coffle.

"I knew him to be dead. But it was as if my dear son Ben were there, running ghostly up and down crying out 'Abu! Pappy!' and I grew faint with guilt and shame that I had not protected his father, or at least stuck with him and the others who had finally accepted me, me and Betty. At that time I was certain that they all were dead. But as you know, as I myself learned later, Quashey had taken those I named upon the sloop, and like Noah was sailing through deep waters, with the plan to pick up members of the umma who had revolted in the northern parishes, that they might head across the channel to that island. That place which they call Montserrat, under Our Lady's protection; peopled by Muslims and rebels from Erin and Brazil and who knows where? All marooned together. With powdered lords like ye, sir, to try to hold them all in check."

"My records show that Quashey was picked up with these others at Cuckhold's Bay, while taking on more traitors," sighs Peter Coote as he flips the split tail of his surcoat up, scrapes his chair back, and finally sits down.

"Yes. That is as far to freedom as they got in mortal life. Never did I see his face again, or Chiva smiling at me with her ivory man o' war grin. Jiba they never took, for she dived overboard to Guinea; and for years I, drowning in remorse, felt that is what I best had done in '51, from the deck of the Falconer. But I have come to feel different, and I will tell you why, sir."

Coote keeps dunking his plume, then scraping and blotting it as he stares toward her shape. The entire front of her is in shadow. The direction of her eyes cannot be seen, though the bright filament of afternoon which leaks through the unlatched shutters casts a ruddy nimbus over the graduated mound of her shawled head and slumping shoulders.

"He was not executed until '76, after that great folderol of fear meant to bring all bondsfolk to their knees forever in Barbados, and to clear the conscience of Christian folk of any doubts about the need for harshest cruelty on the plantations. They dragged him here and there as an example, before . . . But I felt my Quashey's death that morning, when the militia stood us on the steps of the Glebe and shouted in our faces with threats and questions. I tell you, the land itself expressed some great and solemn shift. For there was a hollow silence under everything. In spite of threats and weaponry, the clanking of the slaves' chains as they began to shuffle down the road, the barked orders of the soldiers left in charge to restore order until fresh overseers could be appointed, Rigley scrambling in panic from the jungle where he'd run when his cart was overtaken . . . in spite of all this commotion, a finished silence underlay all. A pallor one could hear, a very . . . abandonment . . . of life from its center; a center which is the focused and unnoticed core that holds together that which is still pulsing. Why can I still not say this? It was as if the stones and grasses, the buildings and the waving trees; as if everything under the sun lay in an empty vault, calm only because life itself had been extinguished. The last breath of something burning with life's orange flame had been exhaled. Further . . . further . . . losing shape, then visibility . . . spreading out smaller than dust motes toward the cold cold stars."

The prisoner relates that she'd not been compelled to attend the final executions in Bridgetown; nor had she been to town during the months when the heads of Chiva, Quashey, Afebwa, Cudjoe, and their band hung along the town wall on iron spikes. Yes, she knew that six were beheaded, eleven hanged, many others burned at stake. She had remained at the Glebe raising her daughter Betty until New Year's, 1680, when her indenture had at last been up. But at the end, because the child was chattel of Lord Cleypole for life (the father having been an African), the Irishwoman had not wished to leave. Had pleaded to stay, a paid servant on the place, to remain with her daughter.

Permission had been refused. Her own record, as well as the record of the Irish as troublemakers in general, had gone against her, in spite of the fact that she knew sewing and harness making as well as sugarhouse and fieldwork. She was ejected twice from hiding places in the woods nearby. Flogged the second time she was captured, though only eight stripes, then driven from the parish by two redshanked militia with gleaming bayonets.

She became a huckster in the parish of St George. "And," she tells Coote defiantly, "I began my trade with three clay pots of rum, stolen by the slaves of Glebe, for which I smuggled them a wild piglet. The piglet was for a ceremony of Bantu bondsfolk from a land where I hear tell there are elephants and tigers; these folk eat bacon, while Quashey and the umma sort of folk do not. Perhaps you know that wild pig runs as freely through the hills here as it does on Ben Bulben. The Portuguese it was who brought the hogs, before the British came. But something that they saw here, felt here, when the last people of the middens were still packing their canoes and rowing off, made them sail away, never to return. The Portuguese were in a hurry. They did not collect their swine. At any rate, I kept one pot of poteen for myself. I drank it for the pain, you see, at night when the market was over and the hell of loneliness tormented me."

"Which slaves would those be, biddy? The Bantu thieves? Name them!" Coote commands, pulling a new page toward himself.

"Ah, gone and buried now. So soon gone and buried. Disremembered. I made mats too, and once I got some coin to clink together in my pocket, I began to be the middle-wench. Cheating everybody, you might say. Or helping everybody, from the other point of view."

"Where was your domicile?"

"I who had been put out upon the ground was familiar with the ground, sir. I could post some poles and spread mat walls and a brush floor in a few hours, wherever I needed to be for the trade. I made my food, I took my drink, I early got hold of a dagger which I strapped to my waist, as those who tried to rob a drunken harpy in her stupor soon found out. I shifted here and there . . ."

Coote rubs his head, impatient, then demands cool water from Lucy, who stands behind him still. "What I want to know is how came you from St John's to St George's, then from there to St Lucy's Parish, where you were apprehended by the troops."

"I wandered everywhere," she tells. "Awake, I crossed this island with my feet. But in a sort of dreaming, I also rambled back to Ireland. Or Montserrat. Then it might be Guinea, and I was in the place where he had come from. Quashey. Except that darling Mama Chiva was there with him. And little Ben. Afebwa too. I would come upon them in a pleasant village, going about their chores, my son walking at his father's heel or tugging at his elbow to show him aught. There were many huts, like up on Slave Hill, and the people spoke a foreign tongue; but when I came among them I was welcome. Not like at a reunion, mind, but like a person who has never been away and whose welcome is taken for granted. I mean that no one made a fuss of me, nor did my husband speak my name or greet me: but the friendliness that sparked within his eyes when he gazed in peace on me before returning to his task! I was loath to leave this family: to spread a mat, unroll my wares, begin the oily bartering of goods.

"Yes, I lived everywhere. In this world, and in a better world, and in the world where their second souls have gone. Happy. Happy were they, including that brave and humble queen Afebwa, who now indeed must watch my darling Ben until I join him once again. If only I can find the canoe they left for me . . .

"And in the marketplace, where I earned what kept me crawling around in this flesh, I heard many things. We are a great gaggle of races at the market, sir. All those who'd signed on from the European islands for seven years, with promise of free land at the end of it—there has been no land for them. But you'd know that. Though some say there's still land being passed to and fro among the wily: enough to make hearts quicken and keep false hopes, like paper notes, in circulation . . . And so the voluntary indentured, freed, found themselves homeless: selling fish, selling stolen forks and blue ribands and filched medicaments to keep their bellies full.

"Then there were others, like myself here, who had not enlisted, but were stolen away, to be put out into destitution. Refused paid service, left to shift or starve in our mock freedom. Many other market folk, however, were the children of those lonely-hearted planters and merchants of Bridgetown: those who had made by-blow increase with African girls—girls of beauty, girls of grace, girls you can feel a kind of royalty rising from, sir, like our Lucy there. These—the largest clan at market—were freed mixed-blooded blacks, or mixed-blooded whites. Many of these see themselves the true heirs of this island. And everyone knew who I was—that I belonged to Quashey's clan here in Barbados. So they reckoned there was a place for me too at that inheritance. So they said."

"Who? Give me names," he almost entreats.

"Arra, how would I know, an old sot like myself, wandering from marketplace to marketplace and sleeping under bushes? It was the story, not the teller, that concerned me. Then, about two years ago, among this polyglot of races, I began to hear tales of the rising of '75. They were talking about things I had not seen: things I'd cowered in a shed with my girl Betty to keep from crediting. They spoke of fires, spread by the after-winds of a hurricane; of angry spirits rising up; of cattle and horses let loose from barns, eyes rolling yellow in the glint of flame as they ran free. They spoke about a slave girl, Phoebe, who ran through the forest with an arsenal tucked beneath her petticoat, and how her panting can still be heard in the woods between the capital and Brighton plantation, as she runs, runs, runs, relaying us to freedom. These murmured rumors stirred my soul to put down the rum jar and take out for the crossroads, looking— well, they spoke, sir, of places up the country by the coast where even in broad daylight there appeared the leader . . .

"Some said they saw him, tattooed bracelets on his arms as he plunged from forest into water, or from strand to bush. But others saw nothing. The thing was, they all heard, sir. They heard a sort of hum or buzzing, but in patches like, so no tune could be discerned. It was not a clear song, not even notes to cobble together. But it was Quashey's, of that I am certain. His eyes and thoughts are loose still, or loose again, still on the Jihad for freedom. His body's bones were thrown in a zigzag heap after they stuck his head upon a spike. But his spirit—can you imagine it, how one morning with the sun it lifted like humble steam from the deserted corpus, ascending, rising up for freedom?"

Coote speaks, his tone inflexible as metal: "Woman. Will you tell me once and for all how and why you came to transport weapons for the traitors we have hanged?"

"I will," says she, simply. Coote finds his writing hand begin to shake.

"A year ago I received word at the market that wee Betty had been sold away to a ship's captain, trading in tobacco. Like my Máire, Betty was taken to be reared for some officer's concubine. Things are heating up, sir, is what I hear. All throughout the colonies, they say, there are objections on the part of bondspeople of every sort. The more objections, the more officers required, is what they say. The more officers away from their powdered wives and pampered children, the more of our own lively young they look for to wind in satin and lay on beds under damask canopies, where spiders nest all winter long, and birds fly through the open casements to eat them up come summer. My husband's last words to me told me how to do my part. 'Heaven lies under a mother's feet,' he said.

"Aye, I know 'twill be long after my own Betty's teeth have fallen from growing her own young—for that's the fate of women, sir—before enough objections will rise up to make a wall of sound. Still. The more I sat at the market among those whisperings and whimpers, jokes and taunts, complaints and blame, hatred and scandal, apparitions and histories and plans, the more I weaned myself off of the rum. Because I began to hear patterns—no, a patchwork—not of meaning so much as surges of feelings, callings, desires, that make up our lives. Patchwork patterns of a freedom I, and perhaps you, have never known."

"What are you on about?" Coote sputters sternly.

"Freedom to and freedom from, sir. Freedom from being another person's thing to gain the sour rations of survival, rather than rising up to our full statures and filling them, every inch, scab, gland, and hair. This is the freedom Quashey and them died living, in his Jihad." Coote sees the sweat run down her skinny neck: she raves. "Bishop's in thrall to Archbishop, Duke to his King . . ."

He averts his eyes. She is very ill. Her mind is rambling the darkest tunnels where the human mind ought never go.

"Biddy . . . madam . . . this is not necessary . . ."

But she continues, panting.

"I wandered and wandered, listening with younger ears, as if I had the ears of Máire and of Betty, my living daughters, who in a better time would have shared hearth and understanding with their Mam. I listened to the sweat of people who from pot gang to field accident to a cold pallet were valued slightly above beasts only because they could hold the instruments of harvest between their fingers and obey complex instructions, while beasts could not. I saw people lulled, like myself, into sullen confusion by a few jars of rum, a bright bit of clothing, a promise not to sell their best-loved kinfolk away. And I saw people who'd been refused all of these, as punishment."

"Who? Who did you carry the guns for?" A curl of warm wind blows the stink of her toward him. He is shouting.

In a bell-like voice she answers, "Paudi Iasc."

"You idiot!" he grates. "Stop your rambling and make some sense. I don't want the name of some redshank clapped into the Arlington stocks thirty years ago! Tell me who you carried those bloody guns from and to!"

A definite pride rings from her voice. "I have told you. 'Twas Paudi Iasc himself. Returning that silky morning in his log boat, the Maroon told the one he called Bat Fish about the wife of Quaco, a woman who had his same 'fish-colored' hair. And one day, even before the leaders of the Jihad were executed, a message came to me. From the headlands of St Lucy, the parish across the waters to Montserrat—to Bridgetown, where they were taken from me, I carried what arms and maps I could. First a black man was my connection, then an old granny; but the last sir, was one like yourself."

"English!"

"No, sir, or yes, but when I say like yourself, I mean a

gentleman, sir. The sort you'd think would be happy with the way Barbados is run as is. But who can say? There are those here who are greedy, sir. Then again there are those born with the spleen of conscience and a heart for brotherhood, no matter what their class. The Quakers up in St Lucy are like that. I met some. They seem to stand fair and tall, though they could stand like silk-swathed puppets. Others do . . . In the end, sir, I think there are two kinds of folk. People who look up, wanting to see themselves in their high-placed betters; and people who find the best of themselves upon the midden of the humble poor."

There's a pause; she is seeking something through scarves of fever.

"If you've the strength to philosophize, biddy, you've the strength to tell me: Where can we find Paudi Iasc? Tell me, and I swear it shall go easier with you . . ."

"Freedom from. And freedom to follow the cold milling stars in new directions, or to lose the self in the red moon of the hearth, a child's life burning like a small safe flame in the next room . . ."

A knock sounds tentatively upon the outer door. Then another. "Lucy. Answer that," says Peter Coote.

She complies. She returns, leading the wiry Scots lad the Governor sent those several weeks ago with a parchment inviting Peter Coote to become his man at Speightstown Gaol. The door, held open to admit the youth, admits as well the purpled weal of evening. On the freshening breeze comes a faint sound like small fine bones, clacking together, as if chimes were hanging in a tree in the fruit garden.

Eyes on the ground, the lad calls loudly, "Sir. The Gov'nor has sent me."

Coote holds forth his hand expectantly, but there is no scroll.

"His Excellency's spoken with the widow, sir. Them shirts ye ordered. They been paid for by the Gov'nor. You need only fetch them first thing in the morning . . ."

Another fragile gust of sound, as if strung shells were blowing backward, inhaled into one another. "Another way," the prisoner mumbles, "to see it is that they're all our ancestors. Quashey had his own, and I have mine, you with your family crest and this lad from the crofts, those who piled up the midden on the St John's River—of course everybody comes from his own clan. But in some other way, all the ancestors are ours, and we are theirs—they pick us out and call on us. Yes, if you asked me why I carried pistols in with my papayas, 'tis because Afebwa is as much my ancestor as any Daley. And I have come to know that I too will become everyone's ancestor. So I must choose the right road for the progeny I've mothered: I have chosen where to set my mother's-feet. That this inverted paradise, sir, might become someday that garden-heaven, where people are at peace and plenty. Free, to discover their very destinies."

Rising, Peter Coote says, "Thank His Excellence for me," and searches for a small coin.

But in his rote and piping voice the young man goes on, "You are to come for tea upriver at the mansion once you've got the shirts, says the Gov'nor, sir. After you have disposed of the old project. There is a new matter for you to start upon, says he. That is all, sir." The lad ducks back through the door into the dusk. Bare feet slap down the road. The tinkling has stopped.

"Lucy, get the prisoner out of here. Make her a posset, get her an extra covering. The night is cool, and in her fever she has lost her senses. But I . . . I am done with her."

In the garden the stiff young fruit trees spread their blanket of lacy shadow. Shutting the door after the messenger sucks the last mote of light from the office. "Send Daniel. I need a lamp," says the Apothecary. When one comes he will take down the journal where his mercantile hypothesis rests, and write the confused and disillusioned computations this investigation has led him to. Eventually he will grow tangled, melancholy, frustrated. He will never consider changing the hypothesis.

WALTER MACKEN

"THE PASSING OF THE BLACK SWAN" from
CITY OF THE TRIBES

I T WAS LATE afternoon when she started for home.

The sea was ruffled, and heaved like a sleeping giant under green blankets.

There was just sufficient wind to fill the old brown sail. It caught the sail and billowed it, and the black boat sidled over the waves, gently, like her namesake. Her black breasts were gently rounded, like the bows of the Viking boats of long ago on which she was modelled.

She was nearly a hundred years of age.

From a distance she looked just the same as all the other black puckauns which sailed the bay after the elusive fish, and even when you came nearer to her, she belied her age. She sailed so sweetly, *The Black Swan* did, and she looked stout. It took a keen ear to hear the groaning of her tarred timbers, the odd lurch of the age-ing keel, and the hidden places where the implacable able seawater had found a crack and seeped to destroy. All that.

There were three men manning her at this moment as she headed for home.

Three generations.

The father, his son, and his son, too.

The father was very old.

At the tiller he was, sitting there holding the worn stick in his old hand. A very old hand. The flesh was loose on it, but still firm.

His fingers were gnarled from decades of weather. His legs in the rough blue cloth of his trousers were bent and thin. His body was curved, and he looked small in the blue high-necked jersey and the navy blue reefer jacket. Only the eyes in his head under the black broad-brimmed Connemara hat were still young. They were blue and startlingly clear in his old face, a worn face, a sort of ivory brown from exposure, and looking delicately brown behind the short snow-white beard and moustache and the jutting white eyebrows.

His eyes were wistful and his lips were tight. He avoided meeting the eyes of his son or his son's son.

They were uncomfortable and unconscious of the contrast they presented to the old man, showing in themselves and their dress the slow march of civilisation.

The son was a fine man in his prime, over forty. He leaned his body against the side of the boat, his feet resting on the fish boxes, one strong arm across his chest and the elbow of the other arm resting on it, to hold the bowl of the brown pipe he was smoking. He was dressed just a little differently to his father. The same coloured clothes, but he wore a plain double-breasted mac and the cap on his head was a peaked sailor's cap. But the high-necked jersey swelled on his great chest. He had a big face. The muscles on the sides of his jaws were prominent, and his skin was the colour of teak, and there were weather wrinkles around his eyes. Grey eyes. Very firm.

He was idly watching his son, who was just as idly coiling rope on the forecastle.

Even bending, the young son was promising bigness. You could see that from the swell of his thighs pressing against the cloth of the overalls he wore. Yes, overalls. Of blue cloth, of course.

And over that an ordinary tweed jacket, much the worse for wear, shiny with washed fish scales and tarred ropes, and on his head he wore a plain tweed cap. He had the blue eyes of his grandfather and the shoulders of his father, and he was smoking the butt of a cigarette.

His lips were red and his skin was clear, the down of his teens barely left behind him.

He was uncomfortable, too, and cast a look now and again at the old man at the tiller, a worried look.

And for some time they sailed, no sound within but the swish of the water being pushed aside and the creak from the swinging sail on the blackened mast and the wind in the ropes and the cry of the wheeling seagulls above them, attracted by the glint and smell of the dead and dying fish.

It was a particular evening.

Late August it was, the season of sunsets and hunter's moons. The sky above was clear, and all around a pattern of small clouds girdled the world. Behind them the sun was blazing to death behind the islands, and the clouds were coloured, multi-coloured, and if you had been on the sea ahead of them and looked back you would have seen the boat and the men in it as black silhouettes. Ahead of them, where at the end of the bay the land had shaken itself free of the clinging town, in the east there, the moon was about to poke its way into the twilightened sky. You could just see the tip of the top of it, gigantic. Where the sky wasn't coloured from the sun, it was green, crab-apple green, and green-grass green lower down. The evening star was beginning to glint, too, and the winking light of the lighthouse ahead of them was beginning to, take on significance.

Oh, a very lovely evening indeed, one for contemplation, and wonder, too, at the glories that God could create from a blank canvas. Had things been different, they would have been sunk in contemplation, because most men who go to sea have learned while at sea to talk only the minimum, and not about silly material things. They have to leave that for the land and the pub in the evening with the mumble of men's voices, or the clatter of crockery in their own homes.

But things were not different.

They were all tightened up inside with the things that were unsaid and had to be faced now. Every wave that the boat rode brought them nearer to the end of it, and the decision of it. The two younger men were surprised that the old man hadn't talked sooner. Maybe he wouldn't talk at all, they were thinking That would be good, or it might be worse in a way, because concealed suffering only festers. So, although outwardly calm enough, the stomach muscles of the three of them were very tight.

And then the old man spoke, just as they were coming up on the small island where the lighthouse was built. The sun was gone at last, and their faces were in shadow, unlighted as yet by the climbing moon. He spoke then because perhaps he wanted them not to be able to look at his face and see the emotions working on his countenance. It is a fallacy that helps all of us, believing that darkness can conceal emotions.

"I remember," said the old man, "the first day I ever went out in her, so I do." He had to clear his throat then, to get a frog of rust out of it. They waited tensely for him. "Oh, a long time ago, maybe over sixty years ago, I was very small then, and I remember my father, and he putting the long line into my hand, and the drag of the lead was almost too much for me. I could feel the bite of the twine in my palm. But I held it, so I did, and when I felt the twitch at the end of it, I hauled, hand over hand, and I will never forget, ever, the sight of the green mackerel there on the water. I had caught him, be meself, and I thought then that there was not a greater man than me in the length and breadth of Ireland!"

They listened as he paused, and for a moment they thought, too, of the times they had gone and first felt the bite of a fish-loaded line.

"I loved her then," the old man went on. "You can love a boat more than you can love a woman or your own child. As true as God is there, you can. You can love a boat more than you can anything else in the world after God. People will tell you that a boat is only seasoned timber fashioned by the hands of man and ballasted by the even limestone blocks." He slithered his boot over the blocks now. "But that's not so. If ever anything living had a soul, it is a boat. It was me called her *The Black Swan*, from the sight of them in the river, the white ones, sailing sweetly and without seeming to put any effort into it. She was the *The Black Swan* to me, and we in Ireland know that a swan is a precious thing, that inside the white feathers there is a human shape; every one of us knows that. You would no more kill a swan than you would kill your own mother. Well, she to me is like that, too."

His voice ceased and they could hear the lapping waves.

"She often talked to me. Often when a great sorrow would be on me, when my father died and I was young and I had so many to provide for, when I took her out to sea then for the first time on my own. She talked to me then. She took me to the right places where the fish would be that meant so much to me. As sure as God is in heaven, she did! I wanted in my foolishness to go places other than where my father had gone, thinking like all young people that I knew better than he, but when my hand would turn the tiller to go in my direction, she would go the other way. This is as true as the tiller is in my hand now. I cursed her, too. I hammered at her sides with my hand and my nailed boots, but she wouldn't go. I gave in to her in the end and followed her. That day I took more fish than I had ever done before. You know that, even though you are young, that she would know better than myself. Even though you don't like her now and you are about to kill her, you know that what I say is true."

The son stirred, and took the pipe from his mouth.

"Father," he said, "that's wrong. We don't want to do that. But she is like all other things. She gets old. She has lived longer than a man even. And times are changing. There are different ways. We must move. We have to have an engine. You know she wouldn't take an engine on her now. Listen, listen, can't you! You can listen if you want and you can hear the groaning of her keel."

"She is beyond repair," said the son's son, flatly but kindly.

The old man swallowed his futile anger.

"If you tried to put an engine on her tail," he said, "I would take an axe to her myself and chop her into a million pieces. By Holy God, I would!"

The son shrugged and put the pipe into his mouth again. His own son turned away. It is useless, they told one another, useless to argue with him.

"Why can't you let me have her?" the old man asked pleadingly. "I can run her. I know every twist and turn of her, ever caulk and baulk of her. She would answer to me, I tell you. I would just tell her and she would go where I wanted her to. Can't you see that? When your mother died and the light went out of the sun, I went down to the quay and I went away in her, far far away, and we were alone and she talked to me, and even then it was deep winter and the sea was very cross, but I was alone with her and I came back again, and then my heart wasn't as sore as before I left. She has been a wife to me when my wife died and a father to me when my father died. If I didn't have her those times, I would have died like them, and if you take her away from me now I will die, too. As true as God, I will. What else have I left in life but her?"

"You are silly now," said the son gruffly. "You are speaking like a character in a fairy tale. We cannot run two boats. We cannot afford to run two boats, and you can't handle her alone!"

"But why not, why not, why not?" asked the old man.

"Because," said the son, "you are an old man. You won't admit it. You are nearly eighty. The sea is no place for you. Not any more. You see yourself all the time through the wrong eyes. You are looking at yourself as you were one time, not as you are now. You see yourself still as a tall man, powerful and big chested, but you are not, and that's the truth of it. For your own good and to save the worry that's on us thinking about you, can't you see that you are an old man? That you can't handle a heavy old boat like this alone, not any longer? I don't wish to be brutal, but I must tell you out clear like this, to try and make you understand."

There was a stricken look on the face of the old man.

The son's son spoke then, too, kindly, his voice deep like his father's, but not as strong.

"It's because we like you, Grandfather," he said. "It is no ease to us to have you out here in the cold sea with us. We are too fond of you, so we are. We like you to be waiting on the pier for us when we come home in the evening. When we are out in the cold and the wind and the rain, it is very peaceful to realise that you are at home near a fire, warm and smoking your pipe over the ashes. We want you to live with us for a long time. We don't want to have your death on our minds."

There was a long silence, as they looked at him. Both of them felt that what they had said was totally inadequate, that they hadn't pierced his thinking at all. Because they did love him and they were proud of him. He was the King of the Claddagh, and all men respected him for his goodness and the kindness of him, and for the deeds he had done in the past, and for his great honesty. He was a model on which other fishermen tried to fashion their own sons. That was true. They knew it, and they knew it was a great thing to be his son and his grandson, because all men became respectful when they heard that you belonged to him, but it was so hard for them to explain what they felt.

The old man was going to speak. They awaited his speech anxiously, and then he dropped his head on his chest, so they sighed and turned away.

This is the end then, the old man thought. The end of *The Black Swan* and the end of me, too. He knew that they were doing what they thought would be for his good. He knew what he wanted, too, but he couldn't come straight out and tell them there. In the first place, he would find it hard to put into words, and in the second place, he was misty about it himself. He just had a dim picture of himself and *The Black Swan*, just the two of them, sailing sedately over the water. It never struck him that it would be difficult for him to hoist the weight of the brown sail or to hold the heavy boat in heavy seas. He didn't want to think of that. All he wanted to think about was the two of them alone, on the sea. If the rough came and proved too much for them, two ancients like them, then what did that matter? They would go under the waves, and the water would close over their heads. He would prefer that.

That was the trouble.

He couldn't say to them, "I want to die out there, on a rough black night with the waves vicious." He couldn't say, "I do not want to stay at home warm and smoke my pipe over the ashes. I do not want to go home and wither and rot away to old death under your kind eyes and the eyes of your wife and children. All is tranquil and peaceful, but that is not what I want at all. I want violence and fight even at the end."

He wanted to say to them, "Wouldn't it be far kinder to shoot me, instead of keeping me warm at home and bringing me home a pint of porter in a jug because you thought the walk too much for me? What am I to do all day, while I am drooling over the ashes smoking my pipe? Give me *The Black Swan* and the sea if you want me to live for you. Not the other, not the smothering kindness of your house and the weary waiting, sitting on the capstan at the pier waiting for you to come home again!"

All this, he thought vaguely. How can you tell it to them? How can any man fight against the awfulness of well-meaning kindness?

The boat veered towards the gaping mouth of the docks and turned up where the river and the sea became one. His hand unconsciously guided her in, skilfully avoiding the flow of the river, feeling the rising tide on her tail and taking her across in a sweep towards the fishing boat pier, hearing for the last time the musical creak as the sons lowered the sail, the blocks sighing mournfully.

The moon was shining strongly now, and all over the mouth of the river away from the race, the white swans, hundreds of them, were sleeping with their long necks tucked under their wings.

The boat scraped against the granite wall. The young man leaped for the steps, raced up them with the rope in his hand and tied it swiftly to the stone bollard nestling above in the green grass. The boat shuddered a little and then lay placidly.

The old man sat there, listening to the low, seemingly disembodied voices of the men above questioning them about their fishing fortunes, and he sat there as his son and grandson returned and took the boxes of fish from the belly of the boat, and he sat there as, with the help of the others, they started to strip her.

They took the sails from her, and they took the mast from her, and they broke off her forecastle with their axes, and with crowbars they levered off the iron braces and cleats of her, and they took the tiller shaft from his hand, and they raised the big wooden rudder from the water, and then with their crowbars they took the ballast rocks, so neatly laid, and they tore them from her womb, so that shortly she was riding the water, high and unrecognisable, a hulk of a thing, with the exposed water gurgling inside her, water that was seeping through her wounds.

So quickly it was all done.

The side of the pier was piled high with her guts.

They did it in silence now, too, as if the pain the boat was suffering was being transmitted to them from the slouching despondent little figure of the hunched old man at the back of her.

They consulted then, quietly, and they tied a rope to her bow and connected that to the stern of a heavy rowing boat, and they slowly pulled her over to where the earth rose from the sea in an incline. An old black shed there and rails and a rusty capstan. They lowered the trolley, and they fixed the wheels under her, and they pulled her from the water with little effort.

After that they lifted the old man out of her, gently, and left him standing while they heaved her from the trolley and left her lying on her side, forlorn, useless, on the coarse sea grass.

The son put his big hand on the old man's shoulder.

"Come on home now, father," he said.

"You could do with something warm inside you, I bet," said the son's son on the other side of him.

"I'll be up in a while," said the old man. "I'll be up in a whileen after ye."

They looked at one another worriedly.

"Don't be too long," said the son.

"No," said the old man, "I won't be too long."

They left him then.

When the crunch of their boots on the ground ceased, there was no other sound except the gentle hiss of water escaping from her, that and the muted sound of traffic on the town streets away in the distance and the scream of a mother calling a recalcitrant child home to bed.

The old man stood a while dazed, looking at *The Black Swan*, who had been so lovely. And look at her now! He went closer to her and rubbed his hand along the part where the seaweed and small barnacles and winkles clung to her under the waterline, such a contrast to her body above where the heavy tar gleamed and shone in the light of the moon. He picked at her side with the nail of his finger and the soft rotting wood came away in his hand.

Aye, she was old all right, and withered like himself, but now she was dead and he was alive.

"What have they done to you at all, my lovely black darling?" he asked as he walked around her, resting his white beard on his arms as he looked into her gaping interior. Blackness and rusty nails and nothing, and he saw her as she had been, and as he had been, and a terrible bleakness came over his heart, and he sat down on the wet ground close beside her, his shoulder hugging her rounded breast, and his head sank on his arms then resting on his knees, and the senile tears poured from his eyes.

"Oh God, oh God, oh God," he said then to the night.

The moon shone on them.

The shadows merged them as if they were one and as if in answer to his weeping, the water came from her sides, too, and poured down them. Was it water?

Or was it tears?

The moon climbed high, ageless, and the white swans slept with their long necks under their wings.

JOHN MAHER

THE LUCK PENNY

IT WAS A morning on which a war might have started. The storm the previous night had all but stripped the lime trees, and the ground around the rectory was water-logged. There wasn't a sound of chick or child out on Sackville Square as the Reverend John Drew dragged open the flaking wooden shutters. He suddenly found himself wishing the three women were back again: Judith lolling about on the armchair, her nose buried in a book; Theodora tricking with some embroidery she had been set in Miss Markham's; and Eliza, in the background, calling out commands to Bridget Doheny in the scullery. But now he was alone with himself, with no warm words to soften the uneasy moments between dawn and dusk. And Westmacott's sojourn in Aghadoe had been deferred. His eye fell on the letter lying on the oak escritoire under the bedroom window.

> Lanscombe Terrace
> September 15 1849

My Dear John,

I hope this letter finds yourself, Eliza and the girls in good fettle. It is with great chagrin that I have to tell you that I will be unable now to keep our assignation over the next two weeks.

He made his way down the creaking stairs. In the parlour, he surveyed the cold grate, the books strewn here and there and the half-eaten platter of pork on the table. He watched Bianconi swarm about the room, searching for a warm spot to settle down. It might be possible to do an hour's work before lighting the fire. Perhaps go over the syllable charts and the signs again. He could wrap his legs in Judith's fluffy mauve eiderdown and sit in at the drawing room table. But then that queer sort of sadness, a millstone pulling his soul down to the sinful depths of despond, overwhelmed him again. He stooped to pick up one of the copies of the Darius inscription, from Persepolis.

The legend, written in Babylonian over a palace portal, had sat out the centuries, waiting for the attentions of a woebegone, rheumatic cleric in a small damp town in the Queen's County. In a fit of pique, he suddenly screwed up the copy of the inscription and threw it into the empty grate. No, it wouldn't take much at all. Just a little spark from the box of matches Bridget Doheny had left on the mantelpiece. Then the vain words of a vain king would be sent roaring up the chimney of a vain cleric.

In the gloom of the early morning, it took John Drew a moment to make out the little silver locket lying beside the matches, and the silver chain dangling over the edge of the cold marble.

"She's forgotten the blessed thing . . ."

At first he stayed his hand from the locket, afraid, perhaps, to invoke an even greater evil by touching the thing. Then, he slowly reached out for the locket that contained the little wisp of blond hair. He fancied, for an idle moment, that the little silver locket was still warm from his wife's breast, but the cold metal case rebuffed his fingers, like the books and the script tables had already done. Slowly and deliberately, he set the little silver locket back down on the cold mantelpiece. He stood there awhile, lost between the locket and the scripts on the table—between the heart and the head—with the past washing over him, like the autumn rains that sluiced the choking dust down Sackville Square. He scarcely noticed Bianconi rubbing against his leg, and he certainly didn't hear the child's bony hand knocking on the bare wood of the scullery door at all.

"Dr Drew! Are you in there at all?"

John Drew crossed stiffly into the scullery. It must be one of Bridget Doheny's, come with the kindling. Despite the misunderstanding, Bridget Doheny wouldn't see him freeze. He opened the scullery door to the grubby, wizened little face of a ten-year-old boy.

"I brang the kippeens for you, Mr Drew."

"Oh, yes . . . the kindling . . . fine . . ."

"Do you want them left again the coachhouse wall?"

"Yes . . . by the coachhouse wall . . . that will be fine."

He watched absently as the boy dragged the bundles of damp faggots from the little handcart. How many were in the Doheny house? Eight or nine. Two dead during the height of the hunger, from fever, or so Mrs Tours had told Eliza. Not that he credited anything the Tours woman said. And Eliza was getting far too fond of visiting that quarter, in the dark of night: an unseemly thing for the wife of a minister of the cloth to be doing.

Bridget Doheny's boy smiled a gap-toothed smile at John Drew as they sauntered into the house. While the child set to clearing out the grate and arranging the sticks into a pyramid, John Drew cut a large wedge of bread and covered it in fresh salted butter: bread that Judith Drew had taken from the oven the day before; fresh, salted butter that Bridget Doheny had churned before her little temper tantrum out in the coachhouse. He set the wooden tray on the table and nodded to the boy. Easy seen that Eliza Drew wasn't at home. It would be wash your hands in the yard barrel and eat standing up in the scullery, boy. And maybe she was right at that. Too much familiarity complicated things with them. Hadn't he learned that to his cost the time of the business with one Mr Fox Keegan, all those years ago? He needed to know which way things stood with Bridget Doheny, though. Was the blessed woman going to reappear at all before Eliza came home? What a calamity! Hardly had Eliza and the girls left and Westmacott's letter arrived when Bridget Doheny turned on him and walked out. Misery comes in threes. The boy looked over the heel of bread at John Drew.

"What about your mother, then? What about Bridget?"

"I know nothing, Mr Drew. As God is me witness."

"Didn't she give you any message, then?"

John Drew cut another hunk of bread for the boy and larded it well with butter.

"I only heard her say to me father that she was rale put out."

"Is that so, now . . . rale put out . . ."

"Over them yokes she seen, above in the coachhouse . . . the ould cows' heads and them other yokes . . ."

John Drew thought back to the scene. Eliza had scarcely left with the girls in Willie Hill's pony-and-trap when he heard the clamour of Bridget Doheny in the scullery. Her face was all flustered, as though she had seen a ghost. He couldn't get any good of her at first. Finally, he had followed her out to the coachhouse, where the jaunting car was heeled up in the corner. But she wouldn't cross into the building.

"I'm not going in with them yokes in there, so I'm not!"

"What yokes, Bridget?"

"Them cows' heads and yokes. If I had've known they were there all the time, I would have went long ago, so I would."

And nothing would do her but to burst into tears, throw off her apron and storm out down Sackville Square. Such a scandal! It was all around the town now, of course. The world and his wife would know well that the matter wouldn't be resolved until Eliza Drew returned from London with Theodora. Even then, Mrs Tours would probably have to be prevailed upon to mediate.

There was no point in harrying the boy further, he realised, especially now that he had wolfed down the last of the bread and a large cut of cheese to boot. So John Drew showed him to the door kindly and then went back inside to stare into the fire. When the fire had found itself, he set a couple of damp culm balls on it and stood back to watch the coal smoke rise up the chimney. The house would still be cold without the women, no matter how many fires burned in it. Still, anyone strolling across Sackville Square that morning or coming out of the gates of Terry's brewery would at least know that, despite everything, the Reverend John Drew, among the clutter of rubbings and drawings and script tables that littered the drawing room, had made a fire. As he stood gazing into the flames, he recalled the precise moment, five or six years before, out in the coachhouse, when he had correctly read one of the first cuneatic words on a brick brought back from Mesopotamia.

Nabu-ku-du-ur-ri-usur

Syllables. Not letters. That was the key to it, of course. To think in syllables and, when the strange new Babylonian script demanded it, in ideographs. In ideawords.

The old blackness started sweeping over him then. He saw, in his mind's eye, dry piles of manuscripts with rough cuneiform scripts etched into them, blazing in the hearth. It would be a liberation from the past of ancient tyrants in the desert wastes of Persepolis. A liberation from the hours and days and years of study in dim light, away from the savants of London, in the manse in Aghadoe. But then the moment passed as suddenly as it had come. He knew it would come again, over the coming days though, now that there was no breakwater between him and despair. Now that the women were gone. But he must not give into despair. Must not commit the sin of Job. So John Drew, taking a deep breath, pulled his black frieze coat about him and made purposefully for the coachhouse in the pale midday light to read the brick again.

II: BY STEAM TRAIN TO DUBLIN

On the day before the storm, Willie Hill's man appeared with a bockety old trap in Sackville Square to bring Eliza and Theodora to the train and to bring Judith back out to Willie and Violet Hill's for the duration, so that John Drew and his visitor, Mr Westmacott, would have the peace and quiet necessary to carry on their work. It was all a bit of a squash in the trap with all the baggage. At the bottom of the square, a rust-coloured dray horse snorted in the cold September air as it drew a wagon laden with beer barrels past the gates of Terry's brewery. Theodora lisped the slogan on the side of the wagon to herself.

> *Guinness stout is good, no doubt*
> *In barrel or in bottle*
> *But Terry's Ale will never fail*
> *To quench the thirsty throttle.*

Eliza spotted Waxy Daly, cobbler and gossip, standing talking to a red-faced man in a topcoat near the brewery bridge. Both men nodded as the driver flicked the reins, goading the horse on up the hill past the squat Catholic church. Eliza Drew pulled Theodora close to her, reminding her to keep the new cambric shawl pulled tight, because even in autumn a chill could knock you down, and quinsy was always lurking around the corner at the change of the seasons. Judith, dreamy-eyed and not yet awake, looked out vacantly on the street. They had all dressed by rushlight as John Drew carried their effects out to the gates and their eyes were still stained with sleepiness. Eliza and Theodora could catch up on their sleep on the train to Dublin, but the sleepiness in Judith Drew's eyes was something else. When that dreaming came into her eldest daughter's eyes, it always annoyed Eliza. She felt like shaking her and dragging her back to the world around her. Still, Dr Beatty's School for Young Ladies "especially suited to clergymen's daughters" at

Mount Merrion, in Dublin, would soon bring her back to real life. The summer of idling and losing herself in unsuitable books would be over. There would be regularity, early mornings, a strict diet and a rod of iron for mind and morals. It would stand to Judith in later life, as her own boarding school, in Chiswick, had stood to Eliza.

As they turned down the hill, past the graveyard, Eliza Drew once more ran over all the arrangements she had made. She had set out a special routine for Bridget Doheny, with the "big cleaning days" and the "little cleaning days", marked with an X and a Y respectively, on a sheet of writing paper fixed to the pantry door. The house was to be kept in apple-pie order until she returned with Theodora, ten days later. When Mr Westmacott arrived over from London, Bridget was to take account of any particular needs the English scholar might have and make appropriate arrangements. On no account were the men to be bothered with unnecessary interruptions during the two weeks. Aside from his church duties, John Drew should be free to resume the previous summer's British Museum work with Mr Westmacott. A freshly painted jaunting car with a hunched-up figure at the reins approached them at a crook in the road. Eliza glanced across and caught the eye of Billy White, the postman, who was coming back from meeting the train. A burlap sack lay at his feet. Tidings of good and bad news.

"Are we in time, Mr White?"

"You needn't worry yourself at all, ma'am. Them trains does always be late out . . . on account of filling the boilers up."

"I see."

When they reached the mill, halfway between Aghadoe and the train station, Eliza Drew realised that, in her rush to have the girls ready, she had left her locket in the parlour. All of a sudden, despite her best efforts to staunch the flow of her thoughts, the Belfast days were in her mind again. The cold, damp house at Castle Place and the Union where John Drew had ministered to the poor, flooding into the town from the villages of Ulster, looking for work and sustenance. And the terrible disaster the Almighty had seen fit to visit on herself and her husband, the worst thing that could befall any woman or any man. A thing she would not name. They had placed an advertisement on the heels of the terrible visitation:

Clergyman will exchange living in Belfast for similar in parish in Wicklow or Wexford or similar.

Their flight, like that of the Jews of Egypt, had been a hasty one, with Theodora just a child and Judith fretting for the loss of friends. Of course, it mightn't have been so bad if they had been fleeing to Wicklow or Wexford, though England was what she herself had wanted. But John Drew had been offered only Aghadoe in the Queen's County, and since her objective was to get the girls out of Belfast as quickly as possible, they had accepted Aghadoe. The possibility of a post in the grove of Academe was long gone. John Drew had been considered too High Church for that. So it was Queen's County, where no one could pronounce a "t" or a "th" to save their lives and the winters were wet and just as miserable as Belfast, if that were possible. But at least cholera and typhus had been kept at bay there.

When the trap crossed the railway bridge, it wheeled sharply right for the stone-cut train station at Ballydermot. Eliza called Theodora to settle her bonnet. Conveyances of every make and shape were drawn up to meet the steam train now taking water from the great green water tower. Eliza Drew spotted a few familiar faces. There was Twinkle Jameson, the wax chandler's daughter, and that English gentleman John Drew said had been sent over from Manchester to sort out some new chemical process in the brewery. She smiled at them vaguely as she helped her daughters down from the trap. They were all standing together on the platform, with Willie Hill's man minding the luggage, when she turned to Judith.

"My locket, Judith . . ."

"Pardon?"

"I've left my locket behind. Tell your father to take care of it until I come home."

And then there was a great fuss and a scene as the girls took it in turns to blame one another for the missing locket. Eliza Drew felt an ache cut through her heart. Then she rallied, hooshing Theodora aboard the trembling train, saying decisively, to no one in particular, "Yes, it will have to wait until I come back."

While the engine got up enough steam to chug out of the station, they waved farewell to Judith on the platform. Eliza reminded her, again, to conduct herself appropriately out at the Hills, and to remember that her return to Dublin and school was imminent. She might also look in on her father, the odd day, to check that everything was in order and that Bridget Doheny was carrying out her orders. The locket must stay where it was. Some things, perhaps, were meant to happen. At least, that was what Mrs Tours, the seamstress, made out. In uneasy moments, Eliza Drew suspected that this sort of talk was only a stone's throw from papish superstition, the sort of hocus pocus that, when she was a child, had always roused her father to wrath at the dinner table. Isaac Cameron's sidelocks would bristle with anger as he stared across the table at Eliza, his eldest daughter.

"Reason, child! We are all creatures of reason or we are nothing!"

But wasn't reason, too, subject to the vagaries of vanity from time to time? Eliza Drew took out the tartan blanket and wrapped it around her daughter's legs, to guard against the chill of early morning.

What with the stopping and starting at this station and the next and the unexplained delays along the way, the journey to Dublin took about four hours, all in all. The only thing she was really worried about, though, was that the boiler would burst and shower them with scalding water. Rumour had it that it wasn't as much the heat of the water as the weakness of the boilermakers' rivets that accounted for the awful accidents you read about in the English papers. Luckily, she had managed to avoid Twinkle Jameson. With the exception of a crusty little woman in black widow's weeds, she and Theodora had no one to trouble them for most of the journey. Mind you, the old lady, when she spoke, was full of all sorts of morbid intelligences. Cholera was worse in Dublin than the papers were letting on, it seemed, and as for London! Eliza recalled the dinner in Gusty and Edith Lamb's, two weeks earlier, when they, along with the Willingtons of the Commons, had been subjected to a tour de force on the phenomenon of the disease, its provenance and remedies. The whole table had guffawed at the notion, proposed by no less a figure than Mrs Willington herself, that the sudden reappearance of the terrible disease from the East could be put down to divine intervention. It was Eliza who had brought Gusty Lamb to book for his pompous guffaw.

"And do you have a better explanation, Mr Lamb?"

"Well, I certainly don't have a worse one, Mrs Drew!"

Gusty Lamb's cheery, red-raw face couldn't hide the annoyance of being upbraided by a mere minister's wife, of course. They had all taken turns, as the sherry cobblers were served, at puzzling the thing out. Each had vented his own thesis. John Drew, a confirmed miasmatist, favoured the notion that clouds of contagion were at the heart of the whole cholera business. This would explain the movement of the disease from Bengal, right across Europe and the Lowlands, to the heart of the Empire. Edith Lamb, who was looking distinctly dowdy of late, felt that electricity might well lie at the root of the matter; galvanism was all very well, but it was still an unknown quantity. Which comment gave rise to the biggest belly laugh of the evening, from Philip Willington.

"Why, next you'll have the steam engine in the dock, Mrs Lamb!"

"Who knows, Mr Willington? Who knows?"

They all agreed, in the heel of the reel, that prudence was the most important thing. In cooking food, in drinking from strange sources and in mixing in unsavoury circumstances. Who could tell but that a simple handshake mightn't lie behind the transference of cholera between people? Even then, as she sat listening to the chatter at the table, Belfast had been at the back of Eliza's mind. But were such thoughts ever anywhere else? Mrs Tours thought not. She had said so in private moments, when Eliza Drew called into the seamstress's little house in Pound Street, on the pretext of dropping by to leave in some mending. The upright wife of a Protestant minister seeking solace in the hob philosophy of a Catholic seamstress! If anyone even suspected. . .

When they finally arrived in Dublin, a cold, raw wind was blowing up the river. Luckily, they managed to find a cab on the instant, and soon they were on the quays, past the Four Courts and the canvas-covered book stalls, heading for the hotel. The peace and stability that the Four Courts betokened was soon over-shadowed by what they saw further on. For Dublin's streets were a hotchpotch of horse manure, beggars and a few decent folk try-ing to clear a path between both. Hadn't they heard of crossing-sweepers at all here? In London, at least some effort was made to keep things clean in the better quarters. But that was the difference between England and Ireland: Anglo-Saxon order was endemic to one and Celtic chaos to the other. As the cab turned up from Eden Quay, she thought of her sister Hetty Arkwright in the order and ease of her cosy house in Gower Street. That same Hetty, in front of the parlour fire, surrounded by her reading circle: Mrs Meredith, Mrs Rawlings and Mrs Collier. Charles Arkwright up in the study, chatting with a business colleague over some new project, or sorting out some problem at his corn factor's premises, down near London Wall. The sound of little Albert Arkwright above in the playroom, reliving the Napoleonic wars with the tin soldiers Eliza and Hetty's brother Walter Cameron had given him for Christmas.

When the cab pulled up sharply at the little hotel on Westland Row—recommended to Eliza by no less a figure than Edith Lamb—Eliza Drew didn't move until the porter had come down the steps to help with their baggage.

"You'll be Mrs Drew?"

"That's right . . . are our rooms ready?"

"Ready and waiting, ma'am!"

In a jiffy, she and Theodora were settled in their rooms. But after they had rested and freshened up, there was still the shopping to be done for London. There would be no time the following day, when they had to be up early for the Kingstown train and the Holyhead steampacket. There were presents for the Arkwrights to be got, a couple of other bits and pieces to be tidied up, and then they could rest, once all the chores had been attended to. But first things first, as Isaac Cameron would have it.

GERRY ADAMS

"A GOOD CONFESSION" from
THE STREET AND OTHER STORIES

THE CONGREGATION SHUFFLED its feet. An old man spluttered noisily into his handkerchief, his body racked by a spasm of coughing. He wiped his nose wearily and returned to his prayers. A small child cried bad-temperedly in its mother's arms. Embarrassed, she released him into the side aisle of the chapel where, shoes clattering on the marble floor, he ran excitedly back and forth. His mother stared intently at the altar and tried to distance herself from her irreverent infant. He never even noticed her indifference; his attention was consumed by the sheer joy of being free, and soon he was trying to cajole another restless child to join him in the aisle. Another wave of coughing wheezed through the adult worshippers. As if encouraged by such solidarity, the old man resumed his catarrhal cacophony.

The priest leaned forward in the pulpit and directed himself and his voice towards his congregation. As he spoke they relaxed as he knew they would. Only the children, absorbed in their innocence, continued as before. Even the old man, by some superhuman effort, managed to control his phlegm.

"My dear brothers and sisters," the priest began. "It is a matter of deep distress and worry to me and I'm sure to you also that there are some Catholics who have so let the eyes of their soul become darkened that they no longer recognise sin as sin."

He paused for a second or so to let his words sink in. He was a young man, not bad looking in an ascetic sort of a way, Mrs McCarthy thought, especially when he was intense about something, as he was now. She was in her usual seat at the side of the church, and as she waited for Fr Burns to continue his sermon, she thought to herself that it was good to have a new young priest in the parish.

Fr Burns cleared his throat and continued.

"I'm talking about the evil presence we have in our midst, and I'm asking you, the God-fearing people of this parish, to join with me in this Eucharist in praying that we loosen from the neck of our society the grip which a few have tightened around it and from which we sometimes despair of ever being freed."

He stopped again momentarily. The congregation was silent: he had their attention. Even the sounds from the children were muted.

"I ask you all to pray with me that eyes that have become blind may be given sight, consciences that have become hardened and closed may be touched by God and opened to the light of His truth and love. I am speaking of course of the men of violence." He paused, leant forward on arched arms, and continued.

"I am speaking of the IRA and its fellow-travellers. This community of ours has suffered much in the past. I know that. I do not doubt but that in the IRA organisation there are those who entered the movement for idealistic reasons. They need to ask themselves now where that idealism has led them. We Catholics need to be quite clear about this."

Fr Burns sensed that he was losing the attention of his flock again. The old man had lost or given up the battle to control his coughing. Others shuffled uneasily in their seats. A child shrieked excitedly at the back of the church. Some like Mrs McCarthy still listened intently, and he resolved to concentrate on them.

"Membership, participation in or cooperation with the IRA and its military operations is most gravely sinful. Now I know that I am a new priest here and some of you may be wondering if I am being political when I say these things. I am not. I am preaching Catholic moral teaching, and I can only say that those who do not listen are cutting themselves off from the community of the Church. They cannot sincerely join with their fellow Catholics who gather at mass and pray in union with the whole Church. Let us all, as we pray together, let us all resolve that we will never cut ourselves off from God in this way and let us pray for those who do."

Fr Burns paused for the last time before concluding.

"In the name of the Father and the Son and the Holy Ghost."

Just after communion and before the end of the mass there was the usual trickling exit of people out of the church. When Fr Burns gave the final blessing the trickle became a flood. Mrs McCarthy stayed in her seat. It was her custom to say a few prayers at Our Lady's altar before going home. She waited for the crowd to clear.

Jinny Blake, a neighbour, stopped on her way up the aisle and leaned confidentially towards her. "Hullo, Mrs McCarthy," she whispered reverently, her tone in keeping with their surroundings.

"Hullo, Jinny. You're looking well, so you are."

"I'm doing grand, thank God. You're looking well yourself. Wasn't that new wee priest just lovely? And he was like lightning, too. It makes a change to get out of twelve o'clock mass so quickly."

"Indeed it does," Mrs McCarthy agreed as she and Jinny whispered their goodbyes.

By now the chapel was empty except for a few older people who stayed behind, like Mrs McCarthy, to say their special prayers or to light blessed candles. Mrs McCarthy left her seat and made her way slowly towards the small side altar. She genuflected awkwardly as she passed the sanctuary. As she did so the new priest came out from the sacristy. He had removed his vestments, and dressed in his dark suit, he looked slighter than she had imagined him to be when he had been saying mass.

"Hullo," he greeted her.

"Hullo, Father, welcome to St Jude's."

His boyish smile made her use of the term "Father" seem incongruous.

"Thank you," he said.

"By the way, Father. . ."

The words were out of her in a rush before she knew it.

"I didn't agree with everything you said in your sermon. Surely if you think those people are sinners you should be welcoming them into the Church and not chasing them out of it."

Fr Burns was taken aback. "I was preaching Church teaching," he replied a little sharply.

It was a beautiful morning. He had been very nervous about the sermon, his first in a new parish. He had put a lot of thought into it, and now when it was just over him and his relief had scarcely subsided, he was being challenged by an old woman.

Mrs McCarthy could feel his disappointment and resentment. She had never spoken like this before, especially to a priest. She retreated slightly. "I'm sorry, Father," she said uncomfortably, "I just thought you were a bit hard." She sounded apologetic. Indeed, as she looked at the youth of him she regretted that she had opened her mouth at all.

Fr Burns was blushing slightly as he searched around for a response.

"Don't worry," he said finally, "I'm glad you spoke your mind. But you have to remember I was preaching God's word, and there's no arguing with that."

They walked slowly up the centre aisle towards the main door. Fr Burns was relaxed now. He had one hand on her elbow, and as he spoke he watched her with a faint little smile on his lips.

Despite herself she felt herself growing angry at his presence. Who was this young man almost steering her out of the chapel? She hadn't even been at Our Lady's altar yet.

"We have to choose between our politics and our religion," he was saying.

"That's fair enough, Father, as far as it goes, but I think it's wrong to chase people away from the Church," she began.

"They do that themselves," he interrupted her.

She saw that he still had that little smile. They were almost at the end of the aisle. She stopped sharply, surprising the priest as she did, so that he stopped also and stood awkwardly with his hand still on her elbow.

"I'm sorry, Father, I'm not going out yet."

It was his turn to be flustered, and she noticed with some satisfaction that his smile had disappeared. Before he could recover she continued, "I still think it's wrong to exclude people. Who are any of us to judge anyone, to say who is or who isn't a good Catholic, or a good Christian for that matter? I know them that lick the altar rails and, God forgive me, they wouldn't give you a drink of water if you were dying of the thirst. No, Father, it's not all black and white. You'll learn that before you're much older."

His face reddened at her last remark.

"The Church is quite clear in its teaching on the issue of illegal organisations. Catholics cannot support or be a part of them."

"And Christ never condemned anyone," Mrs McCarthy told him, as intense now as he was.

"Well, you'll have to choose between your politics and your religion. All I can say is if you don't agree with the Church's teaching, then you have no place in this chapel."

It was his parting shot and with it he knew he had bested her. She looked at him for a long minute in silence so that he blushed again, thinking for a moment that she was going to chide him, maternally perhaps, for being cheeky to his elders. But she didn't. Instead she shook her elbow free of his hand and walked slowly away from him out of the chapel. He stood until he had recovered his composure, then he too walked outside. To his relief she was nowhere to be seen.

When Mrs McCarthy returned home her son, Harry, knew something was wrong, and when she told him what had happened he was furious. She had to beg him not to go up to the chapel there and then.

"He said what, Ma? Tell me again!"

She started to recount her story.

"No, not that bit. I'm not concerned about all that. It's the end bit I can't take in. The last thing he said to you. Tell me that again?"

"He said if I didn't agree then I had no place in the chapel," she told him again, almost timidly.

"The ignorant-good-for-nothing wee skitter," Harry fumed, pacing the floor. Mrs McCarthy was sorry she had told him anything. "I'll have to learn to bite my tongue," she told herself. "If I'd said nothing to the priest none of this would have happened." Harry's voice burst in on her thoughts.

"What gets me is that you reared nine of us. That's what gets me! You did your duty as a Catholic mother and that's the thanks you get for it. They've no humility, no sense of humanity. Could he not see that you're an old woman."

"That's nothing to do with it," Mrs McCarthy interrupted him sharply.

"Ma, that's everything to do with it! Can you not see that? If he had been talking to me, I could see the point, but you? All your life you've done your best and he insults you like that! He must have no mother of his own. That's all they're good for: laying down their petty little rules and lifting their collections and insulting the very people. . ."

"Harry, that's enough."

The weariness in her tone stopped him in mid-sentence.

"I've had enough arguing to do me for one day," she said. "You giving off like that is doing me no good. Just forget about it for now. And I don't want you doing anything about it; I'll see Fr Burns again in my own good time. But for now, I'm not going to let it annoy me any more."

But it did. It ate away at her all day, and when she retired to bed it was to spend a restless night with Fr Burns's words turning over again and again in her mind.

Choose between your politics and your religion. Politics and religion. If you don't accept the Church's teachings, you've no place in the chapel. No place in the chapel.

The next day she went to chapel as was her custom, but she didn't go at her usual time, and she was nervous and unsettled within herself all the time, she was there. Even Our Lady couldn't settle her. She was so worried that Fr Burns would arrive and that they would have another row that she couldn't concentrate on her prayers. Eventually it became too much for her and she left by the side door and made her way home again, agitated and in bad form.

The next few days were the same. She made her way to the chapel as usual, but she did so in an almost furtive manner, and the solace that she usually got from her daily prayers and contemplation was lost to her. On the Wednesday she walked despondently to the shops; on her way homewards she bumped into Jinny Blake outside McErlean's Home Bakery.

"Ach, Mrs McCarthy, how'ye doing? You look as if everybody belonging t'ye had just died. What ails ye?"

Mrs McCarthy told her what had happened, glad to get talking to someone who, unlike Harry or Fr Burns, would understand her dilemma. Jinny was a sympathetic listener and she waited attentively until Mrs McCarthy had furnished her with every detail of the encounter with the young priest.

"So that's my tale of woe, Jinny," she concluded eventually, "and I don't know what to do. I'm not as young as I used to be. . ."

"You're not fit for all that annoyance. The cheek of it!" her friend reassured her. "You shouldn't have to put up with the like of that at your age. You seldom hear them giving off about them ones."

Jinny gestured angrily at a passing convoy of British army Land-Rovers.

"They bloody well get off too light, God forgive me and pardon me! Imagine saying that to you, or anyone else for that matter."

Jinny was angry, but whereas Harry's rage had unsettled Mrs McCarthy, Jinny's indignation fortified her, so that by the time they finally parted Mrs McCarthy was resolved to confront Fr Burns and, as Jinny had put it, to "stand up for her rights".

The following afternoon she made her way to the chapel. It was her intention to go from there to the parochial house. She was quite settled in her mind as to what she would say and how she would say it, but first she knelt before the statue of Our Lady. For the first time that week she felt at ease in the chapel. But the sound of footsteps coming down the aisle in her direction unnerved her slightly. She couldn't look around to see who it was, which made her even more anxious that it might be Fr Burns. In her plans the confrontation with him was to be on her terms in the parochial house, not here, on his terms, in the chapel.

"Hullo, Mrs McCarthy, is that you?" With a sigh of relief she recognised Fr Kelly's voice.

"Ah, Father," she exclaimed. "It is indeed. Am I glad to see you!"

Fr Kelly was the parish priest. He was a small, stocky, white-haired man in his late fifties. He and Mrs McCarthy had known each other since he had taken over the parish fifteen years before.

As he stood smiling at her, obviously delighted at her welcome for him, she reproached herself for not coming to see him long before this. As she would tell Jinny later, that just went to show how distracted she was by the whole affair.

"Fr Kelly, I'd love a wee word with you, so I would." She rose slowly from her pew. "If you have the time, that is."

"I've always time for you, my dear."

He helped her to her feet.

"Come on and we'll sit ourselves down over here."

They made their way to a secluded row of seats at the side of the church. Fr Kelly sat quietly as Mrs McCarthy recounted the story of her disagreement with Fr Burns. When she was finished he remained silent for some moments, gazing quizzically over at the altar.

"Give up your politics or give up your religion, Mrs McCarthy? That's the quandary, isn't it?"

He spoke so quietly, for a minute she thought he was talking to himself. Then he straightened up in the seat, gave her a smile and asked, "Are you going to give up your politics?"

"No," she replied a little nervously and then, more resolutely: "No! Not even for the Pope of Rome."

He nodded in smiling assent and continued, "And are you going to give up your religion?"

"No," she responded quickly, a little surprised at his question.

"Not even for the Pope of Rome?" he bantered her.

"No," she smiled, catching his mood.

"Well then, I don't know what you're worrying about. We live in troubled times, and it's not easy for any of us, including priests. We all have to make our own choices. That's why God gives us the power to reason and our own free will. You've heard the Church's teaching and you've made your decision. You're not going to give up your religion nor your politics, and I don't see why you should.

All these other things will pass. And don't bother yourself about seeing Fr Burns. I'll have a wee word with him."

He patted her gently on the back of her hand as he got to his feet.

"Don't be worrying. And don't let anyone put you out of the chapel! It's God's house. Hold on to all your beliefs, Mrs McCarthy, if you're sure that's what you want."

"Thank you, Father." Mrs McCarthy smiled in relief. "God bless you."

"I hope He does," Fr Kelly said, "I hope He does." He turned and walked slowly up the aisle. When he got to the door he turned and looked down the chapel. Mrs McCarthy was back at her favourite seat beside the statue of Our Lady. Apart from her the silent church was empty. Fr Kelly stood reflecting pensively on that. For a moment he was absorbed by the irony of the imagery before him. Then he turned wearily, smiled to himself, and left.

NENAD VELIČKOVIĆ

LODGERS

*Brkić hangs out flags. Fata viam invenient. A hammam for
brainwashing. A book-sized brown bag. A snowstorm rages
and in it Korchagin. Archangels' tracks.*

THE GREATEST LOSERS in this war, after us young people, who
have lost the coming thirty years, are the old people, who
have lost the preceding fifty. That's why Brkić decided to leave the
city. On several occasions he formulated his idea of doing so by
balloon. I shall describe it here in a shortened version.

What stimulated him was the discovery of flags in the cellar.
Piles of flags. Some of them belonged to the museum, and were
intended for public display on holidays. Another pile, consider-
ably larger, was there by chance: Dad had done someone a favour
and kept them safe in his store. A third pile also belonged to the
museum; they were the flags of the Partizan units, which, in the
last war, participated in the action of liberating Sarajevo. Since tri-
colours with five-pointed stars had subsequently gone out of fashion, the bales of bound flags had begun to fill with dust instead of
wind.

Brkić's idea further relied on the Singer sewing machine (the
one Danilo Kiš drew in his novel *Garden, Ashes*), Julio's gas cylin-
ders, and ropes from the Collection of Sarajevo Crafts.

I was present when he asked Sanja whether they had studied maths in her course.

At that moment she was kneeling, pushing the inquisitive Sniffy away with one hand, and with the other brushing the rug, and collecting his freshly shed hairs. The best way of preventing their dispersal throughout the museum was to catch them in flight or just as they landed. Yes, they had studied maths.

Would she be able to calculate something for him?

What?

Could one make a balloon out of flags?

As in everything else, Sanja was thorough. Thanks to her, the problem acquired a definitive mathematical form, in the shape of a bunch of Greek letters pinned to a fractional line. Of the units known to me, the following were mentioned: squared and cubed yards, pounds, seconds, newtons, joules, moles, kelvins . . . The balloon would rise if the air in it were heated. (Pressure and specific density of air.) The balloon would not rise if it were too heavy. (Pressure, gravitation, load weight, canvas, basket . . .) The balloon would rise if it were large enough and hot enough. (Capacity of the ball, energy.) It would not rise if the loss of heat were great. Flags, two hundred flags (surface of the ball), would let air out, but it could be additionally heated. (One cylinder for blowing up the balloon and heating the air, another for topping up and steering the balloon.) All in all, difficult, dangerous, risky, impossible.

Enough for Brkić not to give up.

Mother asked whether there weren't another way?

No. A former Partizan was not about to fill in some Ustasha or Chetnik questionnaires, in order to travel with women and children.

Dad offered to try to sort it without questionnaires.

Did the Director mind about the flags?

No, but it could all look rather suspicious to some people.
Was the Director frightened?
No, but the police . . .
That was Brkić's problem.

In the end Dad gave the flags, and rope, and the sewing machine,
Mother and Sanja took it in turns to sew, Sanja did the smaller
pieces, which Mother then joined together. Julio took it on himself to concoct a burner, Brkić and Davor would see what could be
used to improvise a basket.

Mrs Flintstone, of whom it could be said that she came into the
category of women who spent their youth in a state of pregnancy,
was a guest in our residence today. She didn't, of course, come
because she loves us, but to roast coffee on our fire. Like most
other things, she did this in a traditional way, several hundred
years old, the so-called Siemens-Martin *shish*-procedure. A *shish* is
a can stuck on to a long stick. The can has a little door, which is
closed when it is filled with raw coffee beans. The can is shaken in
the fire and heated, until, on the basis of the aroma, it's decided
that the coffee is properly roasted.

That aroma brought not only me but also Sanja, Davor, and
Brkić into the kitchen. Half-joking, half-sorrowfully, Mother men-
tioned the fact that we had been drinking teas for two days now.
That was for my benefit, because Mother can do without coffee.
Besides, since we've been teetotal (tea-drinkers), she isn't left out.

Brkić then asked what had happened to the sack with Brazil
written on it.

Mother shrugged her shoulders: Julio had taken it away.
How?
The way he brought it. On his back.

One of the strange things connected with my homeland is economics, or more exactly the traffic of goods. On the whole there is none, and everyone regrets that there isn't, but when people talk about it, they talk about cardboard boxes, packets, trailers. It seems that one of the local laws of economics is that the less there is of an article, the larger the units of measure in which it is mentioned. Like coffee. We have been drinking tea for two days, and Julio brings in and carries out sacks. (Units for measuring coffee: *fildžan, džezva*, pan, spoon, mill, eight ounces, one pound, a sack, a trailer, a boat.) We could thank him and Mother for the fact that our supplies of vegetables for the next two years had been reduced to an amount barely sufficient for a month. Julio had exchanged a fair amount for heaven-knows-what, while Mother would probably be able to explain in connection with the carrots and the neighbouring children why, one afternoon sucking, scraping, munching, and crunching could be heard from all the houses round the museum.

I've got it! Julio exchanged the vegetables for a portable stove, a godsend for making coffee, saving fuel and time. Hand on heart, the stove was the loveliest I'd ever seen. But, when we wanted to try it, it turned out that it was not intended for us, but for Sanja's employer. (Sanja does not embroider little pillow-badges any more, but crochets and sews bed linen, tablecloths, and curtains for model furniture for dolls. Her colleague from her student days, the aforementioned employer, had the idea of offering this hand-made furniture to the Western market. He pays so well that envy prevents me from describing all the beauty of the little flowers and pieces of lace that emerge from Sanja's fingertips.)

Description of Mrs Flintstone:

She always wears a plush housecoat of tiger or leopard fur. Under her dressing gown, or as we say in the Bosnian language, *schlafrok*, Adidas gym shoes with four white lines (stripes) on them peek out. Under the gym shoes are nylon stockings. The nylon stockings are then drawn into woollen socks, so-called knitted slippers, and the whole lot is then squashed into mules with fur on them, which, for interneighbourly flights are shoved into old men's shoes.

Mrs Flintstone talks approximately like this: give me a little water, blessyou; eh, thanks, godsaveyou; godgrant the chemist be open nonstop; very handy, *mashalla*; it wasn't me, on my soul; I didn't, godstrikemedead!

She said this last after Mother complained that our canister had disappeared. (The tanker comes once a day. All citizens, including those who have wells in their yards, but who don't have water in their wells, and who gravitate to our pipeline catchment area, leave their canisters on the pavement, in the order they arrived. When the tanker comes, everyone rushes out of their houses, picks up their canisters and starts shoving to ensure no one begins filling up out of turn. In that pushing and shoving, half the water from the tanker gets spilt. Half is poured into several fifteen-gallon barrels. Half is poured through the gate into the yards of prominent people. And half is kept by the driver for his house. How many of those halves make a whole? Not enough, as may be concluded from the fact that after the arrival of the tanker half the canisters from the queue go empty to look for water somewhere else. Dad, who, as a historian is always a step ahead of his times, has already acquired the habit of going to meetings in the Ministry, carrying a gallon canister instead of a briefcase. *Per kanistra ad astra*.)

However, Mrs Flintstone had not taken our canister, as she had not taken anything of what she now had, after the Chetniks had driven her out with nothing whatever. While she was grinding her coffee, she did a bit of grinding of us as well. We heard what she was cooking for lunch, that she had thought that a microwave oven was a "fortable" television set, that in their new apartment she had found a typewriter with a Cyrillic keyboard. Her children were sick, one had dried up, and was inured to medicines, while the other had gone for the runs . . .

Mrs Flintstone wouldn't shove herself up the tanker's arse even if someone drove her with a pistol. Thank god her Junuz went with the van to fetch their water. And why didn't the Director ask for a van for the museum?

Because they didn't need one.

What about wood, what did they burn?

There was still a bit of coal in the cellar.

Handy! Her Junuz had four yards up there at his post, and he'd bring it. She'd heard the Director's a doctor?

Yes.

Fine, *mashalla*. And what about that dried-up one of hers?

He was a doctor of historical science.

Ah well!

Not knowing the real application of the stove-beauty, Mother put a coffeepot on top of it, shoved cardboard and chippings into it, and lit it. The stove melted. Brkić's favourite saying: Everything's possible, apart from a wooden furnace, now had to be adjusted: A tin furnace wasn't much use, either.

Fata (real name Mrs Flintstone) doesn't come round to our place more than seventy times a day. When Sniffy barks at the sound of her footsteps, Dad says *Fata viam invenient* (the Fates are knocking at the door) and goes off to find something to do in another place.

Fata arrives in the same way every time: she comes in, puffs, sits down, puffs, waves her hand in front of her face like a fan, puffs, and then we learn of the terrible thing that has befallen her. Once, while there was still power, the washing machine emptied all its water into the toilet bowl on which she was sitting. It completely, if you'll excuse me . . . sluiced her. Or, she had just put shampoo on her hair, and the water went off. Or, she pulled off a sheet of toilet paper, the whole roll unwound.

Just before the end of a hot spell, as a result of a temporal miscalculation, Dad came back. Mrs Flintstone now knew that he was a doctor of history. I presume that she wanted to make an impression, or to be witty, when she asked whether, by Allah, there had ever been such bestial shelling of a city.

Dad didn't know whether anything like this had been recorded.

Anti-aircraft guns were now active in the marginal areas, and it had also been observed that the Aggressor was regrouping material and technical staff, as well as bringing in fresh personnel, but our lines were impenetrable and firm and the Aggressor would not succeed in realising his criminal aims.

Dad remembered that he hadn't closed the window. I took advantage of his departure myself.

I must observe that certain changes may be seen on Dad.

First, he, too, has acquired accreditation. He wears it on his lapel. That's an external mark of change. The inner change, far more significant, consists in the following: a few days ago he introduced a compulsory watch in the porter's lodge. *Dictum factum.* We keep watch with a notebook in which it is our job to write down all our observations. We are also obliged to have with us, in case of fire or ransack, all the keys to all the rooms. No one is permitted to take anything out of the museum without his permission. Once a day, after supper, Dad reads extracts from the daily newspaper. This evening, after an unexpected lull of several days, the conflict had broken out again. Davor refused to listen to those articles being read.

Dad was surprised, it was courageous to take a stand. However, what was such a brave young man doing here? If he were stationed somewhere, rifle in hand, he would not have to listen.

What, actually, did Dad want?

Davor to sign up for the army.

He had done that once. And served his time.

If he intended to go on hiding in the museum, then let him in future restrain his reactions.

Davor intended to go on hiding in the museum, but this was no longer a museum.

What was it then?

A hammam (Turkish bath) in which brainwashing was carried out by reading newspapers.

Better that than a fifth-column hotbed. It was sad that a radio journalist should approve of what was going on.

He didn't approve.

Silence was approval!

Fortunately, Sanja clutched her stomach and groaned, and we all leapt up so that the birth should not surprise us at table. The end of the quarrel was left for one of the subsequent installments of the series *The bald tear their hair out*.

The birth, of course, was not yet on the horizon. I knew that and was able to observe the whole scene from the height of my objectivity. Dad, Davor, and Brkić took Sanja to her room. Granny stayed to collect the leftovers from their plates, Julio helped Mother to clear the table, and then sat down and rolled a cigarette out of the article Dad had marked.

That same evening I seized the opportunity to mention Davor's gullibility with respect to his wife. Because the twenty-ninth attack of premature birth had ended with him holding her hand and making mini-sandwiches, so-called bitelets, which, in addition to all their other qualities, could be eaten while lying in bed. (When she was full or pleased for some other reason, Sanja began to speak in the diminutive.)

He replied that anyone who had been bitten by a snake was afraid of lizards.

I remembered that the two of them had already been through a pregnancy, and that it had ended badly, but nevertheless . . .

Following my previous note, Davor is now sitting at the table, listening to Dad reading, and making little balls of breadcrumbs. And today will be remembered for the fact that we got our long expected and awaited humanitarian aid.

This consists of a certain quantity of food with which the civilised world wishes to feed the starving Sarajevans. Feed them is perhaps a bit of an exaggeration. This reminds me of the fairytale about Ivica and Marica. I think that the aim of the world is to keep us alive, so that, when the war is over, we will be able once again to take out loans from it and buy whatever will be indispensably unnecessary.

For me the most interesting thing of all that we are given is the so-called lunch packets. They are packed in brown paper bags the size of a book (but that doesn't make them unpopular with the people). The bags contain two or three boxes the size of a volume of poems. In the boxes there are brown bags the size of savings-account books and in them, finally, say, a ham omelet. In the book-sized bag, in addition to the cardboard boxes, there are also little brown bags of fruit-juice or cocoa in powder form, and peanut butter or cheese. And finally, one brown rustling bag, in which there are, no one will believe me who hasn't seen it with his own eyes: matches, chewing gum, hot sauce, salt, sugar, coffee,

coffee-creamer, a spoon, sweets, a freshening-up tissue, toilet paper.

All in all, more packaging than food. You are worn out unpacking it all. What you see in front of you is a heap of bags, boxes, little bags, pieces of paper, you think there's going to be all sorts. But, in fact, what there is is a book-sized bag. Brown.

The aid is distributed to each municipality, and then to each member of the household. For instance, for one person (me, let's say): 170 grammes of peas, 400 grammes of cheese, half a kilo of rice, half a litre of oil. In determining the quantities, account is taken of the packing, so that everything has to be cut, weighed, and poured out. When you finally reach the end, you see that the number of calories expended in the course of receiving the food is equal to the number of calories the food contains. (When I read this to Brkić, he said bravo, I'd make a good communist.)

That same afternoon Mrs Flintstone came round to ask whether we would swap. She had been given food packets with pork in them, and her Junuz didn't eat it. We couldn't help her, our brown bags also had pork and ham written on them. A conversation ensued about the impudence of the western world. Them and their aid. They didn't send what we needed, just what they didn't need.

Julio rebelled. He needed everything in the packet. Even the condoms. They demonstrated that the Americans intended to make Bosnia a condominium.

Mrs Flintstone hadn't had any of those in her packet.

They must have given her children's packets then.

Brkić to Davor: There's no need to deceive people who can be helped to deceive themselves. I remembered this from a conversation the two of them were having about art and direction. It was the evening following the theatre performance. Davor had come to congratulate Brkić. The reader remembers: Julio and Davor produced a performance and exchanged Granny's suitcase. They needed time to do it, because in his nervousness Julio kept dropping the skeleton key.

Finally he lifted the lid. And they saw in it everything that they had themselves put into it. Julio was the first to realise what had happened: Brkić had somehow worked out what they were up to and had changed the suitcases over earlier. They had had the right case in their hands the whole evening and gave it back closed and untouched.

On his barge, Brkić (and Julio, when he was in the country) had been friendly with actors and Bohemians. That barge, as far as I can deduce from their stories, was a kind of private pub. Brkić worked for the Politika printing press and there he published special issues of the newspaper, with news with which he began his jokes. (News: the nationalisation of hard-currency savings, a special tax on the possession of Moskvich cars, the banning of a book, a false obituary— the reader with imagination may conclude what kind of thing could emerge from such plots in such company.) He was also inclined to teach actors to present themselves falsely and thus, as lovers or undivorced wives, to cause chaos in many hidebound marriages.

Brkić made the following observations to Davor on his job as director: First, writers make gods of people, and directors make them idiots. Second, directors are like lichen on a tree, the greener they are, the more quickly the tree withers. When he reads a book, he doesn't see either the book or the words, but a raging snowstorm and in it Korchagin. But when he saw it in the theatre, there was no snow, and no Russia . . .

Brkić wasn't usually so talkative, but when brandy was being distilled, then his simple sentences arranged themselves of their own accord into complex ones.

The distilling of brandy takes place in the atrium, on an improvised apparatus, which in addition to a pressure cooker (so-called Prestige), and long copper pipes, relies on Brkic''s lengthy experience. The raw materials are water and sugar, enriched with raisins and prunes, and in exceptional circumstances freshly picked crushed fruit: mulberries, cherries, rotten apples, and plums regardless of their degree of ripeness.

The Partizans set about distilling the brandy after they had drunk all the supplies of medicinal alcohol. Julio had found this in the first-aid packs, which Dad had found in the civil defence warehouse, where Julio had also found two hundred sterile needles for single-use syringes.

He intended them for one of the strangest trophies in his commercial activity. Two drug addicts brought into the museum a quarter of a yard of asphalt with the prints of two shoes in it. Left and right. They belonged, legend had it, to the Sarajevan assassin of the Austrian Emperor, Gavrilo Princip. The asphalt had been planted into the pavement in front of the Young Bosnia museum, from where at the beginning of this war national fury had uprooted it and flung it into the Miljacka River, from where it had been dragged out again by addicts' intuition.

Julio offered Dad Gavrilo's footprints, but Dad didn't know what to do with them. And he had the shoes somewhere among his exhibits, so, when an appropriate time came, a new print could be made. Julio had no choice but to sell the piece of asphalt to Unprofor soldiers. The tall, blonde, and broad officers who smelled of after-shave and chewing gum, first wanted to buy a *stećak*. But when Dad refused to listen to Julio, the archangel's shoes were exchanged for a box of goods from the duty-free shop at the airport. Among many colourful items, I saw a jar of Nescafé.

The blue-helmets took their souvenir away in a white bulletproof Land Rover, the windows of which, small and thick, reminded one of the eyes of a white-headed vulture. The only subject on which Dad and Davor agree is their anger with the blue-helmets. Dad compares them to a priest standing in front of the executioner at the execution of the innocent, while Davor sees in them a doctor summoned to confirm death, rather than to prescribe medicines.

I feel in their presence like a llama in the zoo. Let them take this as my way of spitting at them.

PETER TREMAYNE

"FEAR A' GHORTA" from
AISLING AND OTHER IRISH TALES OF TERROR

"BLESS ME, FATHER, for I have sinned."

Fr Ignatius had heard the words a million times or more. He could not begin to recall the times he had sat in the dark oak tomb of the confessional box, oppressed by the odour of polished wood, the musty smell of the velvet curtains and the camphor-scented candles, while he sat on the hassock which served as a cushion but which did not ease the hardness of the wooden bench on which the priest was supposed to sit. He could not begin to recall the times he had heard the opening line of the confessional formula echoing from successive shadowy forms beyond the small fretwork grille. Fr Ignatius had served both as curate and priest in the Church of the Most Holy Redeemer, on New York's Third Street, for twenty years. Twenty years of confessions. He reckoned that he was now as broadminded as anyone could be; nothing could shock him after listening to twenty years of sins from countless individuals. He had heard the opening line of the confessional ritual spoken in many tones— truculent, fearful, bored...

"Bless me, Father, for I have sinned."

Yet the hoarse whisper of the voice which came through the lattice held a timbre which made Fr Ignatius stir uneasily. The emphasis on the words gave them an immediacy and a terrible urgency that the priest had never heard before. Fr Ignatius frowned into the gloom at the shadow beyond the grille.

"How long has it been since your last confession, my son?" he asked.

There was a pause and then the hoarse whisper came: "Twenty-five years, Father."

"Twenty-five years?" A priest was not supposed to sound so condemnatory but the words were wrenched from Fr Ignatius in an accusing tone.

"I last made a confession on the first day of August, 1848."

The priest made a rapid calculation.

"Indeed," he confirmed. "Twenty-five years lacking four weeks. Why do you come to make confession now? Why, after all this time?"

"It is a long story, Father."

Fr Ignatius turned, drew aside the velvet curtain and peered into the church. It was deserted. The man had obviously waited until last before coming to the box, waited until the last of the evening confessionalists had departed.

"We have plenty of time, my son," he said, bringing his attention back to the shadow behind the grille.

"Then perhaps, Father, I could tell my story without interruption? In that way I will confess all and you will be able to understand why it is that I have been so long in coming back to the sanctuary of Holy Mother Church."

Fr Ignatius listened to the cadences of the voice and then observed: "You are Irish aren't you? I can tell by your accent."

The shadow gave a rueful laugh.

"Strange, after twenty-five years in New York I fondly thought that I had lost me accent. Is it so obvious that I am not a native of this city?

"What is a native, my son?" smiled Fr Ignatius. "We are all immigrants here."

"But you are not Irish, Father," observed the voice.

"I was born in Austria. My parents brought me here when I was small." The priest hesitated. He had heard of the clannishness of the Irish. "Would you prefer an Irish priest to hear your confession? Fr Flannery is in the presbytery and I am sure…"

The voice was firm. "No. It does not matter who hears my confession. A priest is a priest, isn't this so, Father?"

"We are merely the link to God, my son. Very well. Perhaps you had best begin."

"My name…ah, perhaps that does not matter. When I had friends they called me Pilib Rua, Foxy Pilib on account of my red hair. Among the Irish here I am called *Fear a' Ghorta* which, in the Irish language, means the Man of Hunger. Why I have been given this name will become obvious as I proceed.

"My home was in the province of Connacht, in the west of Ireland, where I was weaned and educated for life. I was sixteen summers in my youth when I ran away form the drudgery of life on my father's croft. It was a terrible existence. We worked on the estate of Colonel Chetwynd, the English landlord who owned our part of the country. And a poor land it was. It was a place filled with poverty and where cold clung to your marrow and the rain was a constant and relentless downpour. There was no hope of improvement in our life for the poor sod which we worked was not ours to enjoy. We could work it but had to pay tithes and tribute to Colonel Chetwynd and if our poor land did not give us sufficient to pay the rent then the Colonel's bailiffs would evict us, throwing us off the land in which our fathers and our forefathers had dwelt for centuries. To prevent those evicted crawling back to their homes for shelter the Colonel's bailiffs would burn the thatch from the roofs. Our small corner of Ireland was no different from any other corner of our poor conquered land. That was why I could not bear to face a future there. So I ran away to sea. I joined the Royal Navy as a means of escaping from the drudgery of my life and voyaged abroad for five years until, falling from a rigging, I suffered an injury which drew me back to my native land.

"I landed in the city of Galway in August of 1848 when the famine was in its fourth year and the dead lay unburied on the roads and lanes of Connacht. Homeless beggars roamed the streets of the city, while others gathered on the quays trying to find a place in the emigrant ships. The worst sight of all was the children...mere animated skeletons, some screaming for food, while many were past crying. They sat or lay, emaciated bundles of bone with scarcely any flesh, with only their eyes...large, round eyes, staring beseechingly in muted suffering.

"I had heard of the extent of the famine in my voyaging. Indeed, I had heard it said that nearly a third of the population of the province of Connacht had already perished from the land by the time I set foot at Galway. Yet it had been impossible to visualise such suffering. As well as the suffering children there were those who had the famine dropsy, with bodies swollen to twice their natural size, the gums spongey so that the teeth fell out, the joints enlarged, the skin red where the blood-vessel had burst and the legs turned black. They peopled Galway city like wraiths.

"Among this swarm of figures from hell rode the well-fed English cavalry troopers and the administrators. Truly, after the centuries of struggle, could it be said that in those years of famine the English had finally conquered—conquered our spirit and our will.

"I walked from Galway north along the shores of Loch Corrib until I turned west and came by easy stages to my village. It nestled at the foot of some gaunt hills facing the brooding Atlantic sea.

The people scarcely recognised me in their plight. Many had died. Indeed, 'twas to a cold and empty croft that I returned. My father, mother, and two young brothers had been dead a year since.

"'Why did you come back, Pilib Rua?' demanded Dangan Cutteen, who always acted as spokesman for the villagers. 'Weren't you better off sailing the seas than returning to this bleak place?'

"I told him my story and how the Royal Navy had put me ashore because I had fallen from a rigging and was no longer any use to them.

"Dangan Cutteen scowled. 'And what are you here but another mouth to go hungry?'

"I was surprised at the bitterness in his voice. He was a man of fierce primeval passions but of equally fierce attachments. He was as hard and gaunt as the granite rocks and withal as protective to those he cared for as the bleak surrounding hills. From Dangan Cutteen I had learnt seacraft by going out with him since I was a sprogeen, scarcely walking from my cradle. Many is the hour we spent in his curragh while he would teach me not only the way the fish ran but also the old ranns and proverbs of our native tongue. In his rich baritone, which droned like the wind, he would sing the wild traditional songs of our forefathers as we fought the currents and the tides of that restless coast.

"Seeing the hurt in my eyes, Dangan Cutteen gripped me by the shoulders.

"'Yerrah, boy, let there be forgiveness at me. I am half insane with fear for our people. Nearly half the village has perished and I am helpless to aid them. The men grow desperate as they watch the old, the sick and the young grow wizened and frail before their eyes. God! God! What a fearsome sight it is to see the old and the young neither crying nor complaining but crawling over the potato ridges, turning sods of earth in the hope that a good potato might remain in the ground.'

"'But why are the people starving?' I demanded. 'It is only the potato crops that have failed, and the oats, grain and barley yield in abundance. Why, coming into Galway, for every famine relief ship that I saw entering port, I saw six ships loaded with grain and livestock and wool and flax sailing for England.'

"Dangan Cutteen gave out a bitter laugh.

"'The people starve because the grain and livestock belong to the English landlords who own the land in Ireland. And we…we Irish are but a poor, crushed and conquered people. We do not have the backbone to rise up and take what is ours that we might live. The English landlords threaten us with eviction if we do not pay our rents, and whole families die of starvation so that the lords of the land have their due.'

"'Surely the politicians…?'

"Dangan Cutteen spat.

"'A curse on their dead ones!' he pronounced. 'There is devastation in the land and what do the lickspittle representatives say? John O'Connell, the son of Daniel O'Connell whom the people hailed as 'The Liberator', rose in the English Parliament and said: "I thank God I live among a people who would rather die than defraud the landlord of rent." Aye, they die, they die, the Irish, in their tens of thousands to feed the English landlords.'

"I heard hatred in Dangan Cutteen's voice. It was a hatred I came to share. Yes, I'll admit that. *An Gorta Mór* left hatred behind it. Between Ireland and England the memory of what was done has and will endure like a sword probing a wound. There have been other famines in Ireland and doubtless there will be other famines to come but the days of the Great Hunger will never be forgotten nor forgiven.

"During the first few days I stayed in my village, I joined with Dangan Cutteen and the others in putting out to sea in the curraghs in search of fish. Yet even the fish had apparently deserted their normal feeding grounds along the coast, perhaps sensing the presence of the terrible spectre of hunger which stalked the land. Several of the women of the village protested at their menfolk putting to sea, for in their weak, starving condition they felt that they would not have the strength to fight its contrary moods. But Dangan told them that there were was only death before them anyway so was it not better to look for death on the water rather than passively wait for it on the bleak land?

"Came the day when Dangan Cutteen ordered the people of the village to gather together. He had decided to make a final appeal to the lord of the land, Colonel Chetwynd, to release some of the produce and livestock he was keeping in his barns. The people walked slowly in a body up the steep road to the great white-walled mansion which was the seat of Colonel Chetwynd's estate. It lay about a mile east of the village. With the afternoon sun slanting its golden rays across it, it looked a beautiful and peaceful place. It seemed a place at odds with the terror that was oppressing the land.

"Colonel Chetwynd was obviously warned of our coming and, as we approached the big house, we saw him standing at the top of the great stairs that led to the main doors. At his side was the weasel-faced overseer of the estate, a man named Brashford. I recall him well. He had been brought over from England to manage the estate for the Colonel twenty years before. Brashford made no pretence at hiding the fact that he carried a revolver in his pocket. I was sure that a corresponding bulge in the Colonel's pocket concealed a similar weapon. Also, posted about the estate, there were half a dozen English soldiers sent up from the Galway garrison in case of trouble.

"The soldiers were there not specifically for us but because there were rumours of a rising against the English throughout the country. I have never known a time when there were not such rumours, although I was too young to remember the uprising of 1798 and 1803. It seemed that the Young Irelanders were determined to make another attempt to establish a republic in Ireland before the year was out and English troops were flooding into the country in preparation.

"As we approached Colonel Chetwynd I saw there was a disdainful look on his fat, bloated features. It was at least six years since I had previously seen the man who was the sole arbiter of our lives and fortunes. He had not changed except that he appeared to me more dissolute, more debauched than before. There was no hunger nor want about his replete figure.

"'What do you want here?' His voice was nasal and he called in English.

"We halted, unsure of ourselves. Then Dangan Cutteen moved forward. He was unused to speaking English and his voice was slow, soft and considered.

"'Why, your honour, we want food.'

"'Food?' Colonel Chetwynd gave a sharp bark of laughter, like the bark of a fox at night.

"'Your honour, we work on your estate. We know you have enough livestock, hogs and cattle, and sheep, and enough grain to keep us from harm. Yet we starve and sicken and die. We are in desperate need, your honour.'

"Colonel Chetwynd grimaced, his mouth ugly.

"'Am I to be a philanthropist, issuing alms out of altruism?'

"'I have no understanding of those words, your honour,' replied Dangan. 'Is there not an abundance of food on your estate?'

"'No business of yours,' snapped the Colonel. 'It is my property and on it depends my income. Do I have to explain the principles of business to the likes of you?'

"'You do not, your honour, for we are not discussing the

principles of business but the principles of humanity. Our people are dying almost daily from *An Gorta Mór*. Our potatoes, on which we rely, are blighted, our own pigs and fowls are long since dead, and now our old folk, the wee ones and the frail and sick are dying. Yet in your barns is food a-plenty.'

"It was then that the overseer, Brashford, whose face was almost apoplectic with rage, interrupted.

"'I know this man, Colonel. Dangan Cutteen by name. A troublemaker if ever there was one. Let me drive these swine from the estate.'

"Colonel Chetwynd smiled thinly.

"'No, Brashford. No. Mr Cutteen has a good argument here. He seems to be stating the law of supply and demand. He and his people want food. We have food.'

"For a moment we stood silently, not one of us sure that we had heard the Colonel aright. Few of us had subtle English and we thought that our interpretation might be at fault. Dangan took a pace, frowning.

"'Are you willing to give us food, your honour?' he asked hesitantly.

"Colonel Chetwynd threw back his head and guffawed loudly.

"'By the pox, no! I am willing to sell you the food. You must pay the price that I would get were I to ship to England.'

"It was then that we realised the bitter humour of the man and a murmur of suppressed rage ran through us.

"Dangan Cutteen did not lose his temper.

"'Your honour, you know that we have no money. We work on your estate to earn for the rents and tithes you claim for our poor hovels. We have to provide our labour to you in order to remain on the land which was our forefathers' land long before you and yours came to it. For this we must be grateful, but the only extra money we have, in a good year, is when we can sell any abundance and surplus from our small potato plots. Since the start of the famine, we have no money.'

"Colonel Chetwynd was smiling evilly now and nodding his head.

"'Then we have no business to discuss, Mr Cutteen.'

"He made to turn away and Dangan Cutteen spoke sharply at last:

"'God forgive you, your honour!'

"Colonel Chetwynd glanced back. 'The question is settled, Cutteen. Business is business. You have no money. I am not a charity. My produce goes to England.'

"'And we are simply to starve to death?'

"'Are there no fish left in the sea?' Brashford interrupted again.

"'None that we can take,' replied Dangan.

"'Then eat grass,' replied the overseer. 'Didn't His Highness, the son of our Gracious Sovereign, Queen Victoria, suggest that the Irish nation could save itself by eating grass, for aren't the Irish people capable of eating anything?'

"The weasel-faced overseer laughed uproariously at his sally and the red-coated soldiers joined in his mirth.

"Dangan Cutteen stood there a moment more, his face twisted in a scarce-controlled rage. 'But Colonel…' he began slowly.

"'Have I not made myself plain, Cutteen? There is no more to talk about. I don't care a damn about your people. Eat the bodies of your dead for all I care!'

"He stormed into his great, rich house leaving us standing there. Had Dangan told us to charge it and set it afire, I don't doubt that we would have met our end there and then. Brashford and the soldiers seemed to sense what was running through our minds for they lined up their revolvers and rifles and stood waiting. But Dangan Cutteen turned away and we followed him back to the village.

"That afternoon lots were drawn as to who should crew a three-man curragh and go to sea in search of fish. Dangan wanted to go and I, likewise, for we were still fairly healthy. But the lot fell to others and these were proud men, these men of the West, and none would change their seats in the boat. No sooner had the black dart of the curragh vanished beyond the headland than a wind came up, whistling and crying like the banshees of hell. The curragh did not return home. By dusk we gathered on the foreshore, silent and ghastly, and we waited; waited until dusk gave way to night. The grey murderous sea was empty of any craft.

"It was in the grey light of the morning that a man from the neighbouring village of Raheenduff came to us to tell us that a curragh had been washed ashore there upside down.

"'They are all away,' the man said of the crew, which is a way of saying in the West that all had perished.

"A strange look come upon the features of Dangan Cutteen then.

"He gave a long sigh. *'Ní chuimhníonn cú gortach ar a coileán,'* he said softly.

"I thought it a strange time to utter the old saying which means 'a hungry hound does not remember its whelps', which is to say that necessity knows no law.

"Dangan beckoned to Seán and Iolar, who were his brothers and closer to him than anyone. 'We have work to do,' he told them and he left without a backward glance to any of us.

"That night I sat in my cabin trying to keep the spectre of hunger away by boiling the edible carrigeen seaweed, which grows along the shoreline, into a soup. I had decided that I must leave the village while I was still healthy and perhaps find a berth on a merchantman bound for the New World. It was true that I felt more remorse this time than when I had first run away to sea years before, for was I not leaving my fellow villagers and comrades to their deaths?

"It was then that there came a sharp rap on the door and opening it I beheld Iolar in the gloom.

"'Dangan has sent me,' he said. 'If you want to eat, there is food to be had.'

"'What?' I cried. 'From where is the food come?'

"'Follow me, Pilib Rua, and you shall see.'

"I was surprised when he led me through the darkened village and up the steep path to the old caves in the hills above the village. Few knew of the existence of these caves for this was where the villagers had sheltered during the devastations of Cromwell, when the English could take the head off any Irish man, woman or child and receive a £5 reward for doing so; a time when the English soldiers could ride down on villages and take off the young men and girls to ship them as slaves to the Barbados. The caves had been our secret shelter in those days.

"I was startled to see the entire remnants of the village gathered in the caves when Iolar led me in. Everyone stood in silent wonder around a great roaring fire. I, too, stared in bewilderment at the great roasting spits that were turning over the flames while on them were cuts of meat which cracked and sizzled as their natural greases dripped on to the fire which cooked them. And the smell…ah, the sweet smell of roasting pork!

"And Dangan Cutteen was there, grim-faced and silent as he supervised the roasting.

"What miracle had he wrought to bring us such a plentiful supply of meat?

"Each person was given meat and each person ate their fill without stinting. Not a word was spoken while we sat and made ourselves replete with the feast.

"Only when the people began to move drowsily back towards

the village did I seek out Dangan and asked: 'Where did the food come from? Did you steal it from the estate of Colonel Chetwynd? If so, we will be in trouble from the English soldiers on the morrow.'

Dangan Cutteen glanced at me without a change of expression on his grim features.

"'The meat came with the courtesy of Colonel Chetwynd,' he said softly. Then he turned away after the villagers, leaving me alone in the cave staring at the dying embers of the fire, staring at the smouldering bones which lay behind.

"It was the bones that first raised some tiny pricking in my mind…bones which belonged to no pig that I knew of. A chill began to run down my spine and sent my stomach heaving.

"Some instinct made me turn towards the back of the cave, seizing a piece of wood from the fire to act as a torch. I held it aloft and moved forward.

"I did not have to look far.

"There, in a heap at the back of the cave, were the blood-stained but easily recognisable clothes that I had last seen worn by Colonel Chetwynd. And by them lay a torn and stained coat that Brashford had been wearing. I stood like a statue, not wishing to believe what I knew to be true. When Colonel Chetwynd had said to Dangan Cutteen: 'I don't give a damn about your people. Eat the bodies of your dead for all I care!' he had sealed his own fate. He had pronounced his own sentence for his crimes against us.

"Such was the horror that overcame me that I fled crying with terror from the cave and did not stop at the village but went to Galway. At Galway I persuaded the captain of a merchantman to give me a berth, working my passage here to New York."

The hoarse whisperer from the shadow behind the grille halted a moment and Fr Ignatius heard the sound of an emotional swallow.

"I have not been able to tell this story for twenty-five years, Father. Please…please…I must have absolution."

Fr Ignatius hesitated. It was a grim story, a horrendous story. But God must be the judge. He was merely the instrument and he was moved to pity for the owner of the hoarse voice; pity, in spite of the terrible tale, for the fault lay clearly not with the man but with those conditions which had forced the man into his grotesque sin.

"Please, Father!"

The pleading tone of the man's voice tugged at his soul. Fr Ignatius stirred himself.

"I will absolve you, my son," he said slowly, "even though the sin you have committed is beyond anything that I have ever heard in my years as a priest. I will absolve you because your story has moved deep compassion in my soul. Before you leave this church you must recite five decades of the rosary and make an offering…that I shall leave to your conscience and God."

The figure behind the screen let forth a deep shuddering sigh. "God bless you, Father, for you have charity of mind and spirit."

"It is God's will to move me to compassion, my son," replied Fr Ignatius, "and I am but an instrument of His infinite goodness and His compassion. Make a good Act of Contrition, my son."

The figure beyond the lattice bent its head.

"Oh my God, I am heartily sorry for having offended Thee. I beg pardon for all my sins. I detest them above all things because they offend Thy infinite goodness who are so deserving of all my love and I am firmly resolved by the help of Thy grace never to offend Thee again and carefully to avoid the occasion of my sin."

The ritual Act of Contrition was recited mechanically as Fr Ignatius had often heard it recited. Yet it fell strangely on his ears for what had gone before had prepared him to hear some more emotional declaration of intent. But he shrugged. The Act of Contrition was said and was meant.

"Absolvo te ab omnibus peccatis tuis nomine Patris et Filii et Spiritus Sancti…Amen!"

He made the sign of the cross.

The figure behind the grille sat with its head bowed for a moment and then came the long, drawn-out sigh again.

"Am I truly absolved in the eyes of God and the Church for what I have done, Father?"

Fr Ignatius frowned. "Do you doubt the rituals of the Church, my son?" His voice rose sharply.

"No, Father. Yet it seems that I have shouldered the burden of this guilt for so long that it is strange that it should be cast from me in a single moment."

"God, in His infinite wisdom, so ordained His priesthood to forgive sins however great," responded Fr Ignatius with pursed lips. "From this moment on your sins no longer exist. You are reborn into the world in the eyes of God as innocent as if you were a newly born child."

There was a silence behind the grille. Then the voice came, sounding almost triumphant. "Then I am reborn as pure as if the last twenty-five years had never existed?"

"Of course, my son."

"It is a wonderful feeling, Father."

Fr Ignatius smiled and was about to gently dismiss the strange confessionalist when the fretwork grille that divided the confessional box splintered into fragments. A thick, hairy arm thrust through towards the priest, the squat, dirty fingers grasping the startled man's throat and choking off his cry of alarm.

Fr Ignatius was aware of the grotesque face in the shadows, the wild staring eyes, blood-veined and burning like the coals of hell. He was aware, too, of the large twisted mouth, the blood-red lips drawn back to show pink gums from which sharp white teeth ground against each other.

The voice was clearly triumphant now. "I am innocent again. But your confessional has not dismissed the craving, the terrible longing...you see, Father, the terror and horror I felt when I ran wildly from that cave, twenty-five years ago, was not at the fact that I had eaten human flesh. It was the realisation that I had enjoyed it. Enjoyed it in spite of the knowledge of what it was. I am innocent again. Therefore I must sin again. There will be others to hear my future confession but now...now I must have meat again...succulent human meat...I cannot live without it!"

JOHN TROLAN

"PROLOGUE" from *SLOW PUNCTURES*

1 JANUARY '78

RED WAS A colour which would have looked good on me ma when she was in mourning, so why she wore it to see in the New Year is anyone's guess. I mean, it wasn't as if she was expecting something. I don't think Joxer noticed. He was preoccupied with more serious concerns, more urgent matters.

Red was the colour of the stranger's lipsticked lips which spat Hail Marys at me brother, Joxer, when he was a child. He remembered them hitting the back of his neck. He remembered the splash and the dribble and the disgust of it all. I remember him shivering, because telling me about it reminded him of the bitterness which had propelled the prayers. How it shamed him down to reluctant knees for the sins of his father and his father's father and the father he himself might someday become. It pressed him there until the lengths of his shins ached from kneeling on blocks of polished hardwood. It held him there until, when it was time for him to leave, cramp forced him to limp. He told me all this before we left the pub; how he would beg the agonised, crucified Christ, who hung, Himself reluctant, all over St Canice's Church in Finglas, to come and rescue a forlorn child.

"You too?" Joxer would address the crosses, young as he was. "Has thou forsaken me too?"

Everyone used to say it: "He should be on the stage."

"Why should he?" me ma would ask. "Sure doesn't he think the bleeden world is a stage."

Bright red is the colour of arterial blood. He told me this too.

Pure Persil white was the colour of the blouse me ma wore to go with her cherry red, two piece suit. She looked fine, contented, sitting back in the fat flowery armchair beside the weary fire. She always looked satisfied with a gin and tonic in her hand. In the other she held a menthol cigarette and, cross legged, she used the cigarette to conduct me da's rendition of "Love Me Tender".

Excitable red was the colour Joxer turned the time he read the magazine article to me from the top bunk. He went white every time he remembered it. He had read out loud the advice, the knowledge Sammy Davis Jnr had got from his experience, that to hesitate only led to a certain change of heart.

Pure white, Joxer told me, is the colour of unbearable pain.

It was an hour since the bells and me oldest brother, Jimmy, felt it was time to perform a number. He clambered on to me aunt Aileen's living room table and launched into a fine impersonation of Elvis. Jimmy did him well. He was only into the introduction when Aileen shouted at him, "Take your shoes off or else you'll mark the table. Remember, you're not too old to have the back of your arse marked!"

Jimmy pushed each shoe off at the heel.

"And mind yeh don't fall," me ma shouted from her chair. "That'd be all we need."

With one hand on his hip ready to push into action, Jimmy sang into a full, uncapped bottle of Harp, "Yuh aint nothin' but a hound dog . . ."

"Oh, me favourite," me aunt Aileen screamed, almost as soon as Jimmy began. She jumped from the crowded settee pleading, "Spit on me, Elvis," while pretending to tear out her hair.

Joxer would have obliged. He would have plopped from the tip of a rapid tongue a wet gollier which might cling between the fingers of the hand Aileen would raise to protect herself, but Jimmy just finished and asked, "D'yeh want me to sing the other one yeh like, the ghetto one? How does it start?"

Joxer walked to the kitchen and I followed. I could tell he was hunting for someone different to listen to him. He cornered me ma's youngest sister, as she sat at the kitchen table sipping a vodka and coke. Me aunt Paula was three years older than Joxer. "Does this not drive yeh fuckin' mad?" he asked her.

She pretended not to know what he was talking about.

It didn't deter Joxer. "I mean, you're oney twenty. D'yeh not think the likes of me and you should have somethin' better to do?"

"Are you on them tablets again?"

"Oh for fucksake! Does it look like I am?"

"Listen, Joxer, I want to enjoy meself tonigh', so don't start goin' on abou' your problems, will yeh? Jaysis! You used to be a great laugh, d'yeh know tha'? Until yeh started readin' all those books tha' is." Paula stood up. "I'm goin' out to have a dance." She edged her way round Joxer's chair and squeezed past me uncle Jack at the doorway.

Jack tried to grab hold of her arse, when he was sure me aunt Aileen wasn't looking. "Happy New Year, Paula," he told her, after clasping a handful, and he walked down the kitchen to the toilet.

Paula changed her mind and came back and sat beside Joxer.

"D'yeh see wha' I mean?" Joxer asked.

"All I know is the reason *you* don't pinch me arse is because of the box I gave yeh the last time yeh done it."

Men were always trying to grab hold of me aunt Paula's arse. It tempted them, the way it squeezed out at the top of her pencil thin skirt. She was gorgeous, in every sense of the word: gorgeous looking; gorgeous talking; gorgeous no matter what she was doing.

Even when she listened to Joxer, when the tone of her voice was derogatory and her eyebrows tightened, her eyes always remained soft, like she cared. I used to ache for that look, but she only ever smiled at me. I would have read every bleeden book in the library, if I thought she would look at me with those deep brown, disapproving eyes of hers. I would have practised being as funny as him if I thought she would laugh with that hysterical shriek she had, like she would when Joxer cracked a joke. She would throw back that bucketful of black hair of hers and say, "Oh stop it, Joxer Daly. You'll have me pissin' meself."

"Have yeh not got a drink, Padser?" Even the way she said me name, compared to his, wasn't the same.

"Get me one while you're out there and make sure me ma doesn't see yeh drinkin'," said Joxer.

He had these little ways of trying to put you down. I was only two years younger, but he went on like I was a kid. "Me ma doesn't mind me drinkin'," I reminded him, "because I don't get sloshed like you all the time and make a bleeden show of meself. Will I get yeh one, Paula?"

Paula smiled at me. "No thanks, Padser. I'm alrigh' at the minute."

I had to squeeze past me uncle Jack on the way back. "I'm watchin' yeh," he said. "There's oney one six pack of Carlin' opened, you're the oney one drinkin' it, so when it's finished, that's it. D'yeh hear wha' I'm sayin' to yeh, kid?" he asked, pinching the cheek of me face and with his big, hairy, ink-purple nose breathing down me mouth. "Who's the bottle of Harp for?"

"It's Joxer's."

"I'm keepin' me eye on you too," he said, slapping the back of Joxer's head a bit more sharply than necessary. "If yeh do your party piece tonigh' and throw up all over me bathroom floor, I'll make yeh lick the cold sick up in the mornin'. D'yeh hear me?"

"You're a great laugh, Jack," Joxer replied, without so much as the threat of a smile, "comin' out with some of the things tha' yeh do. I swear, I don't know where yeh get them from."

The kitchen was quiet, despite the constant traffic flow of people to and from the toilet. Quiet enough to have a conversation. The noise from the singsong in the living room travelled vertically towards the high ceiling rather than horizontally towards the doors, because after a few drinks people tended to throw their heads back when singing. The other door in the living room led to the hall and stairs where younger couples, the twentysomethings, sat and kissed, or argued, or made promises they were never going to keep, and if they did they would regret ever making them in the first place. Upstairs, the children were in bed. The youngest would be asleep by now. The older ones, having made new alliances with cousins, would fight even against sister and brother. Sometimes they would play together. Sometimes too, Jack, convinced that he could hear the ceiling shaking, would visit and bully them into bed, because some things never change. If this didn't work he would bribe them, or at least promise to bribe them the next day, and then tuck them up in bed with a slap and a squeeze, boys and girls together.

"D'yeh want to know wha' my first memory is?" Joxer asked Paula. "The first concept, or thought, or realisation I ever had?"

"Wha'?" Paula asked, after swallowing a sip from her drink.

I was looking at her from the other end of the table, above a half dozen empty beer bottles.

"Tha' somethin' wasn't quite righ' abou' all of this," said Joxer.

"Wha' wasn't righ'?" she asked him, "abou' wha'?"

"All this," said Joxer, with a wave of his arms. "I knew it from the very start."

"Knew wha'?"

"I knew I was bein' lied to. I knew everyone was lettin' on tha' they hadn't a clue wha' I was talkin' abou' when I said tha' there was somethin' wrong. I knew tha' they would fall over themselves in the rush to agree with me when I said tha' there was somethin' wrong with me."

"Is he all in it?" Paula asked me.

I was delighted when she addressed me, but before I had time to reply, before I had time to assure her that Joxer had never been the full shilling, she was rescued by Aileen.

"Wha' are yeh doin' sittin' listenin' to these on New Year's Eve? D'yeh want to depress yourself or somethin'?"

Where she got the cheek to include me with Joxer, I'll never know, but before I knew anything, Jack was singing Paula a Matt Monroe number. I'm sure this depressed her more than Joxer or I ever would, but she would have upset Aileen if she hadn't made out she was loving it. It had a depressing effect on Joxer too. There was nobody else at the party he could talk to; there was nobody else who would listen.

"I'm goin' to roll a joint in the jacks and go out for a walk to smoke it. D'yeh want to come?"

I shrugged me shoulders and let him know I didn't mind. The year before, Jack had caught Joxer smoking a joint and he tried to make him eat it before Joxer had a chance to put it out.

We left the house in Inchicore with Jack warning that if either of us were going to vomit, then we were to wait until we got to Finglas. We strolled towards Kilmainham. Joxer had stashed in the pockets of his combat jacket a couple of bottles of Harp. The thought hadn't occurred to me to do the same and he made me open his with me teeth, after I asked him for a sup of his. It wasn't the joint that was making me thirsty, waiting on it more like. I swear to Jaysis, he could be that tight.

We walked all the way to Kilmainham district court by way of Emmet Road and the South Circular. Joxer washed down a couple of Valium with a bottle of Harp. It was about as rebellious as he could get. That and pissing up against the door of the main entrance to the court. Whatever buzz I got out of the butt of the joint, I got even less joy out of the request I made for him to roll another one.

"One of us has to keep a clear head tonigh', Brud." He was starting to mumble. "I want a witness to all this."

"To all wha'?" I asked.

"To the fuckin' pain I feel."

"Wha' pain?"

"The pain in me soul."

I remember wondering was he talking about one of his feet until, with the usual dramatic effect, he slapped the palm of his right hand hard against the left side of his breast.

"I know yeh won't understand this, Padser, so just believe me. The stupidity of it all, the absurdity, I swear, it crushes me. I carry it across the broad of me back, an unwelcome weigh' of Irishness tha' pushes me down, expectin' me to do quicker and quicker reels and jigs . . ."

He had lost me again. He always did at some point. I'd learned, from about the age of eight, to just listen at times like these, because if you asked a question, made a comment, offered a suggestion, it prolonged things. Though the fucker often checked too. He would ask a question to see if you were listening.

"D'yeh know wha' date it is now?"

"It's New Year's Eve. No it's not," I corrected meself. "It's the 1st of January, 1978, New Year's Day."

"The first day of the new year and me bleeden stomach's at me."

"Is it your ulcer?" I asked him. A duodenal ulcer had been diagnosed when he was twelve. The doctor advised him to stop drinking and smoking, but Joxer didn't listen. Instead, he drank Maalox by the bottle and put the ulcer down to the diet of bread and drippin' sandwiches he had survived on as a child. These were all the more damaging when combined with the worrying he done for the rest of us. Me ma said he only ever tasted bread and drippin' once, and that was because he asked and wouldn't shut up until he got some. As for the worrying, well he had a talent for that all right, according to her, especially when he was worrying about himself. He was that good at it, he could have represented Ireland in the Olympics. When she told Joxer this, me da asked was it an event for the disabled.

Sitting outside Kilmainham court, Joxer went the colour of ash grey. I think at the time I thought it was because he had too much to drink and the Valium wouldn't have helped. It was two in the morning and it was how I expected Joxer to start every New Year. I asked him if he wanted to go back to the party; the alternative was to head home to Finglas. He looked at me with that look in his eye, the one he always got when he was going to do something mad, or stupid.

"We're supposed to be at a party, Padser," he smiled. "So c'mon."

Me uncle Jack's two bed-roomed terraced house was still packed when we returned. The front door was open and the singing could be heard halfway down the terrace, above the muffled clutter of people talking and laughing and bottles and glasses clinking from one end of the stairs to the other. Paddy, me ma's brother, was doing the singing. I was named after him, though I couldn't sing like him. He was always getting tormented at parties, especially from the oul biddies. To tell the truth, he sang that high I never had a clue what he was singing about, but he was capable of making the oul wans cry and, on occasions, had them bawling before so much as a bottle of Mackeson's was opened.

I sat in beside me aunt Aileen on the settee and listened to Paddy finish his song. Everybody got the opportunity to sing. If you were lousy, the others joined in to help disguise this. If you were good, everyone listened. Joxer was woeful, but nobody helped when he last sang a couple of years ago, because he ignored Aileen's advice to do a Cliff Richard number and sang a Leonard Cohen song instead. He was the only person I knew who had never been asked to sing again.

When it was me ma's turn to sing, me aunt Aileen jumped up and fetched the long white gloves she usually wore to weddings. "Here, Bridey, put these on yeh before yeh start."

Me ma pulled on the gloves and began to sing, "Diamonds Are Forever", aiming in the direction of me da. Now and again, when the song demanded, she spread her arms out rather than push them into her breasts and her full attention was given to the rest of the room. She wasn't a great singer, me ma, but because of the songs she sang, it was unusual for anyone to join in. For other reasons, it would have been a shame to stop her.

"Shirley Bassey hasn't a patch on yeh, Bridey," Aileen told her before taking the gloves and pulling them up her own pale, flesh-sagging, freckled arms. Jack spotted her and before she burst into "24 Hours From Tulsa", grabbed the coal bucket which was only half empty and headed for the back yard to fill it. I'd been squeezed beside Jack and was going to follow him as far as the kitchen, but luckily I didn't. Just as I was thinking of it, Paula came in from the hall and sank in beside me. There was nothing in the world that could fill me with the kind of warmth I felt when Paula sat that close. When she began to sing, "Help Me Make It Through The Night", well, Joxer came rushing in from the kitchen, Jack nearly fell over the coal bucket he was that anxious to get back, and even me da straightened himself up in his chair. While her sisters looked on proudly, the men in the room, apart from her brother, Paddy, all looked shifty enough to suspect they were secretly wishing she was singing it with them in mind.

I could tell by the look in Joxer's eyes that he believed it. He was even arrogant enough to wink at her.

When she finished singing, Paula headed back to the hall and friends of hers who Joxer couldn't stand, so he made for the kitchen. Jack was trapped by Aileen who wanted him to jive. Me ma made eyes at me da, an aunt of Jack's began to snore and I swerved towards the coat closet beneath the stairs and opened another six pack of Carling. The party was getting old but wasn't dead yet. Although Jack had kissed and groped everyone he wanted to, it was never over until he sang that he did it his way. I felt like lying down in the closet, especially after I drank another bottle, but I decided instead to get Joxer a bottle of Harp and take it out to him. He wasn't looking well.

I had only opened it and was in the process of getting him to examine me tooth and check how much of it had chipped away when Jack walked into the kitchen and done the worst thing imaginable: he sat down beside us. Joxer looked to heaven; I looked to see how many empty Carling bottles were on the table. He sat closer to Joxer.

"Well," he said, "are yeh still depressed?"

"Wha' are yeh talkin' abou', Jack?"

"Your mother told me yeh were still depressed, tha' it was even beginnin' to get to your father."

"Depressed isn't a word tha' has space in my vocabulary."

"Why? Is it not big enough for yeh?"

"It has no meanin' for me. Depressed! I could just as easily say I'm happy, for all it means."

"So what's wrong with yeh?"

"There's nothin' wrong with me."

"Will I tell yeh somethin' tha' migh' right' yeh?"

"Is there an'thin' I can do that'll stop yeh?"

"A job. That's what'd be good for yeh."

"Wha' are yeh talkin' abou'? I have a job."

"I mean a proper job. If you'd left school like the rest of us before yeh got anny fancy ideas abou' depression, there'd have been none of this."

"None of wha'?"

"You'd have been out of your time now, had a trade and could have been thinkin' abou' enjoyin' your life before settlin' down with a girl."

Joxer looked to me (he would have preferred Paula) with an expression that asked, "See what I mean?" before turning to Jack and saying, "Maybe you should have stayed in school until yeh were older than seven, or whatever the fuck age yeh were when yeh left. Yeh might have had a clue then wha' I'm talkin' about."

I thought Jack was going to give him a dig when he heard that. Instead, he just asked, "Well, wha' are yeh talkin' abou' then? Gimme a clue. If I'm so much of a simpleton, explain it to me. Yeh should be able to manage tha', the intelligent ball of shite tha' yeh are."

"I'm in pain, Jack, emotional pain. The kind of pain tha' crucifies me. It's so fuckin' powerful, it paralyses me. Can yeh understand tha'?"

Wha' would you know abou' pain, when it's common knowledge tha' you're drugged up to the eyeballs from one end of the day to the other? And if yeh really want to know the meanin' of pain, I'll tell yeh . . ."

"I don't want to hear it, some shite abou' havin' to pick berries for your breakfast while yeh walked barefoot, the five miles to school. But let me ask yeh one simple question. Have yeh ever bothered to ask yourself why it is I get stoned from one end of the day to the other?"

"That's obvious. You're nothin' but a bleeden hedonist and all this moanin' and whingin' is nothin' but a pathetic attempt to disguise it. You're a selfish . . . think of your mother and father! They lie awake at nigh' worryin' abou' yeh."

"Who's askin' them to? I just want someone to hear me. I feel like a dummy in a world full of deaf people. I feel . . ."

"*You! You! You!* D'yeh ever think of annyone else?"

"Who else is there to think abou'?"

At this point, Jimmy could be heard in the living room introducing a song he had made up himself. Jack left the kitchen to go and listen to it, saying he was going to ask Jimmy to write one for Joxer. After he left, I looked down the kitchen table at Joxer and watched a strange thing happen. The colour seemed to leave his long thin face and, if this is possible, gather behind his eyes. It began with a sharp breath through his nose. He then scooped his long fringe with a couple of fingers and flicked it back on to his head. Having shaken it with a toss, Joxer split his fringe in the centre, parting it equally to the sides. Hair groomed to his satisfaction, his fingers dropped to the fawny blond hairs above his upper lip and stroked comfortingly. I swear, between one end of this ritual and the other, his eyes changed colour from green to blue and threatened to fill with tears. They almost turned to dull steel grey when me da passed the remark on his way to the toilet, "Wha' are yeh doin' out here, Mr Happy? Bein' the life and soul of the party again?" All the while, Joxer was going the colour of pain.

"And wha' are yeh doin' out here with him?" me da asked me on his way back.

"Nothin'. I'm just sittin' here, Da."

"Well don't forget wha' I warned yeh abou' before. If I think tha' you're takin' anny drugs off him you'll be out of my home on your arse. Yeh haven't the excuse his mother uses of him bein' a difficult birth."

I couldn't always tell if me da was being serious or not. Joxer reckoned every time me da opened his mouth, he sounded like he had just been sucking on lemons and it was hard to soften that bit-terness, especially when he had a face like a slapped arse into the bargain. I have to admit, me da used every opportunity to take a swipe at Joxer and for no apparent reason. For as long as I could remember, the sun shone out of Jimmy's arse, I was never noticed and Joxer was one big problem. Me ma seemed to see things the same way, though with one difference; she was happy while Joxer was a problem. I don't mean by this that she took any pleasure from his unhappiness, but she did seem to have an interest in find-ing the ways and the means to mother him. Joxer, as he said him-self, didn't want to be mothered. Nor did he want to be solved.

The party was coming to an end. I could hear Jack singing how he had too few regrets to mention. Joxer got up and walked slowly towards the toilet. I watched his back as he headed away from me and had no idea. I didn't know at the time, but imagined later, that tears had begun to rush from his eyes and fall from his face. I've recreated it so many times, I've come to believe it. He closed the toilet behind him, still with his back to me. I'm sure that once inside, he gripped both sides of the hand basin as tight as he could and tried to squeeze whatever was haunting him away. When that didn't work, I would never have guessed what was going to happen next. Joxer? He rolled up, as far as he could, the sleeve of the shirt on his left arm and checked the point of entry that the magazine had suggested. It seemed more tender to him than it had ever done, but this didn't deter him. If anything, it only had him tearing impatiently at the wrapping on one of Jack's Gillette blades. The blade was thin, light, a metallic blue, and Joxer pinched the precision piece carefully in the centre before flinging a glance at himself in the mirror above the hand basin. It was a struggle to see through the haze of tears but he saw himself urging back, "Remember Sammy's advice. Don't hesitate." He didn't, but frightened it might be too painful, he only managed to slash a seven stitch gash across the bottom of the biceps on his left arm. He felt nothing but the dark red blood falling like a curtain of warmth. The pathetic attempt enraged him. It was something he knew he would never live down and would be nothing but ammunition for those who delighted in taking pot shots at him. The magazine had said death in two minutes. At the rate the blood was dripping from his elbow down into the sink, Joxer knew he would still be there next New Year's Eve. The anger he felt, the loathing for himself because he couldn't even get that right, helped him lift the blade determinedly; it helped him pierce the skin where the artery was most vulnerable and drag the blade across. Exuberantly, he severed everything: artery; veins; nerves; everything apart from the bone. Bright red blood splashed all over my brother's face.

One thing more than any other always puzzled me: why did Joxer walk back out from the toilet to the kitchen? I didn't see him immediately because my glance had fallen to the floor. It was that time of the morning. Paula saw him first. She had come back to the kitchen to say goodbye. I heard her scream. It was that loud, everything else stopped. The voices; Jack singing; people moving. Even the cigarette smoke seemed to linger. I saw Joxer, his blood pumping out in the direction he staggered towards. I saw him hold the wounded arm up like he was making some kind of sacrificial gesture. Paula's screams were louder and she was trying to pull her hair out as people arrived at the doorway to the kitchen. Jack was first and he tried to turn back, but he couldn't get out because me ma, me da, me aunts and anyone else still there were following in behind. Joxer was falling towards Jack. I couldn't move because in an attempt to get out of the way of the blood, Paula had begun to climb up behind me. I saw my brother Joxer collapse, and when he fell he was the colour of unbearable pain.

Mary Rose Callaghan

Billy, Come Home

Dublin, 16 October

IN THE END, I flew to London alone.

All the way over, I thought of Billy. First as the white-blonde little brother I loved. Then as the man who needed me too much. Poor Billy. What would he look like now? A body, answering the description of a missing Irishman, had been taken from the Thames. The guards were sure it was Billy. It was my job to identify him, then arrange for him to be brought home, as soon as the post-mortem was over. I couldn't bear to think of Billy being alone. Like so many Irish down the years, he had taken the boat over. According to the guards, he had bought his ticket in Dún Laoghaire. It would have been a bumpy crossing. Then the train. A change at Crewe. But why pick Oxford to end his life? Because we had once gone punting there? I remembered that sunny July day when we brought a picnic down the river, nearly six years ago. Maybe it was symbolic to drown himself where he'd been happy? Billy hadn't had a happy life. Never a place of his own. Or a garden. A garden wasn't much to want. He had ghastly parents. A mother who still wouldn't believe he was missing. And a father who had refused to come to England with me.

Billy's illness was a tragedy. Yet I never remember him complaining about his lost life. We both had the same genes, so it could have been me. He was the unlucky one.

ONE

IT STARTED WITH a bag of chips. That's how things go. You walk down a road and meet your fate, down another and escape it. There are so many chances in life. This time a young girl was fatally knifed. It happened near the roundabout in our neighbourhood, a well-known suburb of south Dublin. The roundabout is probably the busiest on the N11, a main artery out of the city, with endless traffic streaming home during rush hour. But the murder was at around midnight, so no one saw a thing.

The story made the next morning's news.

The victim, Mary Connors, was a member of the Travelling community. She was fifteen years old and had been seen laughing and joking with two other girls, while buying chips in our local takeaway. Then they left, presumably for the campsite in a field by the roundabout.

Mary never arrived. She got separated from the others.

Her body was found next morning in the grounds of the nearby Catholic Church—the curate came upon it on his way to Mass. Her beautiful copper hair was sticking out from behind a bush. At first, he thought she was sleeping, maybe drunk, but she had been dead for several hours. There was evidence of a struggle, and blood stained the path to the church. The autopsy reported that Mary had been crawling there for help when she had bled to death.

The country was shocked—another young woman murdered.

There had been a string of violent deaths, mainly of women, and all unsolved. A few were missing. Because of the church and Mary's age, people were reminded of Anne Lovett, a teenager who had died a few decades back, giving birth in front of the Virgin's statue in Longford. There were no other similarities. Mary Connors had been raped, but she wasn't pregnant.

I had booked that very church for my wedding in eight weeks' time. The same curate who found Mary was to marry us—that's

Kevin, my fiancé, and me. The curate later told me he usually went for a walk before bed, but that night he had a bad cold and stayed home. At around 12.30, he heard scuffling and a scream in the church grounds. He opened his door but didn't see anything. It was just kids messing on the way back from the pub, he told himself. If only he'd gone out, he might have saved Mary. Or seen the murderer.

I wish he had investigated. It would have saved our family so much heartbreak.

The funeral was a week later. I saw the old-fashioned, black-plumed horse pulling the hearse through the village to the graveyard. Half the countryside seemed to be following. It was a fantastic turnout, but by that time I was involved, so I looked away.

One thing was certain: whoever killed Mary had planned it. Why else was he carrying a long butcher's knife? The police had no clues, and people were afraid to go out. There had been other murders associated with our area, but all years before. A famous case in the 1960s had riveted the country. I knew about it, even though I wasn't born until the 1970s. A young woman—her name was Hazel—was choked, apparently accidentally, by her boyfriend, Shan Mohangi. Then he chopped her up and put her into garbage sacks. That deed was done in faraway Dublin—a distance in those days before the DART. But Hazel's mother came from nearby Crinken. I'd heard all about her from our ghastly nanny, Bridie. My child's mind had always associated the word *Shan*kill with *Shan* Mohangi. There's no connection, I know. *Shan* comes from the word 'old' in Irish, and the other *Shan* is a man's name. He got off with manslaughter and became a respected politician in South Africa. Everyone's forgotten Hazel, but a few years back a neighbour brought me to Crinken church where her mother was caretaker.

The village is more built up now. There are housing estates on both sides of it. The old Bray Road used to pass through, so it was always clogged with cars, but since they built the by-pass, it's a village again. There are a few restaurants and a couple of popular pubs. It'll never be ritzy like Blackrock or Dalkey, but we're trying. Except for one rough estate, and a few joy-riders and robberies, the area is full of ordinary families with children. Decent, quiet, upwardly mobile people, a few better off. Like most of the Irish, they resent Travellers, but murder is beyond them.

I actually met Mary. On a Monday morning, a couple of days before her murder.

It was the first day of school and the traffic was bad. It's always a nightmare when parents start ferrying their kids, but that's modern Ireland. No one walks anywhere. I was on my way to school, too, but the roundabout was backed up. Cars stretched all the way from the church, so I waited in my battered Corsa, noticing that the Travellers were back.

About ten families had appeared overnight. In the same field as the previous year. Nowadays there are houses built there and the area is walled off. That day, things were strewn about. Caravans parked higgledy-piggledy beside expensive cars and vans had already made tracks in the grass. Junk was everywhere—tyres, old fridges, window frames, a rickety couch, things no one could want. Even a donkey. And litter—empty milk cartons and banana peels mixed up with used Pampers spilling out of torn black plastic bags. It had a Third World look. Angry residents from my estate had probably already been to the guards. They always wanted the Travellers to be moved on. The committee complained every year, yet the Travellers came back.

I didn't do anything *for* the Travellers, but I hated committees.

That morning, people were hooting impatiently, jittery about

being late for work or school. The Travellers are blamed for everything bad that happens in Ireland, but this time, it wasn't them. A
truck had broken down on the N11 entrance, and was waiting for
a tow.

A few cars had made illegal U-turns—there was another way,
back through the village by the old Bray Road: a lovely wooded
stretch, past the cemetery and Crinken church.

I thought about turning too. The news was over, so it was after
nine, but the motorway went right to school. I teach in St
Nicholas's, a community college in Bray—about ten minutes away,
depending on traffic. That morning, I wasn't in a hurry. I was
enjoying the sun, which was brilliant. Besides, I had no morning
classes, so wasn't exactly late. I just had to check my room for the
new term; make sure there were enough chairs, and jars for water.
Then get art paper from a shop in the town. I always bought in
bulk, so I got wholesale rates.

But the traffic wouldn't budge.

I was about to turn around when two small boys started
roughhousing on the pavement. They were from the campsite. You
can spot a Traveller anywhere: there's something about their
look—freckles and red hair. They are said to be the real Irish, who
were dispossessed during the Famine—they took to the roads and
never got back into proper houses—but I doubt this is true. I've
read there are similar nomadic groups all over Europe. These boys
had matted hair and wore muddy wellingtons over their jeans. A
Jack Russell with a string around its neck was yapping hysterically
at them.

"Ah, fuck up!" one of them yelled back.

I had to smile. I'd never heard that version. "Fuck off!" or
"Shut the fuck up!" yes.

The dog ran out into the road.

I watched uneasily. The boys were only about five and seven.

It was a shame they had nowhere else to play. The side of the road wasn't safe, with fumes and speeding cars. It wasn't much of a home either.

The dog kept yapping, the string trailing the ground. The boys ignored this at first, and went on wrestling. Then the bigger one ran after the dog and, catching the string, dragged the animal to safety.

I leaned out my window. "Mind the cars, won't you?"

I was expecting another expletive, but the boy grinned. "OK."

I wondered if he'd ever sit for me. He was right out of Walter Osborne. "Don't let your little brother on the road."

"Naw." Then cheekily, "Gotta euro, missus?"

"No. Why aren't you in school?"

"Don't go to school."

That was the trouble when you moved all the time. No regular schooling.

"What's your dog's name?"

"Spot."

It wasn't original, but kids are like that—conventional. Billy had once owned a Spot. I could still see that dog. It was a yapper, too, and ugly, with a bald patch on its back from some dog disease. But my brother had loved him. Which reminded me to ring Billy and arrange for coffee. I hadn't seen him for two weeks and felt guilty.

The boy tried again. "Give us a euro."

I shook my head.

At last, the tailback inched forward. At that very moment, the dog wriggled free and darted back into the road. The smaller boy chased it, running in front of the crawling cars to the other side of the road.

A van came off the roundabout.

There was a screech of brakes.

The child was hit. I saw it all in my rear-view mirror.

I froze. Was he badly hurt?

No. He stood up, rubbed his eyes, then staggered and sat down again on the curb.

A few cars pulled over on to the soft margin. I went to his aid, along with the passenger from the car in front of me. The van driver got out, too, ashen-faced and moaning, "Jesus, I didn't see him."

I was sorry for him.

It had happened so easily. A group gathered, as the child looked around groggily. I bent over him, trying to remember my first aid.

"Are you OK, pet?" I asked.

People stared from cars.

"I think he's OK," I reassured the driver.

The little boy howled. His face turned from white to red and tears streamed down his cheeks.

A girl came out of one of the caravans. It was Mary Connors, although I didn't know it then. Her hair was copper, a darker shade than the boys', but she had the same freckles. She was in high heels and was bulging out of tight jeans. The heels sank into the grass as she crossed the muddy field, so she took them off and, carrying them, ran to the child.

She sat down beside him. "Michael, yer all right now."

Too young to be his mother, I remember thinking. A sister or some other relative.

"Yer fine now, Michael."

The dog kept on barking, and the other boy looked on helplessly. Someone rang the guards.

An older woman appeared from one of the caravans. She had a weather-beaten face and was dressed in a black leather jacket. Obviously the mother, she hovered anxiously over the child. The guards screeched up—the station was just nearby. Two of them got out and took details from the van driver. A few witnesses told them what they'd seen. I said it hadn't been the man's fault, that the boy had run on to the road after the dog.

The child tried to stand up.

"He should stay sitting," I said to the woman.

She told him to stay down and he obeyed, but insisted on hugging his dog. It had stopped barking and was licking him, which the kid didn't seem to mind.

An ambulance came and took him and his mother away. They left the dog, which upset the kid. I remembered Billy and his dog, so offered to drive the dog with the other kids after the ambulance. Luckily the hospital was just on the other side of the roundabout.

"Thanks, missus." The girl put on her shoes. Her socks were ruined.

"It's Angie," I said. "What's your name?"

"Mary Connors."

I'll always remember her smile. Hard to describe in words, but it just lit her face. I loaded up the car with the girl, the elder boy and the dog, which he held in a drowning grip.

The truck was gone and the traffic was normal now. I waited my turn for a gap, then circled the roundabout to the hospital exit.

Despite all the bad press for hospitals nowadays, the Travellers were treated well. There was no queue; I suppose it was the time of day. The child was lying on a trolley when we arrived. A nurse at the reception desk had taken charge and was writing details given by the mother. As we went into the waiting room, the nurse smiled curiously at the bedraggled dog, which nobody objected to. I left for school, grateful things hadn't been worse.

It's considered unlucky in Irish folklore to see a red-headed woman first thing in the morning—that was according to our caretaker. I met him afterwards in the school car park. When I told him about the accident, he said to watch out.

I just laughed. You make your own luck. Anyway, I didn't see Mary first. It was her brothers, and one of them had the bad luck. As a race, we Irish are amazingly superstitious; a Kerryman is even more so. The caretaker kept up his daft predictions, but the kid would be OK, I felt sure.

I looked for him when passing the campsite over the next few days, but never saw anyone. The caravans were still there, but the camp was deserted.

I felt a bond with Mary, since we both cared for younger brothers. Except there were just two years between Billy and me. I had been an adult child, pushed into a carer's role. I think it affected me. It made me a worrier.

EVELYN CONLON

SKIN OF DREAMS

O N THE NIGHT of 20 November 1940, Harry Tavey made his
way to the *céilí*. It would not have been a regular night out
for him, but Nicholas Cantwell had asked him to play, and it was
always best to oblige the person who had taught you your first
tunes. And a bottle of stout or two, which the Keenans always
gave, would be very welcome. A little stout went well with tunes,
just a little. The bicycle ride was slow up the hills, the wheels reluctant to loosen their grasp on the frozen patches of the road. But
after the hills, the going was easy. He had to switch on the flash
lamp on the flat, so that he didn't ride into the potholes or splash
his new trousers. They weren't exactly new, but were new to this
level. They were the trousers of his last, recently replaced, suit.
They had just been demoted to this sort of wear. Some of the potholes sported a veneer of thin ice. As Harry crackled over one, he
could have sworn that he heard a shot. Probably the ice. But there
was another one. A clear bang. *What an odd time for someone to be
shooting. What could you see in this dark? You'd need lights at the back
of your eyes. Shooting at rats maybe, but how could you see them?*
When he got to the house there was already a steady lap of conversation, and some people were testing out steps. At least three
women tried not to look at him. Two fathers wondered what the
chances would be. Harry Tavey was a handsome man, a good
worker and a nifty fiddler. It was also most likely that he would

inherit a substantial farm of land. The rumbling excitement in the room put the shots out of his head; he had meant to remark upon them, meant to wonder with someone who could have been shooting at that hour and what.

Harry sat down on a seat, opened his fiddle case and bantered his way into the next reel. They played "The Cup of Tea" and "Peter Street", "The Skylark" and "Maud Miller", "The Stick across the Hob" and "Richard Brennan's". The dancers danced the Ballycommon set, the Cashel set, the Siege of Ennis and the Haymakers' jig. He should have told somebody about the shots. But what with one thing and the other, settling into a tune, sliding into the next, remembering notes, the tucking of his fiddle into a groove in his neck, the leaning of his head to one side as, at last, he could flow with the sound of long hours to come, he forgot. And every now and again, he allowed himself to think that he was being watched by the dancers, or at least one of them. It was a satisfying thing, and even if he had no nerve when it came to women, at least he could string airs together. If only he had the words, he certainly had the thoughts. But if a tune could be overdone, and it could, you can be sure words could, too. No rush, there was plenty of time. When the dance was over and after the woman had waited in vain as long as was decent, the musicians gathered their instruments and left the house. It was hard to leave the room, cosy now with the heat of the just finished dance evaporated from the middle of the floor but still hanging in the corners. On the cold cycle home, Harry heard the tunes. They had colours, black, white, red, purple, and they were still rhyming with the noise of feet beating. Even the frost could not kill the sound that tumbled in his ears for the first few miles, then slipped out to waft through the hedges, and across the fields, eventually sounding like distant clapping in the hills. He slept well.

In the morning he rose early to exercise his greyhounds and to get himself in working order before facing into a day's labour with his cousin, whose continuous cheerfulness could, in all honesty, be sometimes hard to take. It was better to have some solitude first. The music last night had never been dense, unlike the freezing cold this morning. He stepped out over the land, the greyhounds trotting in front of him on their leads. As he went from field to field, he took the opportunity to count his uncle's sheep. He also brought a straying bull, which had wandered on to a neighbouring farm, back into the field. At the end of the third field, his hounds now on the loose with no cattle in sight, Harry noticed that some of the bushes he had used to block a gap had been pushed aside. He climbed up, wondering how on earth that had happened, and then he saw, on the other side of the hedge, a body. It was a woman's body, and it appeared to be lifeless. Beside it sat a small black dog. The dog growled at Tavey, but that was the least of his worries at that moment. Harry swivelled on his heel and rushed home. He told both his uncle and his aunt, who were still in bed, of his discovery. He then left immediately to tell the guards. He told the guards that, because of the dog, he could not go near the body to check whether it was dead or whether the woman was asleep. He said that he knew that it was a woman because of her dress and her shoes. He did not say that he recognised it at once as that of his neighbour Moll Graney. He was not sure, never became sure, why he did not tell them this.

The doctor who examined Moll Graney found a cartridge wad wedged in her hair. Her coat had been torn, but the rest of her clothes were not damaged. Although the coat was buttoned, there was blood on its interior—an odd discovery, one whose significance and puzzlement was overlooked immediately. The doctor also believed that Moll had been shot in another place. He realised, by the position of her legs, that the body had been lifted, probably away from the place that she had been shot. He felt that her legs had been artificially placed one on top of the other and certainly were not in the stance of a woman who had been shot at that spot. But no matter what the doctor said, the cruel fact was that this body had been placed on this farm where Harry Tavey, whose movements were well known because of the exercising of his grey-hounds, would inevitably find the body first thing in the morning. This simple fact hurled all suspicions directly at him.

Harry Tavey, his cousin, his aunt and uncle all gave rigorous descriptions of their movements. None of them led in any way to any evidence that anybody on this farm was involved in the murder of their neighbour. But suspicion is a gnawing thing, and the forces of law and order do like to believe that they will solve crime. It was an easier thing to do, to boil the suspicion to some kind of ready-made mix, so that this death would not hang over this place as a huge question mark for ever. Harry Tavey was brought to court. Harry Tavey was charged. There did not appear to be any evidence for this charge to remain. However, before the batting of too many eyelids, Harry Tavey was removed from his place to Mountjoy Prison and away from the useful petty rumbling of facts in his neighbourhood, the sound of which might in fact have thrown up another name, or at least thrown his out. In a newspaper report that Maud diligently read in the National Library, the history of events was recorded as if no people wondered and wondered and wondered, and as if no people whispered and said it could not possibly have been him, the facts didn't fit. The neighbour who spoke to Maud, years later, said that nobody believed this was going to stick.

"We neither believed that he did it nor that the case would be continued. We were a bit shocked to find that it was going to a court in Dublin, but we thought that, traumatic as this might be, everything would turn out all right in the end and Harry would be back here soon."

They also had ideas as to who might have been involved. Moll Graney's life had caused many anxieties in her local community, none more active than those of the fathers of some of her children. And there were visitors to her house who would prefer never to be known. Indeed, among them was a guard in the station where Harry Tavey was brought to be questioned. And to complete local frisson, Moll worked occasionally in the garda station.

"I have great crack altogether down at the guards," she said often.

There were a lot of people who would not have wished Moll Graney to say a lot of things. Harry Tavey was not one of those. And worse than that, there were growing children, whose resemblance to local men was becoming startlingly apparent as they became older. She lived a dangerous life, this woman alone, feeding her children. A dangerous life and a dangerous death.

When the Mountjoy Prison door closed on Harry Tavey, he tried to think of tunes. He tried to think of weather. He tried to think of farm work. But the only thing that would stay in his mind was the door and the sound of the lock hitting into place. And yet, as he sat on the bed to think his way through the next few months, he did believe that nothing of any real harm would come to him. He did believe that a man cannot be found guilty of something he did not do. He did believe that he would soon be back home.

The questioning of neighbours continued. Those who said the things that made it impossible for Harry Tavey to have committed this murder were left aside. Those who suggested otherwise, by innuendo and overenthusiastic agreement with what they thought the questions meant, were taken seriously. Those who had no reason to like outsiders were believed more than those who saw the man, who played tunes with him, who played hurling with him, who walked with him, who had an occasional stout with him, who talked with him. The gathering of these comments was like a hurricane happening behind Harry's back, who, while he sat in Mountjoy, was completely unaware of the storm taking shape. And even worse was to happen.

Two guards visited the hardware store in Cashel, where most of the ammunition used in the New Inn area was purchased. They inspected the firearms register and pointed out to staff that it contained no record of any sale to Harry Tavey's uncle, on the date that they mentioned, of cartridges of a type that they also mentioned. They suggested that on their next visit they would see such an entry. And Maud saw the entry. She stared at it disbelievingly. The clear crossing out of another man's name, not even erased to the extent that she could not read it. Above it was scrawled exactly the information that the guards had given to the staff in the hardware store. This any person can see to this day.

The black winds edged closer and closer together. Men who had heard one shot, two shots, at times when Harry Tavey could not have been in that area were not believed or had their minds changed or had doubts kneaded into them. Men who could not, because of the direction of the wind on the day, have heard any shots from the spots on which they were standing had now suddenly heard an exact lucid sound. This is the place where certainty is no longer certain. If Harry Tavey had not moved quite happily into the first reel on that night, if Harry Tavey had drawn breath when he arrived in the house of the dance, if Harry Tavey had turned his head around and said to the next man, "I thought I heard shots tonight, just when I was passing Reilly's hedge. Who would be out shooting at that hour of the night? Sure, you could see nothing." If Harry Tavey had said that, to any one man, then things might have been different.

So he thought, as he sat in his cell. Then he thought so many things, so many things that could prove that he did not do this, and yet there was no one in this place to hear them. In good moments, when he had shaken himself up and told himself to get through this strong, he knew that his neighbours would be fine. He knew that they would piece another story together. And it was this knowing that held the saddest truth of all. It was this knowing that sent shivers up Maud's spine as she tried to go to sleep at night.

As Harry Tavey sat on his bed, lay on his bed, walked in his small cell, an uncontrollable story was growing outside, an edifice of lies was maturing into fact. *And it remains to this day*, Maud thought.

At the court in Green Street, Harry's aunt and uncle, cousin, and a few friends huddled together, as if caught in a snow storm of half-truths that fell from the mouths of those who gave evidence. As his defence chipped and chipped at what they knew to be untrue, the friends sometimes galvanised themselves with the consolation that was creeping into their bad dreams. But they knew little of the law. They knew little of the place they were staying. They had never stayed in a bed and breakfast in the centre of Dublin before this. The food in cafés near by was strange. Harry's aunt's varicose veins were playing up. But they could tell what wasn't true, and in their innocence believed that so, too, could the jury. But that was not what happened on those days, in that place, at that time. The jury believed what the others said. Harry Tavey was found guilty of a murder that he did not commit. His aunt and uncle had delayed over the last cup of tea at lunchtime and were coming up the street when two neighbours approached them. They seemed to be walking on the sides of their feet and were ashen faced. The wails of Harry's aunt may still be heard on the corner of Green Street if a person listens closely.

Harry was put into a van and brought back to Mountjoy.

"But it isn't true," he repeated to himself, as if the words could save him. Harry moved into his cell and again worked on himself to believe that an appeal would succeed. But the appeal did not succeed either. In the days that followed the appeal failure, guards from outside the locality still visited the scene, still asked questions, still wondered about odd pieces of evidence that clashed completely with other sworn statements. They had great questions; they felt in their bones that a wrong verdict had been created. But the neighbours closed their doors to new questions. They wanted this horror gone from them. They wanted someone to be blamed. They wanted to put that night, that morning, these weeks, behind them. They wanted never to speak of it again. And it was easier; a person from outside the neighbourhood was always a better bet than one of their own. Those who knew he was innocent then travelled to Dublin to meet the minister for justice. But it was too late. The die was cast and the outcome was already written. Harry Tavey prepared for his own unjust death.

* * *

Although Maud pored over the huge question that lay across the spoken words of those who gave evidence, she knew that nothing could change the exact sequence of events. Although she could see with absolute clarity exactly what was right and what was wrong, there was no way to make this thing not have happened. She became lonely in a ferocious kind of way.

DAVID FOSTER

"THE DRY AND DUSTY ROAD" from
THE LAND WHERE STORIES END

YOU MIGHT THINK it strange, a woodcutter meeting a saint, but the Promised Land had saints by the score in the days before cars and telly. Every part of the kingdom had a saint. Some had two, which meant supernumerary saints had to sail off to unknown parts. They were a peripatetic lot, familiar with icebergs and volcanoes. Some lived alone as hermits, while others were cenobites, like Finn.

Finn was the saint who had saved the woodcutter from Galahad's mother. He probably didn't remember that but I hope you do. If not, it might be better for you to go back and start the book again. The minute Finn appeared among them, people forgot their grievances, for saints see right through your liver and lights into the depths of your being. What they see there is your soul wrapped in your personality, that is, something resembling a pearl surrounded by an oyster of ignorance and misery.

Finn liked his monks to construct the most beautiful books on the skins of young calves. These books concerned what Jesus Christ had had to say to the fairy folk, a subject on which Finn, at that time, was the world's greatest expert. Nothing like these books had ever been seen in the Promised Land, and while most people couldn't read they did admire illustrations, affording Finn the pretext of educating them in Christ. While people's attention was diverted as they admired the multicoloured letters in the books, Finn would gently lead them on the dry and dusty road. And that is a road, we are assured, that has never failed an honest heart.

"Tell me about yourself," said Finn, "but make it brief I pray. We have many a mile to walk before we rest this day."

It wasn't one of Finn's better days. Nor was he looking, as he spoke, at the woodcutter whom he addressed. As he assisted the contrite woodcutter off his massive knees, Finn looked to where the pale boy was playing head-butts with the white calf. And as he gazed, Finn's scarred face assumed an eagle's glare, for here was a man who sensed at once this boy's special promise.

Overcome with the feeling of relief men often report when they meet a saint, a feeling some liken to a spigot being pulled from a barrique of wees and poos, the woodcutter hastened to recount his life in the customary sequence. He hadn't gotten to his first meeting with the leprechaun when the saint raised a hand, and when a saint raises a hand, ignorant folk fall silent. It should be recalled the woodcutter had actually been a saint himself, for a bit, but folk on the dark and stormy road are torn this way and that, and as often reduced to the level of an ass as joined in union with The One. Such is the nature of the dark and stormy road. Think hard before you persist with it. If only the woodcutter could have retained his key or even his crucifix, he might have been able to speak with the saint of what he'd seen in the Land where Stories End. Unfortunately, that land was a fast fading memory to the woodcutter, a glib tale that lost more lustre each time it was told. Why, it even slipped the poor woodcutter's mind completely, on occasion. At present, he was more inclined to focus on how he'd lost his carpentry set. The monk to whom he had been speaking, the monk who had given him the bread, whispered something in Finn's ear, and Finn nodded, though never once taking his eyes off the boy Galahad.

"We are all sons of the king," said Finn, "for such is our curse and our blessing. But our king is ill and we cannot make him well through our undressing."

At this point, he pulled out a bere bannock, broke it and offered it to his monks. It was rare to see a saint eat, as they deprive themselves of food and sleep.

"I wouldn't mind a bite of that," said the woodcutter, miffed he hadn't been offered any. "In exchange I'll tell you about this meadow, which is not as it appears. A witch lives here and I was thinking of her as you spoke, my friend, for like yourself she wants to cure the king but she would do it by undressing. I wonder where she can be? She tells me she never leaves the clearing."

The saint whispered something to a monk who wore his long hair in a mullet, before wandering off to the river to pray up to his neck in cold running water. Another monk then asked what had been said in order to write it down, for everything the saint said was dutifully written down.

"He says we cannot see her as no woman can be three. No woman, says Finn, can be a saint's daughter, a maiden's mother and a fool's confidante. He says she's in the king's pay and that each full moon a steward comes here, to pay her one black pearl."

"Then let us," said the woodcutter, rising, "let us look for her treasure trove, for she told me, may God be my witness, she never leaves the clearing. We have men enough here to mount a thorough search, so let's begin. There's nowhere here she could have spent that treasure trove. You start here, sir. And you start there, sir, and I'll start here."

"Wait," said the monk with the mullet, "you haven't heard the full story. Before taking her pearl, she demands it dissolved in red wine then drinks it down her."

"Drinks it *down* her?" The woodcutter couldn't believe his ears. Certainly, there was no point in mounting a search for pearl.

Finn was in the river, up to his head in the cold flowing water. They watched him raise his arms over his head as he asked The Lord for guidance.

"Look!" said a monk, and when they looked, there was the boy, sucking on the cow. Inspired by the calf, he would then butt the cow's bag in order to increase the flow and, as he did, the calf, on the other side of the cow, would do the same.

"You'd think they were meant to suckle four," observed a monk, "for see how they have four quarters? Goats have only two."

"Like your dam," came the jibe, and the monks again laughed heartily. The woodcutter hadn't thought these holy men would be so brash. He felt both let down and disappointed, partly because of their unseemly levity, mostly because that stupid witch had pissed away all those pearls. If it was meant as an effort to cure the king it was certain to fail, for had not the king himself told the woodcutter every time he counted his pearls he found he had more than before? You wouldn't cure him of wealth, if greed were illness, by drinking his pearls.

Whenever Finn, as now, went off to battle the Old Enemy, his monks would start to tell each other dirty jokes and scribble rude drawings. The woodcutter hoped no monk would do a dirty thing with the witch. As things stood, he was now skeptical of the dry and dusty road, but what he had failed to appreciate, was that what is safe is tedious. Success on the dry and dusty road is slow albeit certain. The big drawback of the dry and dusty road, is that men only live a certain time, and their consciousness is diminished by the fact they sleep so much. None of these monks had made much progress on the dry and dusty road, true, but a saint who achieves his sainthood on that road never loses sight of the Truth, whereas a saint who achieves his sainthood on the dark and stormy road is in constant threat of being again reduced to the level of an ass. There are many, many dark and stormy roads, half a dozen dry and dusty ones, but only one sure, safe and immediate method of finding the Truth, and that is never to have lost it in the first place. Carnal ignorance, the bright and sunny road, is, however, just for boys, and furthermore, it is given of God, so we don't go out in search of it.

"Why don't we grab him," said a monk, "and take him into our company? He could make a fine monk and that way, we'll gain merit in healing a future king."

"Finn says no one is to touch him," said the monk with the mullet, whose name was Bran. "We have more need of him, says Finn, than he has need of us. He is a maiden, one of the one hundred and forty-four thousand undefiled of women who, when the Lamb stands on mount Sion, have the Father's name upon their forehead. Unless we too are found with that seal on our forehead upon resurrection, we shall not sing before the throne of God and the four beasts and the elders."

"What's Finn doing there?" said the woodcutter, all this having gone over his head. "I have to be going shortly. Much as I've enjoyed your company, I've got to get back to my clachan. Furthermore, for your information, that child is my adopted son and I shall take him with me when I leave. He'll be too busy to do the devil's work, cutting wood for me."

"You'd better move fast then," said a monk, "for there he goes. Yes he's off."

Galahad was indeed scampering over the clearing, running like a hound and the calf after him. It happened while the woodcutter was taking leave of the monks. There was Finn, doing battle in the river, lips moving in prayer, and there was the wild, tiny child, running like a hound over the grass. Before the woodcutter had a chance to move, the boy had disappeared, and there was the calf, standing on the clearing's edge, looking back at the cow.

"He won't get far," shouted the woodcutter, setting out in hot pursuit. "I know this forest. I'll have him back here, soon as you like, but we may go straight to my hut. Cheerio, it's been a pleasure, and thanks again for the bannock, lads. Delicious. Give my regards to the saint and tell him I haven't forgotten how he saved my life."

The cow imagined the woodcutter was running towards her calf, so she got upset and put a crumpled horn in the woodcutter's cape. The monks roared laughing at this, and the woodcutter grew so embarrassed he got up from where he'd been tossed and walked quickly on, without so much as a backward glance. Later, inspecting his cape well out of sight of those wretched monks, he saw the cow had ruined the one item of value he possessed. This made him all that more determined to find Galahad.

All that evening and all that night he searched for the boy, to no avail. Once he thought he heard the tiny bell-ring of a laugh, but he never saw the child, although he searched both far and wide. At dawn, bruised, defeated and still smarting over the hole in his cape, he took a final glance at the clearing just to see if the boy was there. He wasn't, but Finn, as it so happened, had emerged from his night-long vigil, and was settling down, dripping wet, to talk to his monks about what God had said. He smelt, as a Celtic saint should always smell, of attar of oak.

The woodcutter wondered what Finn would have to say, so he strolled over and sat next to the monks. The cow was bellowing, calling Galahad to breakfast.

"Fellow warriors in spiritual warfare," declared Finn, "hear now the Lord's Word. The Lord is righteous in all His ways and holy in all His works. We shall continue to celebrate Easter on the Sunday between the fourteenth and the twenty-second day of the moon, following John the Evangelist and Polycarp, who taught that Easter is the fourteenth day of the moon, if that day be a Sunday. We shall *never* shave the crowns of our heads behind the tips of our ears. We shall drink beer and beer only, co-warriors in spiritual warfare, for beer is our sacrament. Beer is the blood of our Saviour. Beer, fresh and effervescent as the promise of Salvation. Beer, made from the living waters that flow across this kingdom, and the corn that grows where trees were cleared to allow for the growing of corn."

"Alleluia," shouted the monks, as they hated the taste of red wine. "Hooray," shouted the woodcutter, as the saint was endorsing his vocation.

"I went to Rome once, co-warriors. It is a habitation of devils and the hold of every foul spirit and a cage of every unclean bird. All the houses are built atop each other in Rome. The Pope wears gold and precious stones and pearls. The monks don't know how to sing. It is horribly hot in summer."

"We're not going to Rome then, Father."

"No. But we cannot return to a monastery if it means drinking red wine. Not if it means presuming a ring of hair makes a crown of thorns. Not if it means celebrating Easter between the fifteenth and the twenty-first day of the moon."

"Where shall we go then, Father?"

"We shall go as far from the Rule of Benedict as we can. We shall go to a desert."

The monks sat quietly. All they could hear was the burble of the running water in the river, the rumble of a distant thundercloud, the cooing of the wood doves in the forest, and the fluttering of some little moths over some late heather flowers.

"Do we set sail, do we, Father, in search of a desert? For we have no deserts here."

"What is a desert?" inquired Finn. "Does any co-warrior know?"

Bran put up a hand.

"Yes Bran?"

"A place where there's no water, Father. A place both dusty

and dry. A place like the Sinai in the Holy Land of Jesus Christ Our Lord."

"A good answer, though not the whole truth. All men have access to a desert, for a desert is a place where men can ignore the call of the Promised Land, in order to achieve resurrection as one of the one hundred and forty-four thousand to be saved when the Last Trump sounds. We cannot do that here. The Promised Land is too crowded with women, ogres, and villains. We shall have to find a desert in which to continue our war on He Who Mocks at All Good Things."

Various monks proposed a variety of fastnesses, among them offshore islands, but these were occupied, it appeared, by agents of the Holy See.

"What about the islet in the middle of the lake where the women live under the water?"

"There's a hermit on it."

"We could go to the middle of the forest, Father. No one would find us there."

"How could we live in the middle of the forest? Where would we grow corn for beer? How could we stop the ogres from stealing our sacred books? Don't be stupid, Findlug. I mean to establish a monastery where monks eat at the same table, but each will have his own cell, there to wage warfare from compline to the rising bell. A desert is not a place where there is no chance of waging war. No, it is a place where spiritual life is made more easy through mortification. God, in His river, spoke to me of a fairy isle on the Edge of the World, that is not visible to humankind save once in a millennium. On a certain day in a millennium, should a man emerge from the forest, he sees before him an apparition of a village of wooden huts. And should that man be clean of sin, he sees, offshore, a fairy isle. And if a fairy boat can be found and a fairy man to row it, who's to say that mortal man could not set foot on

Innisfinn? For that, I'm told, is to be the name of the isle. I'm also told that when a mortal man sets foot on Fairyland, a spell is broken."

Here Finn stared at the woodcutter and the woodcutter stared back. You cannot get to a Fairyland on the dry and dusty road.

Douglas A. Martin

Branwell

H<small>E GOES OUT</small> to be with men. Together they share drink. The promise of coming again is a resurgence towards the next day, the next night he'll be here.

He'll drink himself to death.

Men strangle each other in the shadows, all around him, and all he wants to do is fall to John Brown's feet again, one last time.

* * *

Fires burn through the night, in dark recesses where men come together to suffer themselves among themselves.

On his knees, he sketches, a being fallen, holding up hands empty and chained.

On his bed back home, he sketches the pugilists in the paper. He's only sketching now. His heart beats uneasily. He can listen to it, listing, in his chest, some nights, thumping harder, stumbling, trotting, accompanying him loudly trying to sleep.

He imagines one of the men in the bar taking him around the neck, with a dullness in his head, wrapping his fingers there, and throttling. Or he thinks of the shot from their father's gun, how the bullet would enter all at once, welcomed if he could still be there to feel it.

If he pulls his pencil across the page just right, the red nectar appears, rewarding sight. The hairs on his arm cast themselves in warm tints from the light that cracks through the glass.

He might earn his drink by drawing for it.

A fine oak was not to come out looking like a lily from a hot-house, the son a Miss Nancy, a milksop. He's not some fop.

He holds onto the twist of the sheets like someone's little white hand, as his reddish whiskers grow in more fully. He's seldom even up to shave. His lower jaw, around his lips, his chin, cheeks go chestnut. It grows in longer. His pencil makes longer lines. His hair falls down more over a sweat-soaked forehead.

The sheets come apart in his hands.

The door to his room was locked and shut. It's the largest room in the whole house. He had a chair there behind it. Could he be hiding anyone in there with him. Only Emily knows the secret knock.

He tells her how he'd once gone into her room at Thorp Green, Lydia's. Emily would not be able to believe how the mistress's bed had been held so grandly within the four wide mahogany pillars, polished so your face would light up in them. He'd chased the young boy around in there. And then, just as a joke, they'd slipped down into the red sheets of the bed. No light would reach them under there. They were in their cave. At this time of day, the sun was so high up in the sky.

The red blinds on the windows were left open in there, weren't drawn like the brown in his room.

His room kept all to itself on the edges of the grounds of Thorp Green.

The deep red carpet in the mother's master bedroom made it needless to tip-toe up to the boy to surprise him.

Her walls were the color of the inside of his mouth.

If Edmund comes over to the mirror, and opens up, he'll show him.

What were they doing in there.

He'd moved him down on the bed in a boxing move. The red covers work their way up into a mouth that opens up in a squeal, their strings of sweat and spit, the taste of salt, running, as they held each other down in play. The passion of the moment, let any boy try to instruct another in that. There are ways the animals comfort each other. His tongue in his mouth begins to curl up into snaking shapes, raising itself up, falling back, undulating. There in the bed turning over and over and around, he's been practicing trying to draw out the poison. His body becomes a puddle. He disturbs his body by touching it. He holds it in his hands. He can't fit all of himself into his hands. He bleeds from the mouth, when he gasps too much from the coughing fits. He can touch the red spots to the walls. Emily has come up to clean up after him.

He's ruined the nice, perfumed, satin handkerchief he'd tucked in his pocket at Thorp Green.

Their father at home might die any day now, leaving them all in the hands of the parish he'll no longer serve. They'll find Branwell on the road, panting to catch the breath for his next step, a villager, the parson's son, in such a state, trying to get home, unable, to go on, unable, to take, step the next, step alone. And then at the doorstep he's led up to, Branwell unable to lift his leg, at the last to cross himself over inside.

He sees a welcome death now, every night in dreams, as he faints away under the strain of the alcohol on his system. He remembers his sister hiding her face from him in her coffin. Already, at thirty, he's become an old man. At thirty-one decaying.

Each hour was getting closer. Soon he won't even be able to walk. The skin colored, like old papers that time ate away at.

Everyone in the village said there was madness in his eyes now. There was nothing honorable about Branwell to save. He'd let his hair go uncut. It floated around his face in bed. He was so gaunt, disappearing before them.

He believes he looks more now like one of the characters he used to write about. But he no longer writes. His knee hurts him, lying there. The warm blood grows colder. Over the course of a day, it gets colder and colder. There's no way he's going to be able to finish the poem he was working on, he was planning as a present for his friend Leyland the sculptor.

He has friends in London. He'd been just one among a million men. Men manufactured things there. The edges of the buildings had felt rough under his hands, as he'd trailed along them, as he'd leaned against them. The meeting corners were not yet all smoothed out.

Outside their horses wait for them to finish drinking. Inside the building, he runs his hands over the scaled designs. A bleeding spirit often delights in this here. Yes, men being men, being with men. Their brother, he couldn't just disappear into the labor force. He couldn't just become one of them.

In Haworth, their brother was a virtuoso in the bars, where inside the air is cold, damp, and heavy. It smelled deeply of all of them, leather of their heavy shoes, their puddles spilling, and sawdust there to take it all up. Their mouths open like the door, the air heavy with their breath, as over each other they mill, air virgin everywhere outside of there.

His sisters, Anne and Charlotte, off in London now, are taking care of the business of their books. It must be attended to.

* * *

Two days before he dies, he's still drinking in the village.

Shopkeepers, weavers, the chemist, the postmaster, the village children, they all watched him attempting to make his way down their Main Street.

Look how he walks.

And he didn't seem to be eating anymore, only drinking.

Here, he just needs a strong shoulder to lean on.

Some nights they hear his sister Emily even has to come down to collect him to bring him home to bed.

It's a chronic lung complaint, along with his heart.

Notice how his voice softens, as the frame of his body shakes.

Then hush falls over him.

In the night, a cough violently racks its way through his curtained body, rattling his chest, stomach, shoulders, a pale corpse struggling to still appear walking.

He goes one night to the village for the last time, in what appears to be a new state of calm that's taken over his mind. He insists on going out, though he's too weak to leave the bed, they believe.

Charlotte says nothing.

A drink. All he needs. He walks until his knee begins to give out, scanning the street, the spaces of the lanes, around corners, his widening field of vision, that begins to haze, to blur, then darken over completely in the strain. If someone could just meet him at the top of the hill, just the very top, and bring him a drink, he'll feel better tomorrow.

Friday night he'd gone to the village. That Saturday, all day that next day, he'd stayed in bed. That Sunday morning, while John Brown was there with him, watching over him, he began to die.

He'd done nothing great or good, he says to the sexton, in all his life, his friend grasping his hand. The reality of this sorrow takes him. Nothing either great or good.

John was there with him, while the family was at church. It had been years since their brother had been inside one. Not since William, his aunt. And then they'd all come back. He'd held onto John's hand, their brother, unwashed and unshaven.

He was a man moving through a mist who'd lost his way.

In this moment before their eyes, they wanted to see him again become that little boy they'd once adored.

Was he remembering childhood.

They had all been so much more then together.

He says he sees Maria, losing his reasoning.

They think he's losing his mind.

His limbs shake as if passing through them were some very strong internal breeze.

He sees only himself everywhere, not yet reached.

It's Maria, he says, he's thinking of, by calling out for. Maria, John, Maria.

Their son would no longer fit into one of their arms.

Emily recalls to him the skies they'd stood under, how he'd slip off his mother's lap, they'd all run together outside.

She'd still be there to hold them when they got back.

Charlotte had always remembered the hearth glowing, but she won't remember exactly who it was, playing there with their only boy, on the day Charlotte would never forget, watching from the other side of the door, Branwell with their older sister, mother. On her lap he'd tucked flowers into her hair all light was going out of, they'd collected weeds, but they won't call them that.

He's always been their father's favorite. She can't understand exactly why their father remains more drawn to his only boy, more than any of them. She can't let herself admit she thinks of it.

Still it eats away at her.

As a boy, Branwell had known about their different bodies. A woman would have the patience, he believes, for the pain he doesn't. When his father had placed him under the mask of his hands, hiding his son's face behind them, to see how smart he really was, what he speaks out from the dark behind there, when asked why men and women think differently, Branwell's answer is because of their bodies.

Then Maria had slipped behind their father's hands, so he would see she could answer, too. Prepare for a happy eternity, that's how one was to spend one's time, Maria, intelligent, replied.

Sweat stood out around Branwell's eyes, as if he was trying to turn and unlock something inside himself. He'd turned away on the bed from facing Emily, his chest racked with an internal storming that grotesquely bows him up and back.

They say she is in that place where you no longer felt the need for anything anymore, but Branwell knew she was only in all those words in their heads, words that had been there on paper once. He could feel her in the air over his bed, a stain bruising the air, hovering up to the surface, before retreating back healing. She must be unhappy wherever she's gone. She seems so often to be reaching for him.

J. M. O'Neill

BENNETT AND COMPANY

Edward Burke walked up the narrow gaslit hill that he had known from early childhood. Theirs was the only dwelling-house in the confined street. Here was a world of grain and corn stores—they were scattered all over the city—and the market area and the market streets surrounded it. The old constricted passage climbed up from the parish church of St Michael to a main business street. Nothing had changed since his school-day journeys. He could remember shops open at all hours—fine Protestant shops, well-fed, well-dressed men in supervision. He was teaching their children now. Hardware stores, grocers and vintners, pharmacists, saddlers, photographic studios, specialist bakers and confectioners; and there were Catholic entrepreneurs in growing numbers: millers, building contractors, painters, decorators, shopkeepers, hucksters in the race to keep abreast. There was the barracks of what had been the Royal Irish Constabulary, of course, with its archway and courtyard: Catholics hadn't moved beyond the rank of sergeant.

Edward Burke was looking back over two and a half decades, but things had changed in the last ten years. Civic Guards in flat peaked caps manned the station now; the helmeted constables were gone.

He crossed the busy thoroughfare of people and horse carts and a growing bustle of motor-cars. To his right, the highway went on to cross the city's main street and over the lighted bridge, through an enclave of small secluded mansions, into the country-side. To his left, you passed the places of captivity, despair and final rest before you left the gaslit world: the prison of stone, the asylum of stone, and the cemetery of stones.

Edward walked along the back streets now that were still busy with their small shops and hucksters and street traders. Gas lamps were more distantly spaced, dim beacons in the darkness. A big shapeless woman with an infant suckling her bare breast, a huge pendulous udder, stood before him, barring his way. He could smell her uncleanliness.

"May Jesus and his Holy Mother bless you, sir. A little gift to keep hunger from myself and the child?"

He gave her two pennies.

"God will put your name in his golden book. There's a place close to him in heaven for you."

Her hard weathered face smiled a toothless smile, and he was glad when she moved and took the foul body smell with her. The child was a dressing, a stage property; in a day they passed it from one to another. The money was for drink, an escape.

Edward Burke understood.

He remembered his hall door again, the rattle of chain, the noise of bolts, the streets he raced along as a child. The world of stone-built, tall-storied bastions of storage, six rows of four-foot-square windows, shuttered but without glass; each floor loaded with loose grain and men with broad wooden shovels turning it, airing it, preventing it from heating.

He remembered his small bedroom at the front of the house, the comfort of sheets and heavy blankets. Often there were nights of storm. You could hear the wind buffeting the naked gas flames about, and the interminable slamming of wooden shutters on warehouses: slam, slam, slam, all night, sometimes in unison but mostly in confusion. Sometimes there was the crash and shatter of slates on cobbles.

He thought about it and felt he should be older; it seemed such a long time in the past. There had been a war and a rebellion, executions, murders, burning and pillaging. And there had been an exodus. Many of the Protestant Irish had left. They had always been held apart, and now they were subsumed in distant colonies and protectorates. Good people, too, many of them; they would be missed.

A small boy, he remembered them well: their industry, the crowded shelves of their special shops, the huge stone towers of grain and flapping shutters.

In wintertime, when weird, frightening wind howled through these stone castles and he hid beneath the comforting bedclothes, sometimes he heard the heavy steps of the Night Watch, who would be wrapped in black frieze overcoats and carrying small oil lanterns on leather belts. He remembered the whistles and lanyards, the heavy iron-shod staffs, their great bulky watches, the constabulary helmets. They brought reassurance on wild stormy nights when there must be spectres and witches abroad. They were night workers of law enforcement, from ten o' clock to eight each morning. As they walked their beats they called out, at intervals, that time and place was in good hands. He had heard them often beneath his window: "One o'clock and all is well." Then there was the measured pace as they moved away. They banished the ghosts and goblins of darkness. All is well, all is well. Good friends, gone for ever now.

They handled brawls and brawlers, too. If it was a losing battle, they struck on the pavements with their iron-shod stakes and blasted on whistles to bring Watchers from other beats. They won their battles, stuck prisoners in the clink, the temporary lock-up down where the street narrowed at the approach to the river and the Customs House. In the morning the brawlers would be hauled to the main station that he had passed only moments before. He looked back at it; nothing had changed and everything had changed.

A long time ago; he smiled. The rare horse-drawn vehicle on iron-rimmed wheels that might come down their narrow street after midnight always brought terror with it. The Headless Coach: the driver headless, the horses black and thundering on the cobblestones, and the coach flying past, forewarned the death of someone close at hand. The wind and slates and banging shutters. Times of innocence.

He remembered suddenly the candle-lit house he had left, the bloodied tunic, the act of love or lust. He shivered.

He walked on more briskly on the flagstone pavements. Shops, darker inside even than the gaslit streets, might be open until eleven o'clock. It was still early evening; Catholic church bells rang out, close at hand or distant, to announce rosaries, the ceremony of benediction, perpetual novenas, the impending arrival of a corpse that would spend its last night on earth in the house of God. People were shabby or in working clothes; wild, smeared children ran in small groups to jeer or cheer or pilfer.

A newspaper-boy trotted beside him for fifty yards. "Paper, mister, paper, paper. Paper lastedishoon."

"No."

"Lastedishoon."

It was another way of begging; the thin bony hands held a single paper, creased, stained. Paper, last edition.

"Paper, mister. If you can't read, you can look at the pictures."

An old paper, an old joke. He looked down at the blackened bare feet, the dirt lodged between the toes, then up at the bright eyes. Admiring his persistence, he gave him a penny.

The street noises had become a little less raucous. A funeral was approaching. As the cortège came near, people stopped and stood silent. The undertaker, in a black, cutaway coat and tall hat, led the way. Tired horses pulled the glass-case hearse and a couple of closed mourning carriages; men walked behind the hearse. Some onlookers made the sign of the cross, and there were murmurs of "God rest the dead . . . called away . . . rest in peace."

When it had passed, Edward Burke could see his destination ahead. It was a formerly vacant shop, with a small counter and a long narrow space behind where there were tables and seating-forms. Two paraffin lamps barely pierced the gloom. Brown paper had been pasted on the inside of the thin glass, holding three wooden mullions, for privacy and protection. There was a furtive-ness about the people who came and went. A sandwich board at the doorway said, "Everyone Is Welcome."

Edward entered and smiled to the woman at the counter, saying, "Good evening, Miss Langford."

"Good evening, Mr Burke."

She was a middle-aged woman, confident, well-dressed, wearing a brown warehouseman's loose coat over her tweed costume. She wore a plain, unobtrusive hat, and from a cauldron on a low gas ring, she ladled soup into pint-size tin mugs. When there was space at tables, she handed out the steaming brew and a wedge of bread. The bread was two days old but fresh enough for soup and hungry mouths. A younger woman supervised the tables, wiping them down, and waiting for mugs to wash and leave draining. Mugs had a small value, were portable, needed surveillance.

"Mr Burke," the woman at the cauldron said, "your wife is in the kitchen, just through the glass door."

Lillian Burke didn't look forty-one. She was a beautiful woman, not very tall in stature, but slim as a young girl, with piled-up auburn hair and good skin. She looked at Edward Burke and loved him with her eyes. He took her hand and pressed it.

"I thought I'd call," he said.

"I'm glad, but I can't kiss or hug you now," she said. "That's the trouble with glass doors."

Although she also donated money to many other causes, this soup kitchen was her brainchild. You should give to people, she felt, person to person. They should see that the giver wanted to give and that the one in need only paid for it with, perhaps, a softening of features, maybe a smile. She had rented the shop, opened up its back room, bought cheap tables at a half dozen auctions and the tin mugs that hung in clusters outside every ironmonger's. From her churchgoers came the bread, meat, meat bones and scrag ends and discarded vegetables, too shrivelled for rich tables. She had also bought the three cast-iron cauldrons, with broad looping handles for two persons to grip and carry.

She stood now before a small Stanley range with a tea chest of coal and a shovel next to it. She and her helpers worked three hours every evening from four until seven.

"I feel useless," Edward Burke said, looking out at the ragged street. "Sometimes there are loiterers out there. A lot of whispering sometimes. There could be danger, I feel."

"These are bad times for the poor, Edward. Time to give a helping hand."

"I called to see my mother."

"I wish I could visit her."

"Oh, leave her in her own world," he said.

Standing before this busy young woman who had married him, he was overcome with the shameful thought of close family lust. It was a heinous act of abomination. The thought of their grasping, struggling, turning, was overpowering.

He, Edward Burke, had been the runt of the litter. Perhaps not the runt; he had been an afterthought. His brothers, dead and buried, had been respectively fourteen and twelve years his senior.

He had never thought much about it, but when he was still a small boy, they were reaching manhood. Why had she given birth to him? She had been thirty-six when she was carrying him; not an unusual age at a time of large families and high infant mortality, but for twelve years, since the birth of his second brother, her years of child bearing seemed over. And then *he* had arrived.

He remembered his second brother, Michael, wild, but clever, too, with his skill at sketching and painting. But he was distant from him. He had left school with a record of distinction and was almost immediately in demand for his art work. Travelling theatre, music-halls and operettas needed posters, and he immediately grasped the garish flamboyant style that pulled in crowds. She was scathing: the stuff of erotic hacks and comic-cuts. He became silent and with-drawn at home. Edward, still a small boy, listened to her poisonous tirades: loose living, rubbing shoulders with stage persons who were given to drink and licentiousness, a fine return for the education that was handed to him. He was compared with Francis, a junior law partner before he had gone to fight in France, a person of repute in the city. He was nothing. A drinking womaniser.

He had left, made the journey to London to join the fighting forces, to keep pace with the paragon sibling who had preceded him, but he was rejected for army service. However, posters were needed in London, too, and moving pictures had arrived. He drank heavily and picked classless women off the shelf. His health failed and he died, emaciated, friendless, in a mental hospital in the London home counties. He had surpassed the chosen offspring only in age. It was a year before word had reached his father. He had made the journey to a paupers' corner in a Surrey graveyard, a wild lumpy acre of coarse grass and tussocks, without a single marker.

A grave-digger had said, "Impossible to say where anyone is, guv." He had looked about the stretch of fertilised ground, the tall grass. "We put them down here in blocks of ten or twelve. The office might have a record, but most of them don't have a name."

The office had a burial record of Michael Burke, buried in common ground in the autumn of 1922. His father had travelled back and was greeted in his own house with silence. That same year he had walked with Edward to the cemetery at the city's northern edge, and stood before a four-sided plinth recording a hundred and fifty years of family death: the fresh engraving said, "In Memory of Michael Burke, aged 37, 1885–1922." Above it, more prominent, *she* had had inscribed, "Capt. Francis Burke MC, killed in France, 1917, aged 34."

"My sons," was all he had said.

It was the beginning of his decline; he had died within a year, in 1923. He had been young once, in love, so eager, Edward Burke supposed, to wed his adorable Catherine.

Edward Burke looked at his wife Lillian, who was chopping ends of meat, fat and scrag and arranging a mound of bones on a bare scrubbed table. She turned and looked at him.

"You're so quiet, Edward. Are you feeling well?" she whispered.

"Yes, I'm fine."

"You look pale."

"No, no."

"You allowed yourself to be upset again," she said. "She is a good woman, Edward, but it is difficult to cease grieving. Grief is a dreadful thing. Two sons dead, remember. And then her husband. She is alone."

Yes, alone, Edward thought.

"You call but she isn't ready to meet you yet. It takes patience."

"Yes."

"I'll be home before eight. Hannah will have dinner ready. We'll freshen up and there'll be time to talk. And we can sit at our own fire."

Edward looked around the soup kitchen—the tables, the long seating-forms, the noise, the faces of hunger—and then he looked at her face.

She looked at the half-hunter watch she carried in her pocket. "Go and have a drink," she said. "You'll feel better. It'll drive away that paleness."

He nodded. "Yes," he said. "I'll enjoy a drink."

"Good."

He waved, pushed out through the crowded dining-space; it was murky in a bad light, but the warm smell of food filled the room. The pavement, he thought, seemed a little more busy. Or were people gathering? He crossed to the opposite side and stood at the entrance to an alleyway leading to a church fire exit. The alleyway, in the dark spot between gaslights, had a single light mounted on the wall, distant from him. He felt uneasy.

The noise alerted him. He saw the approach of marching men: young men, mature men, some of them in Sunday best, some of them striving, with little, for respectability, some ragged. They had taken the centre of the road. Rosary beads were evident, and some carried small crucifixes. An enemy would call them a mob, but the zealotry of set faces and eyes would leave him in doubt. These were crusaders, purifiers. The street was crammed. As they halted before the soup kitchen, Edward was crowded, isolated. They dragged a table from inside and blocked the doorway, raised up a lion-hearted champion to stand surveying his believers and the faint-hearted on-lookers of the streets.

The man was in his thirties, maybe older; a navy blue suit, a shirt and tie, polished shoes. His cap was pulled low; he wore glasses and a scarf. He held out his hands, waited until there was almost silence.

"You are Catholics," he thundered; a great, rousing, metallic voice. "First we pray."

He held up glittering rosary beads, made the sign of the cross, recited the Pater Noster while he looked up at the rooftops and the black low-lying clouds that shielded earth from heaven. He called out the Ave Maria ten times and orchestrated the volume of their response. He paused for stillness; the road was blocked, the small traffic was detouring.

He held up his rosary chain of glass beads, and a shiny crucifix that had been dipped in pinchbeck.

"Good friends were in Rome last year," he began, "and Christ's Vicar on Earth walked among them, raising his hand in blessing. He blessed these holy beads that are a hymn of prayer to the Mother of God. We call out, 'Hail Mary, full of grace, the Lord is with thee.' Our humble words of homage. Our faith has survived dungeon, fire and sword. This land, our land, newly recaptured from repression and slavery, is still the Island of Saints and Scholars; and it has been decided, I'm told on good authority, that within the short span of three or four years His Holiness, Pius XI, will come to walk among us. He will walk on the same Irish ground as we, poor banished children of Eve, have walked.

"He will say mass and sanctify the Host, and ask God to bless our nation, to make us worthy of the blessings he has showered on us."

He was silent and the crowd was silent. He was gathering breath and power for his attack. He flung up his hands as if he had been stricken, shouted at heaven beyond the blackness. He was a raging, hysterical demagogue.

"Are we worthy? Do we deserve that the Vicar of Christ should come to visit us? Do we? Do we? Answer me! You stand there like cattle. But cattle have dignity. Answer, answer! Are we worthy? Are we worthy that Christ's Vicar on Earth should come to walk among us? Are we worthy of God's love, or deserving of his contempt?"

Silence again.

Now his voice was heavy with sadness. "I am waiting." He kissed the pinchbeck cross of his rosary beads, held up his hands.

A great shout came from his little army. "No!"

"We are not worthy?"

"No!"

The entire gathering was enmeshed now; they were chanting, beating their hands together. He stood before them, head bowed, the rosary beads wound about his hands. The voice, Edward thought: a hammer on steel.

Suddenly he was upright, a hand raised for silence. It came slowly, unevenly, possessed them.

"Why are we not worthy?"

A shuffling uneasiness everywhere.

"Will I tell you?"

"Yes!"

"Louder!"

"Yes!"

He rolled his words at them like great crushing orbs of stone; he paused, studied them, was unhurried.

"You have allowed your city, a tabernacle of Christ, to be invaded, desecrated, by *apostates*! Those who forsook the infallibility of Rome to proclaim a lewd, sensuous, diseased, lustful, royal dissolute to be head of our Church! Who spurned the holy commands of the papacy. Who live only awaiting eternal damnation."

Silence.

"Who are they? Where are they?"

Silence.

"They are here behind me feeding soup and bread to your brothers and sisters in Christ. And for what? I ask you, why are they feeding your brothers and sisters in Christ?"

A great pause for silence again.

Then almost a whisper. "To take hold of their immortal souls!

To win them over. To cast them into damnation." He waited. "Apostates must be crushed, destroyed, driven out!"

There was a thunderous cheer; he was lifted down from his humble rostrum.

Edward Burke watched. He didn't fear for himself; he was a person of courage, caught in the crowd, tossed about in the heave and sway. He saw the table raised up and flung against the window. The thin glass shattered, the crude peeling mullions snapped. He was trapped tight in the crushes. The vanguard was already at the work of clearance. War cries were in the air, and the hungry were bloodied, beaten and pummelled, chastised for sinful greed. There was the crash of cast-iron. The pendant paraffin lamps were flung against the walls and there was smoke and licks of flame. The crowd was tossed like gravel in a sieve. Edward, in the alleyway, caught a small boy, gave him a shilling, and sent for fire brigade and ambulance.

There were residents and small shopkeepers, and the passing few, too, trapped, crushed, left to stand and stare.

A place buying souls for soup. It would be sinful to touch it. Charity was only for the *very* poor, the totally incompetent, the wretches of society who came down through every generation. The Church and Catholic people, their committees and societies, looked after them.

Edward Burke roared at them. "There are people in there!" He was fighting his way through, past little groups that might be in shock as they stood in gaping wonder at the sudden explosion of violence. Now they were coming to life, moving again.

He saw Lillian, his wife, and the younger supervisor from the tables. They had tied wet towels to cover mouths and noses and were dragging the few remaining staggering bodies to the space outside the doorway where the air was clearing. Lucy Langford, the dispenser of soup, was lying on the floor, blood smearing her face, distressed with smoke inhalation. Then everything was clear:

bodies on the pavement breathing air again, being tended. Lillian Burke and her helper wiped away the blood from the face of Lucy Langford, propped her to sit up and breathe. But she was ill. The bell of the fire brigade was only a block away.

The gathering flames lit up the smoky room and kitchen: tables had been ripped asunder, the legs used to beat the ragged clientele, the huge soup cauldrons were toppled, the chest of coal scattered.

The fire brigade had arrived. The ambulance, old-fashioned but clean, efficient, functional, was a legacy from the British army garrison that had left hardly seven years ago. Both were manned by city crews who had learnt their trade in the days of military occupation.

Lillian Burke came to Edward, gripped his hand. "You're safe and sound?" she asked.

"You?" was all he could say.

"I'm fine, not a scratch," she told him, "but Lucy Langford is shaken. The window, and the table that smashed it, caught her. The bleeding is nothing much, but she may have fallen heavily, and her legs were scalded when the cauldron was toppled."

The ambulance men passed carrying Lucy Langford, loosely strapped to a stretcher and covered in a red blanket.

Lillian Burke said, "I must go with her to the hospital."

"Barrington's?"

"Yes. Taddy will be there, and the matron is a good friend."

Taddy, Thaddeus Bennett, was her brother. He had attended at College of Surgeons in Dublin and then returned to his home town.

Lillian said, "I'll go then. We'll meet later at home. The day had a lot of trouble hidden for us. Whenever you arrive Hannah will have dinner ready for you. I'm sorry, Edward."

"I'm glad you're all right," he told her.

He watched as she and her supervisor of tables were helped on the step of the ambulance, the doors closed, and it growled away into the distance.

Steam and smoke coloured the soiled air; firemen in belted tunics and traditional helmets were flattening and rolling up their hoses, removing stand-pipes, sealing off valves. They examined the burnt-out shell of the shop. A job finished, they took their regal seats on the fire engine and drove away from the combat like gladiators.

The smell of the fire would last for days. Edward pondered the speech-maker, hearing the ring of metal in his voice.

Tom Phelan

"Wednesday in the Fifth Week of Lent – 7.20am" from *Iscariot*

THE ONE THING the priest hated doing was giving out holy communion. Most communicants stuck out their tongues and waited for the circle of bread to fall from his fingers like a gleaming snowflake. But there were the few snappers and suckers who, like greedy fish, snapped the blessed bread with their long lips and left the priestly fingers glistening with saliva.

For a man who had no compunction about gutting a fish or paunching a rabbit, Fr Keegan's aversion to other people's saliva bordered on the pathological. On the terrazzo floor inside the altar rails he shuffled along, reaching in and out of the polished ciborium. He kept glancing to his right, looking for the silhouettes of the snappers and the suckers.

The Gilligan woman was the worst, with her great upper lip and protruding chin. She was an ugly lamprey hiding behind a rock, waiting for her prey. Every time the priest recognised her profile in his peripheries, his memory provided him with the remembrance of the time he dislodged her upper dentures as he snatched his fingers away from her descending horse lip. The sight of those stained choppers and the sound of their clattering onto the silver-plated paten which the altar boy was holding under her chin, stirred droplets of acidic sweat in the pores of Fr Keegan's body. He had used his alb to get rid of Mrs Gilligan's spit, but the glare which he had blasted at her had gone unnoticed. She had been too taken up with the recovery of her false teeth. As the altar boy strove to keep the paten level, Mrs Gilligan's thick, embarrassed fingers had pushed the ugly things to the edge. In one great grasp she had recaptured the dentures and, in one great slamming of her hand to her mouth, had made them disappear.

But Maura Gilligan had learned nothing, and she still lunged and snapped.

It was Wednesday in the fifth week of Lent, and Fr Edward Keegan was in his thirty-second year of sidling along the inside of this particular set of altar rails. For the first two years of his priesthood he was loaned to a parish in Manchester diocese in England. When he came back to Ireland, he had been sent to the village of Davinkill, an outpost of the parish of Duneamon. It was unheard of for a priest to be left in the same place for so long and Keegan's fellow clerics never tired of trying to tease out of him the reason why succeeding bishops had not transferred him. Even when his colleagues hinted that the authorities had buried him in Davinkill to support a nest of secretly sired brats, Keegan had not satisfied their adolescent inquisitiveness.

A new silhouette moved into the corner of Fr Keegan's eye, and his brain flashed a warning to his body. But it was only Paddy Dillon, he of the one long front tooth, coloured like a piano ivory exposed to turf smoke for a hundred years. Paddy Dillon was neither a snapper nor a sucker. He was ugly, with sour and meandering wrinkles, hairy nostrils, hairy ears and breath strong enough to stagger a stallion. Every morning Dillon had fresh cuts between the swaths of beard he had missed with his razor.

As he neared Paddy Dillon, Fr Keegan took a deep breath, then held it as he carefully placed the communion wafer beneath the toothy stalactite onto the longest and narrowest tongue in the parish. The priest was repelled by the tongue; it reminded him of the red, glistening connecting rod of a plunging bull. Keegan found it easier to look at the dull blackness of a horse's penis than at the rawness of a penis that looked like a freshly scraped and oil-dipped carrot. Every time he travelled into the countryside, he risked exposing himself to the sexual activity of the indigenous animals. Even on the streets of the village it was not uncommon to see dogs at it, the hindquarters of the all-consumed male pumping as much out of nervousness born of the fear of being interrupted by a hob-nailed boot, as by the instinctual drive toward orgasm. And there was a deeply buried image in Keegan's memory of a man's penis bobbing in the light of an oil lamp, the penis glistening with the blood of the raped vagina from which it had been hastily removed.

Despite the image which Dillon's tongue evoked, Fr Keegan was always relieved to see him at mass. Paddy Dillon was the local pyromaniac; he was also an alcoholic, and the village thief. One December, Dillon had got into the presbytery by breaking four panes of glass, and the wood in which they were set, with a shovel. He had made off with an armchair, making his getaway with the loot in the priest's wheelbarrow along the main street. The local Guard had not had to call upon his Holmesian talents to track down the criminal, and Paddy Dillon had eaten Christmas dinner in the slammer, as he had planned, the misery of his equally demented wife and children forgotten.

When he neared the end of the altar rail, the priest brought his mind back to his sacred duty. He placed the host on Mrs Culliton's non-threatening tongue. There was a stain on her head-scarf, the same one she had been wearing to mass for the last two years. How could she not notice it?—the stain, black like the blackness of old axle grease. Fr Keegan believed Mrs Culliton would be serving her family, and the community, better if she stayed at home in the morning and washed her litter of six boys.

The priest's peripheral vision sent out another alarm, and he

198 • BRANDON TWENTY-FIVE

stopped breathing. Two places beyond Mrs Culliton was the one-eyed head of the knacker and gravedigger John O'Brien, that disposer of carcasses both human and animal. It was the anticipated odour perpetually upwafting off John O'Brien which had closed down Fr Keegan's pulmonary system. When John O'Brien cut up animals which had died of sickness or accident, the smell of the decaying meat permeated his clothes and skin—even his breath had the smell of death.

The priest placed the consecrated host on O'Brien's tongue, and wondered, as he had wondered many times before, how Maura Gilligan and John O'Brien could fornicate with each other, she being so ugly and he being so smelly. Both sinners tried to disguise their voices when they came to confession, but his stench and her breathy saliva rattling against the wire-mesh divider betrayed them every time. They must have given up sex for Lent, Keegan thought, because since the beginning of the penitential season, both had been attending daily mass and receiving communion. There would be more than one resurrection celebrated on Easter Sunday.

With the soft sibilance of the altar boy's slippers trailing him, Fr Keegan made his way back to the other side of the sanctuary and to a fresh row of communicants. He appeared to be looking at the green and black terrazzo as he swished along in the purple vestments of Lent. But the shapes of the kneeling people were flashing by in the corner of his right eye as he scanned the line for snappers and suckers.

Fr Keegan was in good shape for his fifty-seven years. His back was still straight, keeping his frame stretched to its six feet and two inches. He had lost none of his hair which, although nearly white, still maintained its short, sharp-crested waves. His spectacles were rimless, even though their style was one of long ago.

The priest looked clean. He smelled clean. He felt clean. He liked the feeling of being clean. The uncleanliness of the general populace made his cleanliness stand out like a house on fire in the dark.

The sacerdotal sphincter tightened as Keegan neared the end of the altar rails. The shape of Maura Gilligan's hat in the corner of his eye had that effect on him.

When he had not seen her in the usual place in the first row of communicants, he had thought she had decided to come to the second mass at noon. He had also hoped that she was sick, maybe even dead in her bed at home, reeking of dog dung. Instead, here she was, lubricating her lips for her lunge at the Lord. Keegan began to prepare himself mentally for his encounter with the lamprey.

Mrs Gilligan was kneeling in the seventh position from the end of the line, and, until he had given her communion, Fr Keegan knew he could think of nothing else. He wished he could overcome the aversion which was so pronounced in his dealings with this woman.

Fr Keegan began to shuffle his way back along the line, the well-trained altar boy keeping one step ahead of him. The flesh of the priest's lips and nose began to work itself into a defensive posture as his tormentor's hat approached. Because he was aware that this involuntary contraction of his facial muscles was apparent to the casual visitor, Fr Keegan felt vulnerable, the way he felt vulnerable when somebody was standing behind him at a poker game.

Of their own accord the priestly eyelids squeezed forward, and Fr Keegan looked out on the world through blurry slits. By the time he reached Mrs Gilligan the world had faded from sight, and there was nothing left except for the hairy lip and chin, the wide, wet tongue protruding, the tips of the yellowed dentures hanging there, already caught in the grip of gravity and slowly slipping down. With the anxiety of a child escaping the closing jaws of a nightmare's monster, Fr Keegan delivered the body of his God into Mrs Gilligan's glistening interstice, and his fingers came away from the encounter without a trace of the communicant's bodily fluids on them. It was going to be a good day.

The feeling which coursed through the priest's body was similar to the satisfaction of winning a Sunday-night poker hand, especially when that vacuous Monsignor Johnny Rabbet had a lot of money and self-assurance in the pot. So relieved was he, that Fr Keegan was unaware of the identities of the next half-dozen parishioners. It was only when he gave communion to Dervla Donahue that his mind come back to what he was doing. His index finger brushed against Mrs Donahue's lower lip, and he was aware of a new sensation, one which was faint, wispish and thoroughly pleasant. But then Dervla Donahue reminded him of Tony Donahue and Tony Donahue reminded him of Kit Foley. Their names shot a thin line of anxiety through his being and, like a needle slipping its way through a tomato, it disturbed the pleasant feeling as effectively as a breeze blowing away the taunting perfume of a passing woman.

Keegan continued down the line, his hand flashing between the gleaming ciborium and the open mouths.

It had taken him many years to put a name on the elusive pleasantness which Dervla Donahue stirred up in him. The name had fallen out of the dark one night when he was lying awake, without his even being aware he had woken up.

Secure contentment. That was it! And around the edges of the feeling was the faintest tinge of sexual excitement. He had never given voice to this stirring of the flesh. And, most certainly, the priest had never spoken to Mrs Donahue, or anyone else, of the erotic shadings in the penumbra of the secure contentment.

Above all else, Fr Keegan was discreet in word and deed. As the repository of the sins and secrets of the parishioners, he was only too well aware that the walls of all the houses in the village were full of peepholes. The peepholes were not the ones bored through wood or concrete. They were the holes in people's faces. It was through these holes that people often spoke ill of each other, and in speaking ill of each other they revealed many secrets. There was a more dangerous dimension to the peepholes which came into being in the atmosphere of one-upmanship which existed late at night in the public houses. Then the peepholes were not only enlarged, but the magnifying glass of alcoholic exaggeration was slipped incautiously across the openings.

Fr Keegan, like all the other residents of the town, knew at a glance who frequented the public houses. Those who took a pledge at the time of their confirmation not to drink wore a pin in their left lapel. The Pioneer pin was the great class divider in Davinkill, and the Pioneers lived in dread of the enlarged talk which emerged from the drunken peepholes in the pubs. The only fear the drinkers had was that the Pioneers' daily prayer for their conversion would be answered.

The sins and secrets which Fr Keegan heard in the secrecy of the confessional were often encountered at a later date in the form of gossip on the streets of the village. This supported his views about the peepholes, and it fostered his paranoia about discretion. If he himself had an overwhelming need to externalise a feeling, he did not express it in words. Instead he wrote it down and immediately burned the paper. This, he believed, was as good as lying on a psychiatrist's couch.

In the top of his eyes, Fr Keegan saw Saint Willie Gorman approaching the altar rail, saw him limpingly emerge out of the shadows of the nave into the edge of the chancel's brightness. As he placed the consecrated host on a flat, white tongue without noticing the face of the owner, Fr Keegan wondered if there was a place in the *Guinness Book of World Records* for Saint Willie

Gorman's limp. From five feet nine inches, Saint Willie Gorman shrank to four and a half feet with alternating steps, and then sprang back again to his apex. It had to be the deepest limp in the world. It wasn't that Saint Willie Gorman had been born that way or that one of his legs had been shot off in the war. There was something wrong with his back, something which no doctor had ever pronounced on because Saint Willie Gorman accepted all of life's ills as visitations from God.

Saint Willie Gorman had spent six years of his youth in a contemplative religious order, where he had developed his own peculiar brand of piousness. He had also developed deafness in one ear. The affliction had proved to be a sign from God that the future saint did not have a vocation to the priesthood, for how could a monk with one deaf ear hear confessions in confessionals designed for priests with two good ears? The vocation to priesthood had been abandoned for a vocation to sainthood. The deafness had eventually caught up with his other ear, and Saint Willie Gorman was now without hearing. But, lest anyone think he was annoyed with the God who had so mercifully granted his handicap, the Saint beamed out on the world through an idiotic grin. He perpetually looked as if he had just had a satisfying bowel movement, or had just heard that some man in Dublin, whom he did not know, had won a million pounds. In his quest for sainthood, Saint Willie Gorman depended so much on the will of God that he was rat-arsed poor, and he, his wife, five daughters and two sons lived in divine squalor.

In the top of Fr Keegan's eyes, Saint Willie Gorman grinningly disappeared as he came to rest at his four-and-a-half feet height and waited his turn to kneel at the altar rail.

Along the line of opening and closing mouths, Fr Keegan sailed like a dutiful bee visiting clover. He only wished he possessed the enthusiasm for the tongues which the bee had for the stamens.

The altar boy's gleaming paten floated from chin to chin, ever ready to catch a falling host; never touching the chins or wattles of the communicants, nor collecting bodily oil or flecks of dead skin. Since whatever landed on the paten would have to be disposed of later by being scraped into the chalice and washed down Fr Keegan's gullet on a flow of water, the priest appreciated the altar boy's steady hand.

Keegan was mildly surprised to see so many people in the church on this blustery morning at the end of March. The faith was alive in Davinkill. Despite all the backbiting the people engaged in, the Catholic faith was the glue which held them together. It gave them a social unity enabling them to face any obstacle thrown across their path. Whether it was a disastrous wet harvest, an epidemic of blood murrain or an invasion of the village by proselytising Jehovah Witnesses, their common beliefs brought them through.

When the priest administered the Blessed Sacrament to the last communicant, he silently sighed. He had escaped Gilligan's grasping, disease-laden lips, and he had avoided the saliva of all the lesser suckers and snappers.

He turned away from the communion rail and ascended the altar steps, the front of the alb clutched in the crook of his left pinkie, hitching it up to avoid tripping. With a little cymbal-like clash he placed the lid on the ciborium, pushed the sacred vessel through the nun-embroidered silk curtains hanging inside the tabernacle, genuflected, stood up and locked the tabernacle doors with the gold-plated key.

Automatically following the rubrics he had learned in the seminary, and which had been polished to a high sheen with years of practice, the priest purified the altar boy's paten, the chalice paten, his own fingers and the chalice.

Without consciously directing them, his fingers dressed the

consecrated golden cup with purificator, pall, veil and burse. When the awareness of what he was doing came to him next, Fr Keegan was standing in front of the missal with hands outstretched in an attitude of prayer. He continued to move and bow and pray until finally he raised his hands toward the ceiling and called down God's blessing on the standing congregation. It was in the lifting of his arms in this last blessing a year ago that Fr Keegan had unexpectedly felt the first restrictions of age in his upper limbs. He had always thought he would feel the first encroaching limitations of age in his golf swing.

Kicking the hems of his soutane and alb out from under the toes of his shoes, Fr Keegan came down the altar steps. With the stem of the covered chalice grasped in his left hand and his right hand flat on top to keep the burse from sliding off, with his sweeping eyes, the priest picked out Dervla Donahue in the nave; immediately he saw Kit Foley lying in the damp morning grass where he had left her, her bent right knee making a little tent out of the tail of the sergeant's overcoat. With the same urgency he would use to beat a stinging wasp to death, Fr Keegan shook Kit Foley out of his thoughts. He did not know that every time he reinterred Kit Foley in his memory, his head slightly snapped in and out of alignment; nor, for all his knowledge about the village and its inhabitants, did he know that the people of Davinkill spoke often about his nervous twitch, and speculated, sometimes using their scatological and sexual imaginations, on the reason for its frequency.

When he reached the bottom of the steps, the priest turned back to the altar and waited for the altar boys to stand. They all genuflected in unison, and Fr Keegan followed the double line of boys off the altar. It was because he had been thinking of Kit Foley that he remembered Ken Considine was on today's list of homebound communicants. He frightened himself when he felt the word "shit" slipping through his lips.

As one of the chief suppliers of criminal candidates for the imperial gladiatorial schools, it was inevitable that I would have frequent contact with Quintus, the procurator of the games. It was through this contact that the threads of fate binding Julia and Valentine were drawn more tightly together.

Julia was late reaching puberty; she was fourteen when she first menstruated, at least a year behind her contemporaries. Desso had prepared her for the flow, but still the first bleeding evoked a drastic change in the girl's behaviour. Whereas before she had been an unfailingly cheerful child, full of life and curiosity, now she became moody and depressed, rising late in the morning and spending long hours of the day sulking in her room. She lost her appetite and became dangerously thin. Or so I thought. In any case, I became concerned for her health, and once, in the company of Quintus, when he commented on the weakness of his son, I mentioned that my daughter, too, was frail. He was immediately curious. Why he might be interested in the health of my child I did not know. He volunteered to send his personal physician to examine her. I accepted only because it was wise to accept anything Quintus suggested. I had no wish for Quintus to have contact with Julia. He was a man with a reputation for soiling any girl who took his fancy, no matter how young or inexperienced, and he had the power to make these abominations happen without consequence to himself. Quintus was a man who took what he wanted from the powerless, leaving wrecked lives in his wake.

And so it was that Valentine came to our house. He was gentle and well-spoken, not at all the sort of person I associated with Quintus and his circle. He apologised for intruding and gave me to understand that Quintus had *insisted* that he come. We talked for a bit, and our conversation turned to Alexandria and Theophrastus. It was with some happy surprise that I recognised in Valentine the boy who had been present at Julia's birth those many years before. Immediately, my misgivings disappeared and I invited him to examine Julia. I told him of the changes that had accompanied the coming of her menses and led him to her room. Desso, Julia's nurse, came with us. Julia, of course, did not welcome our intervention. She huddled into a corner of her bed, her knees drawn up under her chin. Her dark eyes glowered under long lashes. It took Valentine only a moment to realise that she was blind.

He spoke quietly. "Julia, I am Valentine. I am a doctor, and your father has asked that I have a look at you. He is concerned for your well-being."

I added, "Valentine was present at your birth, Julia. In Alexandria. He was assistant to the doctor who brought you into the world."

She spoke nothing but wrapped her body more tightly with her thin white arms and shrank against the wall. Her eyes seemed to dart about the room, as if she were looking for a way of escape, but of course Valentine understood that she saw nothing. Her fine dark hair was uncombed. The bedclothes in disarray.

"I don't want to inconvenience you," said Valentine. "Perhaps we could talk. I am sending your father away. Your nurse . . .?"

"Desso," I said.

". . . Desso will stay with us."

"Please go away," Julia whispered.

"Yes, I will, of course, go away if that is what you wish. But can't we at least have a talk first? You father is leaving . . ."

"I know he is leaving."

"Yes. Desso is with us . . ."

"Please don't condescend to me," said Julia sharply. "I know who is here."

And that was the last of what I heard. I resisted my curiosity and left them to it. Valentine was with Julia for half of the hour. When he emerged from her room I queried him.

"I did not examine her physically," he said. "We talked. Or rather, I talked and Julia occasionally responded." He smiled. "She was not forthcoming. She is a strong-willed girl, even in her unhappiness. She is angry that you brought me here."

"Is she ill?"

Valentine considered for a moment. "No, I don't believe there is anything *organically* wrong with the girl, nor does there seem to be any unbalance of humours. She is confused and frightened. I believe it may have something to do with the onset of her menses, the realisation that she is no longer a little girl. She is frightened of the city and homesick for whatever place it was you lived in the country. Make sure she is confident of your love. Help her find a friend if she doesn't have one, a girl of her own age. Encourage her to go out."

None of what Valentine said was particularly useful. He merely stated the obvious. Julia showed no interest in the few friends she already had. She refused to go out. Certainly, there was no reason that she should not be confident of my love. And so Quintus's illustrious physician departed, and I put him out of my mind.

Two days later a Gallic pony was delivered to our house. It was from Valentine, and it would be the last I would see or hear of him until he was placed in my custody two years later.

XXXIII

Did something pass between Julia and Valentine during those few moments they spent together, some ineffable communication that would make their amour inevitable? There was no sign of it then from Julia. Only later, much later, did she tell me that Valentine's voice had lodged itself in her ear—*Perhaps we could just talk. I am sending your father away.*—lodged itself there and continued whispering during all of the following weeks and months until they met again—*Perhaps we could just talk. I am sending your father away.*—and always she sought to invent a face for the voice, until finally Valentine's dimly remembered voice and the voice that spoke to her in her religious ecstasies became the same voice: *In a short time you will no longer see me, and then a short time later you will see me again.* And the pony? Why would a physician, out of his own purse, gift my daughter with the animal? Something about his interview with Julia had lodged itself with Valentine, too. Perhaps he did not realise how much my pretty daughter had caught him in her spell. Did her image, dishevelled upon the bed, lovely in her dishevelment, trouble *his* dreams, too? When he saw her again, in his cell at the Tiberian Prison, I recognised in his startled eyes the re-emergence of something lost, now found.

There is no way to explain these things, these choosings by Eros. Fate, we say: the gods, the stars. Or accident, silly chance. Explaining love is best left to poets, not to philosophers or astrologers, or, least of all, to the father of a wounded heart. The pony, of course, was Julia's salvation. It took our garden as its domain, and I arranged for fodder to be brought from the imperial stores. There was hardly room in our small space to ride, but Julia loved to climb upon the pony's back and lay her body along its neck. She named the pony Mel, for I told her of the animal's honey-coloured coat. Occasionally, on days when I was not occupied at work, we would lead the pony out of the Pinciana Gate into the countryside north of the city. There Julia could ride to her heart's content, with no equipage but a bridle, and between herself and Mel there developed a mutual affection that alleviated her unhappiness and sent her flying back into her carefree childhood, with her hair streaming in the wind and a pony for her eyes. Once I borrowed a horse and we rode together to the sea. On the long soft strand, she galloped with abandon and took her pony deep into the licking tide until she felt the warm sea on her calves and thighs. The sun warmed our faces, Tyrrhenian breezes cooled our bodies, and the tumult of the city was forgotten as I waited, holding my steed by its bridle, as Julia galloped along the shore. I felt that if her moment of happiness could be extended for ever, I would surrender my own future happiness for that prospect.

XXXIV

The garden of Quintus was vastly more spacious than our own. It stepped in terraces down the Esquiline Hill. Nothing so ordinary there as a Gallic pony. To the imperial zoo came animals from all over the world, and Quintus had his pick of these for his private garden. Peacocks from the East with regal fans. A pair of red deer from Germany. Monkeys from Africa. Hedgehogs from Britain. These many animals wandered among the fruit trees and flowering plants that overhung the pools and streams that kept the garden cool even in the heat of summer. Eight aqueducts brought hundreds of millions of gallons of water into the city every day, but little of this immense supply found its way to private houses, and none at all into the homes of the poorer sections of the city. But Quintus and other high officials had as much water as they desired. The cisterns of his palace were always full. These fed the basins of the atriums and peristyle, which overflowed into the garden streams and pools and finally emptied their contents, still clean and fresh, into the sewer at the foot of the Esquiline Hill.

The apartment of Quintus's wife Lycisca opened on to the highest terrace of the garden, where blackbirds and nightingales sang in a netted courtyard. It was here that Valentine first visited his "patient". He had been apprised by Quintus of his wife's "complaint". But he had also been advised by Quintus to treat Lycisca without her knowing that it was her husband who had sent the physician to her. When Valentine was ushered into the courtyard, Lycisca was being read to by a female slave, the poetry of Ovid. He apologised for interrupting her and introduced himself as Quintus's personal doctor.

"For what does Quintus need a physician?" asked Lycisca. "He has never been ill a day in his life."

She was an attractive woman, some years older than Valentine but much younger than her husband. She wore a gown of yellow silk, and her hair was braided with blossoms from the garden. There was firm resolve about her mouth and eyes, which were inclined to intimations of smiles but gave little away. Her most striking feature, observed Valentine, were her long and graceful fingers, which moved continuously against the silk of her gown as she spoke.

"He wishes to make me available to his family—to yourself and to your son—and to his servants and slaves," replied Valentine. Then added hesitantly: "In case of need."

"What you will mostly be asked to do is abort his many illegitimate offspring," said Lycisca without a trace of embarrassment or irony.

It was Valentine who was embarrassed. He glanced involuntarily to the slave girl. Lycisca caught his gesture.

"Don't worry about *her*," she said. "There is not a woman in this household whom Quintus has not debauched at one time or another." That flickered smile, the flowing fingers. "I have long since ceased to keep track of the mistresses he keeps in apartments all over town."

"I know nothing of that," said Valentine.

"Well, you will know about it soon enough," replied Lycisca. She shooed away the slave girl and spoke more intimately. "Where are you from?"

"Cyrenaica. By way of Alexandria. I have been in Rome for eleven years."

"It doesn't show."

"What?"

"You seem much too naive to have been in this city for so long. No one in Rome blushes. You blush."

Lycisca rose from her couch. She smoothed her gown against her legs.

"Come," she said. "Let's walk in the garden."

Valentine found that he was pleased to be near her. She was unlike any woman he had known before—confident, intelligent and subtle, regal in the way she held her head and shoulders. Her breasts were full and firm, her belly flat.

"What does Quintus want of me?" she asked.

Valentine shook his head as if he did not understand.

"Again," she said. "Blushing. You need not be embarrassed. Quintus is always suggesting that there is something wrong with me because I do not share his insatiable appetite for perversity. What has he told you? That I am frigid? That I am nonorgasmic?"

They stopped by a pool as two tame red deer came up to Lycisca. From the folds of her sleeve she took out small lumps of sugar which she fed to the animals.

"He asked only that I treat any complaints that you might have."

Lycisca laughed, for the first time out loud. "I assure you, dear Valentine, that I am in the best of health—as you can see. It is Quintus who could use a doctor—to cure him of his concupiscence."

"Why do you . . .?"

"Why do I stay with him?" It was not the question he was about to ask, but it was appropriate. "The answer is obvious. Look around you. I want for nothing. For all of this I need only put up with his occasional connubial maulings. The question you might rather ask is, 'Why does he stay with me?' And the answer to that is also obvious. It was *my* family who placed him in his position of power. And *my* family has the power to ruin him."

"You need not fear that I will betray your confidences," said Valentine, suddenly apprehensive.

She touched his cheek with a long finger. "How did a person such as yourself get mixed up with Quintus? His friends and accomplices are usually as priapic as himself." She paused. "Why have you never taken a wife?"

Was it that *obvious?* wondered Valentine, but he answered honestly, explaining himself as best he could.

Lycisca laughed. "I've never understood philosophy. Ideas are such insubstantial things. Daydreams, really. Sooner or later one wakes up and realises that what seemed so real was only an illusion." She spread her hands. "Why would anyone prefer the *supposings* of philosophers to flesh and blood? The Christians, for example; they are so eager to surrender their lives for an idea, giving up *all of this* . . ." She stroked the deer's fine downy nose. ". . . for an illusion of immortality. And you, Valentine, give up the satisfactions of a woman's love for the abstractions of Epicurus."

"Ideas are perhaps more substantial than you think. I have spent the past dozen years reading Greek philosophy. Mathematics, astronomy . . ."

"Tell me, Valentine, what did philosophy do for the Greeks? Rome made short work of them. I have Greek slaves." She laughed. "Greeks comb my hair, bathe me, dress me. And I haven't an idea in my head of mathematics or astronomy."

"Rome couldn't exist without an idea—the *idea of Rome,* if nothing else."

"Rome is not an idea," she laughed. "Rome is Quintus. Rome is steel and stone. The Caesars *invented* Rome. Not out of an idea, but out of marble. This city has a dozen gates, and what goes in and out of those gates are not ideas, but material things, weighty things, things you can hold in your hands." She gently cupped the deer's face in her hand.

Valentine was silent. The appropriate arguments to refute Lycisca hesitated at the tip of his tongue. He thought of a dozen relevant quotes from Epicurus and Lucretius. But he was silent. He was silent because suddenly his philosophy did seem weightless. It was not the profundity of Lycisca's cynicism that silenced him. It was the force of her beauty. Not a girl's beauty. She was not *pretty.* Her beauty was hard and sure. It showed in the way she held the head of the deer, firmly, possessively. It manifested itself in the unembarrassed curve of her exposed breast when she raised her hand to her hair. It showed in the golden straps of her sandals and the matching paint of her toenails. It showed in the refractory light of her eyes that seemed to burn his cheek.

"What do *you* want, Valentine?" she asked.

He walked away from her and sat down on a bench of fine black granite. *What do* you *want, Valentine?* No one had asked him that question before. He had not even asked it of himself. If anyone other than Lycisca had asked the question, he might have answered: *I want to master the healing arts because the secrets of human health are hidden in the world. I want to understand warmth, cold, dryness and moisture, and how these reside in the atoms, and how to achieve balance in their mixture and expression. I want to understand the innermost machinery of nature, by close observation and reflection.* But he understood that if he answered thus to Lycisca she would laugh, and he knew that she would be right to laugh. Even as he rehearsed the answer in his mind, he had begun to laugh himself. The words did not match the person he had become. True, he still bought books compulsively, but they mouldered on his shelves like gold shut up in chests. He had not performed an anatomical dissection in years. He now spent more time at the baths and in the forum than at the practice of his craft.

She came and sat beside him on the bench. He was suddenly conscious of intense fragrances of orange blossoms and another plant he did not recognise. She pressed his silence. "Do you *know*, Valentine? Do you know what you want?"

He thought that she might be offering herself.

He returned the question, "Do *you* know what *you* want?"

She laughed without hesitating. "Oh, yes. I want to wake in the morning in cool silk sheets. I want to look in the mirror and like what I see. I want to feel warm water sluice down my legs when I step from my bath. I want a pretty girl to be waiting with a clean dry towel. I want her to braid fresh flowers into my hair. I want a handsome young doctor to sit beside me on the bench. I want Quintus to stay away from my bed."

And what would I answer? thought Valentine. *I attend the baths for hygiene's sake only. I eat and drink to be nourished. I have committed to memory the three books of Galenus, but I have no real patients to treat. If I look into the mirror, I see a man who has grown soft and unprincipled.*

Lycisca leaned toward Valentine so that she almost whispered in his ear. She said, "If Quintus saw us sitting here he would know immediately that I desire you, and your life would be forfeit." She stood up and smoothed her gown against her belly. "I would seduce you, Valentine, but I like you too much to wish you dead. An unusual sentiment on my part, since I am used to having what I want. In that way, I suppose, I am like my husband."

"What makes you think I am seducible?" It was his first gambit in a game she was defining on her terms.

She looked at him with bemused condescension. "*Every* man is seducible. I have not yet met a man who does not think with his cock. You are all so terribly predictable."

"Perhaps I am the man who is the exception to your rule."

"Then you would be either a eunuch or a child, and therefore of no use to me at all," she said. She turned and walked back to the courtyard. He was bewildered as he saw her go, her golden feet flashing on the marble steps. He knew that he had been inextricably drawn into her life. And he knew that an affair with Lycisca would be a dangerous sport.

PJ Curtis

The Lightning Tree

Nᴏɴᴇ ᴏғ ᴜs, especially Brian, were prepared for what was about to unfold. How could we know that the result of our activities—the healing and curing of the sick of body and soul—could bring about or be the cause of such pain and suffering for our family?

It happened like this.

Fr Murphy, a simple, good, decent man who cared for the welfare of all his flock, was at that time our local parish priest. Soon after Mary Ellen's death, when I had moved back home, Fr Murphy was joined by Fr Tobin, a young priest from across the Shannon, to help out in the three parishes. You could see from day one that this new priest was cut from different cloth than that of the kindly old Fr Murphy.

Where Fr Murphy was easy going, understanding, compassionate and forgiving and had a way with the ordinary man or woman, Fr Tobin's attitude (not to mention his sermons) was severe, proud and haughty. His general surly demeanour won him few supporters and fewer friends as he moved among his new parishioners.

He had not been too long in the parish before he heard of the our family, of the cure we possessed and the reputation we had for healing the sick who came to our door. While he never visited the house or, for that matter, spoke directly with any one of us, it very soon became clear from his weekly sermons what this priest's thoughts and feelings were regarding our various healing activities.

There was not a single Sunday that he would not denounce from the altar those among us who, in his words, "were slipping back to the old religion" and "going back to godless paganism", as he put it. There was not a single Sunday when he did not make pointed mention about those among us who knowingly turned our hearts and our souls from the grace of God.

Worse still, he loudly proclaimed, there were "certain individuals"—and at this he paused and glared long and hard in Brian's direction—who were putting their souls in mortal danger by engaging in dangerous, non-Christian activities. These he listed as the casting of "spells and incantations" and the healing of dumb animals and Christian beings through the administration of unholy mixtures, potions and other magical concoctions.

Such behaviour, so the priest pronounced, was nothing short of heretical and could only find favour with Satan and the powers of darkness. This, so he informed the congregation, was what he had witnessed since his coming to this place.

"A flock going astray!" he said. "A flock in need of a Good Shepard to guide them back to the paths of righteousness and away from the influence of heretical thought and actions. I know who these heretics are among you! And so do you!"

Standing on that altar, he looked and spoke like a man possessed.

"As an ordained priest and as shepard of this flock, I tell you now it is my intention to root out those among you who would put their souls in peril and embrace these powers of darkness."

I can tell you it was a silent, sober congregation who left the church that day. Though no one person uttered a word to us, everybody attending mass that Sunday morning knew to whom it was Fr Tobin's remarks were aimed.

At this stage, Fr Tobin and Brian had never actually met face to face. However, the priest's sermon on the Sunday following his confrontation with Brian at the Kilfenora fair was direct and to the point.

"There is a man of this parish. . ." Fr Tobin's voice could barely conceal his rising anger. ". . . who sits here among us today. A man who sits here in this house of God as he does every Sunday. A man who calls himself a Christian! A man who calls himself a Catholic! Yet this man, by his own actions, mocks and laughs in the very face of the good Lord who laid down His life for this man and for all here!"

Fr Tobin's face was red as a turkey cock, and he fairly spat out his words. You could have heard a pin drop in the church as the congregation held its breath.

He continued his tirade and his words echoed around the church.

"This man—not to mention others of his family—dares to place himself outside the embrace of Holy Mother Church and her saints. This man dares to call down healing power through magic spells, unholy litanies and dark incantations! This man dares to dispense a special grace—that of true healing—which only Jesus or his Holy Mother—and NOT MAN!—can dispense."

Here he paused and his words fell to almost a whisper.

"I tell you today that this man is in league with the devil and places the salvation of his very soul in mortal danger. This man, unless he renounces all his attachments to the practice of the Black Arts, unless he repents, begs for God's forgiveness and comes back to the fold this very day, is on the road to hell!"

At this, Brian arose from his pew, moved out to the aisle, turned his back on the priest and walked out of the church. I felt the entire congregation stop breathing. Even Fr Tobin fell silent and turned back to face the altar to continue the saying of the mass.

Mass over, Robin and I walked home together in silence and in dread to find Brian seated by the fire, his face a deathly pale and a glass of *poitín* in his trembling hand.

"Did you hear all that?" I had never seen Brian so distraught and overcome with emotion. "Is this priest in full command of his senses? How can I be in danger of loosing my soul? How can that priest say that I—you too, Mariah!—get power to heal and cure from Satan and not through the goodness of God? Our potions and herbs come from God's good earth and are available to all who would seek them. How can this be bad? Do we not make the sign of the cross over each and every one who comes to us for help? How can all this good that we do for those who suffer be evil?"

I had never seen Brian so visibly upset. He was silent for a long while, and then he spoke words that I hear in my head to this day: "I will not return to mass nor set foot again in that church while this priest remains in this parish."

Knowing Brian to be as determined as a man could be, I knew he meant what he said.

Robin and I could only agree with him that the priest's attacks were unfounded and unfair. However, we both pleaded with him, for his and all our sakes, not to take such a drastic course of action, for it would lead only to greater trouble with the priest and the Church.

I counselled—indeed begged—Brian not to take this route and instead to meet privately with Fr Tobin to discuss their differences of opinion.

"Talk to him, Brian!" I pleaded. " Talk to him and show him you are not what he accuses you to be. None of us are."

I urged him that if he could not convince Fr Tobin then he should go to our parish priest, Fr Murphy. He, I knew in my heart, would be both understanding and forgiving. After a while pondering on this, Brian promised he would go first to see Fr Murphy and he would do it the following day.

True to his promise he did go to the parochial house to talk with Fr Murphy, only to find that the priest had, that very day, been taken into a nursing home suffering from a severe pneumonia. Taking Fr Murphy's place as parish priest till his return to full health, so the housekeeper informed Brian, was none other than Fr Tobin.

Brian returned home that evening in very low spirits, and in the days that followed he refused to see any callers and kept very much to himself.

Sunday morning came, and as he had threatened, Brian did not attend mass that morning; nor did he attend the church on the Sundays that followed. Brian's absence was well noted by the congregation, and especially noted of course by Fr Tobin, who continued to denounce Brian from the altar each and every time he stood to make his sermon.

The priest's continuing attacks, coupled with Brian's continuing absence from church, resulted in the turning away of many old friends and neighbours from the family. Our regular night-callers stopped their *cuairds* to the house. I would hail local woman friends or acquaintances on the road, only to see them draw their shawls about their heads and turn their eyes away from me, in fear, so I learned later, that I might put the evil eye on the poor deluded souls. Many reacted in the fear and dread that any social contact with Brian, Robin or myself would result in the bringing down on them of the wrath of this priest. Some truly began to believe the priest's accusations that Brian was indeed in league with the devil. What other explanations could there be for his unusual, and unexplainable, powers?

It was a hard and bitter time for us, and for Brian especially, I can tell you!

But worse was yet to come.

Some month's later, on an overcast January day of cloud and sleety rain, we had a visit from Thread-the-Needle John, the hawker. Every three or four months, Thread-the-Needle John—some say he was a wandering Jew, some say he was an Indian or Pakistani, and others say Armenian—would arrive on his ass and cart to sell us the little items, nick-knacks and the like, we could not get in the village shops.

I remember, as children, we would rush to greet him with whoops of joy and delight when his cart was sighted on the road approaching the house. He would tether his donkey to the forge door, unload his battered old leather cases, and there on the kitchen table would lay his treasure trove before our bulging eyes to tempt us to buy, which usually we did.

One leather case held hardware: spoons, forks, knives and scissors, thimbles and sewing needles, shirt and coat buttons, collar studs, nails and tacks, spectacles, hand mirrors, combs, candles and candle sconces, pens, ink, notebooks and writing paper, perfumes, soaps, spices of every scent, colour and taste.

The other leather case was packed with hard and soft fabrics: tweeds, velvets, shawls, coloured hair ribbons, woven waistcoats, stockings and shoelaces, sandalwood vanity boxes, rings, bangles, broaches and necklaces, and even coloured balloons, Christmas crepe decorations and other gimcracks that Santa Claus himself might bring the wee ones on Christmas Eve.

For countrywomen who lived in isolated places and rarely saw the inside of a shop from one end of the year to the next, there always were so many luxuries in Thread-the-Needle's treasure chests to lure and tempt the woman of the house. He rarely, if ever, departed our house without some item of fabric, jewellery or fanciful bauble and money changing hands.

On this particular day, he had completed his business transactions and was about to continue on his way when he turned to me and said, "Oh, I nearly forgot. I met the postman on the road yonder. He gave me this letter to give to you."

The envelope was addressed to Brian, and it lay on the kitchen table till Brian returned home that evening.

"I saw Martin the Post on the road earlier. Did he call?" he asked.

"'Thread-the-Needle was our postman today. There's a letter for you, Brian," I said as I lit the oil lamp and placed it on the table so as to illuminate his reading of it. I watched as he picked up the letter from the table; slowly unsealing the envelope, he sat down to read the single-page letter. In the pale glow of the lamp, I could see he had turned white as a ghost.

The letter was from Fr Tobin, and its contents spelled out a dark sentence for Brian and indeed for the whole family.

Fr Tobin's letter, written in small, sharp lettering, stated he was writing as acting parish priest and also for and on behalf of His Grace the bishop. It went on to point out that, due to ignoring the many warnings issued from the altar to the family, and especially to Brian, to cast aside the works and pomps of the devil, now at last had come a day of judgement.

Brian had been singled out of all of us and—so the letter continued—because of his straying from the path of righteousness, was to suffer the most severe penance that could be meted out by the Church. He was, from that day on, to be refused entry into the house of the Lord. From this day onward, he was to be refused the sacraments and forgiveness for his sins. He was to be denied the grace of God till it pleased the Church that he had purged himself of his sin most grievous and abandoned all heretical thoughts, deeds and actions and returned to fully embrace the One True, Holy Roman Catholic and Apostolic Church.

That was the general gist of the terrible letter.

Excommunication!

My blood ran cold. I had never thought I would read such a sentence in my life. And to think it was now being issued to my own brother!

Under the light of the oil lamp, I read and reread the letter. Still the words rang steely cold like funeral bells tolling some terrible end.

So here, at last, was the day of reckoning. We well knew that there were many—especially this priest—who had difficulty with much of the healing and many of the cures we had brought about over the years. We knew, too, there might be a price that Fr always said that one day we may have to pay for possession of this gift of healing. To be admonished from the pulpit was one thing. However, to suffer such banishment from the Church and separation from the congregation was the ultimate sanction on a soul.

"This cannot be right or just," Robin said after I read again the letter aloud. "Is this the reward earned for bringing ease to the sufferings of the poor people who crave it?"

"What are we to do?" I asked Brian.

"Do?" he whispered the words. "What you will do—what we will do is carry on as we did before. I will not refuse any poor soul who comes and asks for my help. I know in my heart of hearts I do not commit any sin, little or great, when I bring relief from sickness and suffering to those who ask it of me. I believe that it's no sin to make use of the gift of healing, which surely is a gift for good and not evil. I know in my heart that all power for good comes only from the Lord, Who is good and great and merciful. It is with Him I will make peace, not with a cleric who would judge me wrongly."

With these words, Brian crossed himself.

For a long time that night we three sat in silence, each with our own thoughts, emotions and prayers.

Brian did just as he resolved he would do. While it fairly broke my heart to witness what he was going through, I have to give him credit for the strength and courage of his resolve. From that day on, as he had promised, he did not set foot inside the church for as long as Fr Tobin remained as priest to the parish, though he well knew what lay ahead of him. Few got on the wrong side of the priests without paying a terrible price. Those who did fall foul of the clergy had little option but to flee the land to England or cross the Atlantic to the Americas.

"These priests lead us around like blind sheep. They wield too much power," Brian had often remarked. "Remember Fr saying how they destroyed Parnell back in the '90s when they brought him down with slander and lies so they could put their puppet into parliament? Well, in my opinion, this priest is cut from the same cloth as those plotters."

Brian also now well knew that he had to look at his future and consider the options open to him. Should he remove himself to safer ground, or stay here in this place and face the consequences of his actions?

"Would you consider America?" Robin asked him one night. "They say the clergy don't have as much say or sway over the people there."

"America?" Brian shook his head. "No! I've made up my mind. To run will be to admit my guilt and as good as an admission that the gift is tainted in some way. Or worse, a gift from Satan and not from God. No, I'll stand my ground. I was born here, and I'll die here. Neither Cromwell's armie nor the Great Hunger could shift our forefathers from this place. The priests won't shift me. I will stay, and to hell with the consequences!"

But the whole affair was to take its toll. To be cast out and barred from the house of God was a terrible weight for any good-living person to carry and endure from day to day. This was especially true at Easter and Christmas Day or the funerals of friends and neighbours.

He resigned himself to his banishment from weekly mass attendance. A social banishment was also in force. In the days that followed, Brian's heart nearly broke to witness his oldest companions and neighbours turn their eyes from him when he approached them on the road or in the field or in the village street. Only Tom Cullinan, Tim Grady and a few others—good, true and especially brave friends to the family—remained staunch to the end. Tom especially never stopped visiting the house on *cuaird* or to offer help with work in the meadow, garden and bog.

Still, it was not an easy time. Those who had fallen sick or were in need of the cure were fearful to call to the house in broad daylight. Now they would come under the cover of dark night to consult with Brian or with me in the outhouse forgebarn by the light of a candle or lantern.

In the meantime life went on, and Robin and I regularly attended mass and tried to be as good as Christians as we could. Though we were always aware of being viewed as suspect and guilty of the charges laid at our feet, at least it was some small consolation to all that Fr Tobin had now ceased his tirade of accusations towards us personally.

Though poor Brian found light and spiritual solace and comfort in his own way, we could see that this cross he had to carry was beginning to show on his features and on his spirit. His quick smile and good humour had dimmed and were now replaced with a grave and despairing air, which he carried as he would a great weight. We noticed the lines of care about his eyes and the streaks of grey now running through his hair.

It sorely grieved both Robin and me to see our brother in this troubled condition, and it broke our hearts to witness his terrible sufferings of body and spirit. Our pain was in that there was nothing we could do to ease his pain, nothing we could say that would bring solace to his heavy heart and troubled soul. We could only be there to offer our silent support and pray for an early end to this sorry affair.

What of Fr Tobin? Even when Fr Murphy eventually returned from the sanatorium to take up again his post of parish priest, he continued to work alongside his superior as priest to the three parishes. But a leopard does not change his spots, so it is said, and Fr Tobin never did win the love, the respect or the regard of his parishioners, only their grudging tolerance, fear and distrust.

Five years or so later, he contracted consumption after a visitation to a house that carried the disease and soon after fell sick. He spent his last unhappy days in a sanatorium in Limerick city. It was told later that as his sickness progressed and he realised the seriousness of his situation, he pleaded that his carers send for Brian the Healer, the only man who might cure his terrible condition, to attend him in his hour of need.

It was Easter Week, a few days after the Easter Sunday of 1916, when Brian came home with a spring in his step to relate the news that was on everybody's lips. There had been an uprising of the rebels in the General Post Office in Dublin city.

"A great Rising of poets and peasants alike, so they say. There are many dead, but the talk is of freedom at last for Ireland!"

"A Rising, you say? We've risen before," Robin said sourly. "Where did it get us?"

"There was a Clareman, Peadar Clancy, involved with the rebels at the GPO. There is great talk of a general rising, and I hear in the village that Bertie Hunt is rounding up as many local men from the three parishes as want join the Volunteers to fight the foe. He's fair determined, so they say, that this great rebellion should spread to all parts of Ireland, and all parts of Clare."

"War, fighting and rebellion: do ye men ever get enough if it?" I said.

"The tide may be changing. This one could sweep the country." Brian ignored my comment and added, as casual as you like, "Oh, by the way, I hear other news in the village. . . of Fr Tobin. He died last week of the consumption in a Limerick hospital."

"Good rest his soul," I crossed myself.

Brian crossed himself, too.

JOHN B. KEANE

THE BODHRÁN MAKERS

FR ALPHONSUS DONLEA had been asleep for two hours when he felt the pull on his shoulder. His first reaction was to shrug the demanding hand away and turn on his side. The hand would not go away, however. It kept pulling and dragging and nudging until he was obliged to respond to it.

"What is it?" he called out drowsily from his broken slumber. He could not, of course, see Canon Tett's towering frame looming over him. Although it was one o'clock in the morning the Canon was fully dressed. He had not gone to bed. He had waited by the range in the kitchen from eleven o'clock onwards which was the time Nora Devane had retired for the night.

The Canon had fortified himself every so often with sweetened cups of tea from the full teapot which Nora had left on the range. He had passed the time between the hours of eleven and one reading the *Messenger*, his favourite religious publication, a forty-eight page compilation of stories, poems, prayers and serials, all with a decidedly Catholic slant. It cost only two pence and because of its flimsy paper cover, red in colour, it was easily folded and pocketed. The Canon considered it ideal reading whenever he found time on his hands. When eventually he discarded it Nora Devane painstakingly withdrew the leaves and divided each into two equal parts. These she hung in a bleak outdoor W.C. which served as the curates' toilet. It could be that she intended the bisected but still readable

pages to serve as reminders of their priestly calling as well as fulfill-
ing their primary toilet roles. Old newspapers cut into approximately the same size supplemented the *Messenger* contributions.

"God be with the youth of me," Fr Butt had once confided to
Fr Bertie Stanley, "when the great outdoors was my toilet, a
hundred square miles of mountain and moorland and no one to
interfere with you save a frightened deer or a loping hare."

Eventually Fr Donlea managed to open his eyes fully and lift
himself upright on the bed.

"What's the matter?" he asked as soon as he recognised his
caller.

"There's nothing the matter, Father. Just get up and come
with me."

"Is it a sick call?" Fr Donlea asked as the Canon turned away
without answering. "Has there been an accident?" he called out
anxiously as he listened to the Canon's footsteps descending the
stairs.

"Ours not to wonder why!" he spoke to himself as he hastily
pulled on his trousers before instituting a search for his shoes. He
found one under the bed and the other on the tiny dressing table
honeycombed from the depredations of woodworm. He had but
barely fastened his collar when he heard the booming voice of
Canon Tett calling him from the foot of the stairs. Hastily he
combed his thinning hair and dipped his hands in the ewer of stale
water which dominated the dressing table with its attendant basin,
chipped and cracked.

"What in God's name is holding you up, Father?" came the
irritated voice of his parish priest.

"Coming, Canon," he called from the doorway as he fumbled
through his pockets to make sure his car keys were on his person.
At the foot of the stairs the Canon was waiting. Awakened by the
uproar Fr Butt had appeared in his pyjamas at the head of the stairs.

"What's happening?" he asked of the junior curate. Fr Donlea shrugged his soldiers and hurried to join his lord and master.

"Is anything up, Canon?" The query came from Fr Butt.

"Nothing that you need concern yourself about," the Canon threw back matter-of-factly. "Go back to bed like a good man or you'll miss your beauty sleep."

Fr Butt stood mystified at the head of the stairs. It could hardly have been a sick call. There was an extension from the doorbell attached to the wall directly over his bed and he would have been the first to hear. In fact it was his night for sick-call duty and this puzzled him all the more. If it had been an accident the Canon would have instructed him to contact the Civic Guards and doctor or at least ordered him to be on the alert. There had been a time when he might have lain awake wondering and worrying about it but the years had inured him to the Canon's mysterious ways. He returned to his room and was asleep in minutes.

"Your car will do nicely, Father!" Canon Tett informed his junior curate.

"Of course, Canon," Fr Donlea returned obediently, "but is it any harm to ask where we might be going?"

"No harm at all, Father. Just bide your time and all will be revealed as the man said. Meanwhile get your car out and let us be on our way."

"Yes but which way?" Fr Donlea persisted with his questioning.

"In God's name will you get the car and don't be standing between me and my bounden duty!"

Fr Donlea hurried to the curates' garage, a whitewashed decrepit building which had once been a stable. As they drove northwards through the square on the Canon's instructions Fr Donlea could not help but wonder about their eventual destination. He knew it would be a waste of time putting further questions to his parish priest. When they came to the junction of Healy

Street and Carter's Row Fr Donlea eased his Morris Minor to a halt.

"I await your instructions, Canon," he announced in what he hoped was a formal, yet respectful tone.

"Go on out the main road," the Canon returned stiffly, "and turn off for Dirrabeg. You know where Dirrabeg is, Father?"

"Oh yes, Canon. Fr Butt took me on the grand tour the day before yesterday and I also made the rounds of the entire parish a few times on my own."

"Very well if you did," the Canon cut in. "Just take it nice and handy now until you come to the crossroads and then douse your lights. Dirrabeg, you see, is a very curious place, full of curious people and we don't want anyone to know our business."

During the short period since he had taken up residence in the presbytery, Fr Donlea had experienced several occasions of perplexity, all motivated by Canon Tett's devious and inconsistent behaviour. Even without the advantage of a briefing from the senior curate Fr Donlea's first impression of the Canon was that of a gruff and coarse old man who should be out on grass. He had known others like him, had in fact served under parish priests just as old and irascible. Yet, for all their senility and contrariness they had been basically good priests, shrewd administrators and, as he knew from personal experience, excellent confessors.

The trouble with them was that they had grown hardened against all forms of change and were suspicious of reform even when this was advocated by the bishops. They became dictatorial from isolation. There was no arguing with such men but he had to concede that there was much to be learned from them. What puzzled him most was their inexhaustibility and their eagerness, despite age, to remain in the firing line, ready for any form of confrontation. Fr Donlea envied such priests their unshakeable convictions. For Canon Tett there was no doubt, no shady area, no wrestling with conscience. For him it was right and wrong, right and left and black and white. Such men did not lie awake at night vainly endeavouring to distinguish between what was really bad and really good. They slept the sleep of the just. Their faith was unshakeable and their rules unbending no matter who suffered in the process. It wasn't that they had become blinded to what was happening around them. Canon Tett was aware of nearly everything that happened in his parish. He was not totally insensible to the need for intervention in certain delicate areas such as the all too numerous cases of extreme poverty and want. He was prepared to pay appropriate lip service but he would never harass his better-off parishioners into coming to the aid of the less well-off. To him token assistance was in itself sufficient. Industrious, good-living people could not be expected to give continually of their hard-won resources.

"Slow down, Father, and turn off your engine. The fall of ground will see us to our destination."

"What is our destination, Canon?"

"Keep your eyes on the road like a good fellow and you'll know soon enough. Content yourself with the knowledge that we are about God's business this night. Be grateful that you have been chosen to act on behalf of the Father. Ask not why you are here but be glad you are here and be prepared to act on your Father's behalf."

The Canon's recital became somewhat mumbled as the car moved slowly and noiselessly down the incline which would take them into the yard in front of Bluenose's abode. At first Fr Donlea refused to believe his ears when he heard the faint strains of music. How, he asked himself, could there be sounds of revelry in such a remote place at such an unearthly hour? He lowered the car window and listened. Outside the night air sped past almost noiselessly, its icy breath fanning the car's interior.

"Close the window, Father, we don't want to get pneumonia."

The command came from the Canon who had ended his rambling homily.

"Just a minute if you please," Fr Donlea returned. "I'm almost certain I hear the sound of music."

"Of course you do, Father, and so do I."

"But how? Where?"

"From our destination," the Canon retorted with a chuckle.

Fr Donlea did not close the window at once. The music was unmistakeably traditional, full of that strange mixture of life and antiquity. He found himself pursing his lips and silently breathing the music of the reel, and reel it was. He knew that much about traditional music. It seemed to him that a drum of some kind was the major feature of this rustic ensemble. He had no doubt identifying a fiddle, maybe two. There was also a melodeon or piano accordion; he could not be sure which.

Fr Donlea hailed from a quarter of the diocese where there never had been a wrenboy tradition. He had never seen, much less heard a bodhrán. After a second, curter injunction from the Canon he reluctantly closed the car window. Even with the window shut the music was still to be heard, its volume increasing as they neared their stopping place. As they alighted from the car in Bluenose's yard Fr Donlea could only conclude that some sort of hooley or American wake was in progress or perhaps even the concluding stages of a wedding celebration. He began to revise his opinion of the parish priest. How thoughtful of him and how kind to invite his curate along! He wondered if the Canon made a habit of visiting late-night rural celebrations without the knowledge of his senior curate or housekeeper. The younger priest felt a warm glow for having being considered as a trustworthy companion on this secret and most welcome venture into the hinterland. So this was the Canon's Achilles Heel, a sojourn among the countryfolk who valued the traditional way of life. The visit, no doubt, was his way of endorsing their fidelity to ancient standards. Willingly he followed the Canon across the yard and into the kitchen. Following in the Canon's wake, he was amused and surprised by the vigour and enthusiasm of the dancing couples. Countrified and uncultured they might be but there was a certain dignity in the way they disported themselves. Most of the men were drunk to be sure; he deduced this from their wild yells and glazed eyes. Some of the females were quite attractive, carrying themselves with poise and composure despite the extreme physical demands of the dance and he felt that without them the whole affair would have been a shambles.

As yet neither he nor Canon Tett had crossed the threshold and they could not be seen by the kitchen's inmates. None, save a pretty little girl wearing a light blue coat, was as yet aware of their visit and she, or so it was apparent to Fr Donlea, was so overcome by their presence that she seemed to have lost all power of speech and movement. After a while they were spotted by Johnny Hallapy who was in the act of transporting a bucket of porter from one corner of the kitchen to the other.

He advanced at once towards both newcomers and, dipping his cup into the sudsy content of his container, brought forth a brimming cup which he presented to Canon Tett. It was only then that Fr Donlea became aware that something was amiss and that the Canon's visit was more in the nature of a raid than a ratification.

The moment Johnny Hallapy tendered the cup the Canon smashed it from his hand. It fell with a crash, its contents spreading frothily over a floor already wet from the same carelessly-conveyed liquid. The smashing of the cup was the signal for which the Canon had been waiting. It suited his purpose ideally. He advanced into the kitchen, his right hand raised aloft, his eyes burning with the zeal of conviction. Behind him at the door a bizarre comedy, unseen by all save Patsy Oriel, was being enacted.

Undeterred by the Canon's rejection, Johnny Hallapy thrust his hand into the depths of the porter bucket and produced a second cup, this one was cracked and without a handle. He handed it apprehensively to Fr Donlea. By Johnny's childish reckoning it was only proper that the second priest should receive the same treatment as the first.

Fr Donlea looked around and about desperately trying to ignore his would-be benefactor. The lad could have been no more than seven or eight, should have been abed hours ago, had no right to be posturing in a positively adult environment with a cup of stout at this unearthly hour of the morning. He looked downwards chastisingly and noted the perturbed look on Johnny Hallapy's sleepy-eyed face. The brimming cup was still extended in his direction. Fr Donlea hesitated. There is something happening here, he told himself, which might well have a great bearing on mine and this young fellow's future. He accepted the cup and swallowed its contents without taking it from his mouth, wiped his lips and returned the cracked beaker to a grateful and mightily relieved Johnny Hallapy. It was a moment that Johnny would never forget. Meanwhile, after a brief but paralysing silence imposed by Canon Tett's unheralded entry, the kitchen surrendered itself to bedlam. Shrieking women ran for their coats, crushing, bruising and knocking each other aside in the frantic scramble to escape the eagle eye of the Canon. Minnie Halpin slid silently from her chair by the hearth and would have toppled into the fire in a dead faint had not Monty Whelan observed her perilous position. With the aid of Daisy Fleece he succeeded in lifting her back on to the chair where she lay sprawled and helpless. Her husband Fred knelt by her side while all who could made good their escapes.

The men who had been involved in the dance had drawn their coats over their heads to hide their identities before escaping through the back door. The musicians, Trassie Ring, Mossie

Gilooley and Donal Hallapy stayed put on the stairs, Donal still beating gently on the bodhrán which Bluenose had so lovingly made for him. As soon as the Canon's back was turned Mossie Gilooley and Trassie Ring tripped noiselessly down the stairs, Trassie to take up her position by their father's side near the hearth and Mossie Gilooley to find his wife who had fled screaming into the night without cap or coat the moment she discerned the Roman collars.

When the Canon had raised his hand to claim attention the majority of the revellers had disappeared. The few who remained sat or stood silently, still overcome by the shock of his arrival. Bluenose and Delia stood together at the door of the dining room; Rubawrd Ring and his daughter Trassie stood nearby; Nellie Hallapy had joined Donal on the stairs. The town party sat by the hearth still ministering to the rapidly recovering Minnie Halpin. Seated on his turf sod beneath the stairs, Patsy Oriel also remained; he sat impassive and imperturbable, looking into the bowl of the pipe which he had just withdrawn from between his teeth.

Fr Donlea stood with bowed head, hands clasped behind back, a despondent look on his tired face. He had grown suddenly weary. There was silence now save for the barely audible drumming of Donal Hallapy's bodhrán. The sound, if anything, served to stress the silence. The Canon spoke as if he were leaning against the altar of the parish church.

"How dare you abuse the Sabbath, you ungodly wretches?" was his opening admonishment. "Here it is, two o'clock in the morning, with the first mass only five hours away and drunkenness rampant. How often have I told you that you may not hold these porter balls when they intrude on the Sabbath Day, the day especially set aside by God for worship? Have I not spoken from the altar of your parish church repeatedly on this subject or am I speaking to myself? Why have you deliberately flouted my decision on this question? There are other days in the week yet you deliberately choose the one day forbidden by your parish priest. What are you doing here?" The last part was addressed to Monty Whelan.

"It is none of your business where I go or what I do after I leave school," Monty replied.

"Isn't it now, Mister Whelan? We shall see about that. Remember that any behaviour on the part of my teachers likely to arouse concern or give scandal is my business and I will always make it my business because the school children of this parish must come before all else. I will say no more about this now but I expect you to come and see me after school on Monday. I shall have something to say to you then."

"Say it now," Monty Whelan demanded.

"Not now." There was a menacing chill in the Canon's voice. "This will keep till Monday and make sure you present yourself at the presbytery as soon as school finishes."

As the Canon spoke his eyes took in the others in the kitchen. He noted the defiance on the faces but it did not deter him. His eyes rested finally on Daisy Fleece. The Canon surveyed her coldly and hostilely from head to toe before looking her in the face. She did not bend or deflect her head as he had anticipated. She returned his look without flinching until he was obliged to look elsewhere.

"If you have any sense now," the Canon addressed himself to Bluenose and the others, "you'll stop this tomfoolery and go to your beds. It's past two o'clock in the morning and you'll be entering the Church of God in a few short hours. Do not, under the pain of excommunication, enter my church with the sign of drink on you. Go on along with you now and prepare yourselves for the Sabbath."

Nobody moved. From the stairs the drumming of the bodhrán

increased in volume. The Canon turned, anger flashing in his eyes, his face contorted.

"Stop that infernal sound," he shouted. "Stop it at once or I'll put God's curse upon you."

Donal Hallapy placed the cipín behind his ear and placed the palm of his right had on the surface of the bodhrán. Still the sound persisted, infinitely fainter now, almost inaudible.

"Put that thing from you!" the Canon commanded. There was no response from Donal Hallapy. His eyes were fastened on the hand which covered the surface of the bodhrán. There was no movement from the hand but if one drew close and peered intently one might see that the fingers rippled almost imperceptibly on the goatskin. From a distance the rhythmic beat must seem to be generated by the instrument itself.

Fr Donlea wondered at Donal's expertise. There was no movement from the hand that he could see and yet the muted, haunting, rippling tattoo persisted. Sometimes it seemed to come from a distance, yet all the time, vaguely sinister, it pervaded the kitchen, creating a strange tension. He noted too that the eyes of the man who held the bodhrán had closed. Yet he wasn't asleep. His body was too taut for that. A look of uncertainty had crept over Canon Tett's face. For once he was speechless. The uncertainty became transformed into puzzlement and from puzzlement once more to anger.

"Put that infernal contraption from your hand!" he called.

Donal reacted by snatching the cipín from behind his ear and belting the bodhrán with a ferocity and speed which alarmed Fr Donlea. From where the curate stood the man with the bodhrán seemed to be possessed. The vibrant drumming filled the kitchen; it was almost deafening. The Canon placed both hands over his ears as Donal Hallapy with unbelievable dexterity wrenched the fury through the medium of the drumbeats from his being. Suddenly the drumming stopped. Donal opened his eyes and placed the cipín once more behind his ear.

The silence which followed was unnerving. The Canon removed his hands from his ears, the anger once more dominating his features.

"Throw that barbaric instrument away from you at once," he called out to Donal.

"It is not a barbaric instrument," Delia Bluenose flung back. "It's a drum made by my man Bluenose and the likes of it was never made before."

"It is barbaric," he thundered, "and as well as that it is the devil's drum."

The devil's drum. The phrase was whispered by Delia Bluenose in awe and terror. It was here that Bluenose intervened for the first time: he stepped into the middle of the kitchen and faced the Canon.

"Listen to me, Fr O'Priest," he cried with his fists clenched. "Listen wrendance-wrecker and joy-killer. Just as sure as your Christ and mine is the King of Kings so is the bodhrán the drum of drums!"

"Drum of devils," Canon Tett shot back unchastened. "Come on!" he turned on Fr Donlea, "our business here is finished and scant help you were to me may I say."

In the car there was silence until they reached the crossroads which would return them to Trallock.

"Where did your tongue disappear to?" Canon Tett spat out the words. "You stood there like a danged dummy and let me do all the talking. What in God's name happened to you?"

"Nothing happened to me Canon. I was unprepared that's all. For the life of me I cannot see what right anybody has to upbraid those unfortunate people. All they were doing was drinking and dancing."

"All they were doing!" The Canon spluttered. "All they were doing," he barked, "was flouting God's law and you say I haven't the right to upbraid them. This is my parish, Father, and while I'm in charge I will speak out against debauchery of the kind we saw tonight. Now drive your car and don't let me hear another word out of you."

Fr Donlea drove silently, his eyes fixed on the road ahead. The whole business, in retrospect, seemed to him like a bad dream. Fragments of the scene flashed before his mind as they drew into the suburbs, the shocked faces of the people present, the terror of the fleeing women, the haunting sound of the bodhrán, the face of the youngster who had offered him the drink, the Canon's attack on the teacher and most vividly of all the old man's definition of the bodhrán. The Canon might have ended the dance but the bodhrán player had stymied him and the old man's answer had rattled him. How will I ever justify my visit when I meet those people again? Fr Donlea thought. I was party to a monstrous intrusion into the private activities of a whole community of people. I participated in their humiliation in the name of the Church and by my silence I betrayed them.

"May God forgive me," he said aloud. "May God in His mercy forgive me!"

ALICE TAYLOR

HOUSE OF MEMORIES

THE MORNING OF Jack's funeral, Kate woke before dawn with a throbbing headache. While she lay in the darkness as David, deep in sleep, breathed evenly beside her, her feet were stiff and she felt like a block of black ice. Since she had seen Jack lying in the field, she had been enfolded in a wave of desolation. She had tried to function normally, but her legs and hands had become wooden and her mind had lost its coordination.

In the grey of the early morning her pain was unbearable, and because she did not want to wake David, she slipped quietly out of bed and went downstairs. She lay on the couch in the warm kitchen and let a wave of unrestrained sobbing wash over her. It was a relief to go with the tide of grief. When it abated she was drained but calmer. The yellow rays of dawn were filtering into the kitchen, and when she opened the back door the garden was full of golden light. As she walked down the path, the light encompassed her, and all around white butterflies rose from the flowers and filled the garden with their delicate fluttering. Jack and herself had shared great days in this place, planning and digging. Now she felt his spirit close to her.

She ran her fingers along the fronds of a tall moist fern and remembered him carefully planting it after digging it off one of the ditches in Mossgrove. He knew that she loved ferns, and one of her fondest memories of childhood was of playing hide-and-seek with Ned under the huge ferns in the glen behind the house. "It's good to have a little bit of the homeplace in your new garden," Jack had told her as he lovingly planted the fern into a shady corner under a young chestnut that he had already transplanted from his own acre. Now as she looked around, she realised that most of her flowers and shrubs had been nurtured from seeds and slips by Jack. He had green fingers and loved to grow from seed, and many of the young trees around her garden he had brought on from tiny seedlings with constant care. "Your garden should surround you with friends," he often told her as he brought in yet another little slip from Sarah or Agnes's garden. Now, as she looked around her, she felt the comfort of all the loving that Jack had given her through this little place. He would always be part of her garden.

She sat on the seat under the beech tree. The early morning sun slanted through the surrounding trees, turning their dew-laden leaves into sparkling halos, and a lone blackbird covered himself in silver spray as he hightailed across the grass. Kate felt that she had never before seen the real beauty of this place. Its tranquility soaked into her distressed mind and a calming peace enveloped her. A phrase that Nora had recalled yesterday came back to her: "Where there is sorrow, there is sacred ground." Because now, even though she was in deep pain, she also sensed she was in a sacred place. *When someone you love dies*, she wondered, *do you go a little bit of the journey with them?* Were Jack and herself now in a new place? Though parted in the physical sense, was there in these early days after death a new spiritual union? Here in her garden, where Jack and herself had worked together with earth and stone creating something beautiful, would there always be part of them here together? She felt his intangible presence all around, enfolding her in a delicate cobweb of kindness which she knew might not last but at least gave her peace for now.

Later in the church, as she knelt between a grim-faced Peter and a silently weeping Nora, her sense of peace prevailed. From where had this blessing come? She had no idea, but was just grateful to Jack that he had come to her rescue and was helping her through this black time. Was he telling her that now she would have to take his place and be the one to help the young ones cope? Was she now to be the comforter of the family? She doubted that she was up to it. As her mind wandered around in questioning circles, she suddenly became aware that while everyone else was now sitting she was still kneeling. Nora was squeezing her fingers, trying to bring her back to reality, and Peter was frowning at her. As she sat down between them, she heard Fr Tim talking about Jack.

"Maybe sometimes we could be accused of waiting until someone dies before we acknowledge how great they are, but in the case of Jack Tobin, I think that we all realised that he was one of the stalwarts of this parish. A hard-working, honest, kind man, who loved this place and all of us. To Jack we were all as good as we could be, and yet he never perceived us to be saints; but he was very tolerant of our weaknesses because he had the biggest, most generous heart in the parish. Everyone in trouble went to Jack, and he helped in the soundest, simplest, most straightforward way he could. Jack saw solutions where some of us saw dead ends, and his approach was all about application to detail and hard work. As he used to say himself, he knew the seed and breed of the whole place, and what he thought you should not know he kept to himself. Jack was an honourable man. He loved and shared the life of the Phelans through four generations and buried five owners of Mossgrove in his lifetime. He was the backbone of their life, and today they mourn him as a grandfather and father figure and loyal, loving friend. And yet his going, though sudden and unexpected, was just as he would have wished it, out in the quietness of his beloved fields where he was totally at home with God and creation. As a man lives, so shall he die, and Jack died exactly as he had lived."

As she walked down the church after the coffin, Kate raised her eyes and looked at the sea of surrounding faces, and many looked back with tear-filled eyes. How many of these people had Jack helped in his lifetime? Often when she came to his cottage late at night, there was a neighbour with him deep in conversation. Now they were all here to pay their last respects to this kindly man who had helped them though hard patches of their lives. She was glad to see that Danny was under the coffin with Peter, Shiner and David. It would mean so much to Danny and probably come as a surprise to many people unaware of Jack's recent effort to help him salvage Molly Barry's homeplace. Jack had been the peacemaker who had seen them through the feuding years with the Conways, and now before he left he had planted the seeds of future peace between Peter and Danny. For Peter to have Danny shouldering Jack's coffin was an amazingly generous gesture brought about, she felt sure, by some indefinable urge that Peter himself might not be able to explain. Jack was the source of that inspiration. *Is it possible*, she wondered, *that Jack gone from us is going to be as influential as Jack with us?* Now he had all the answers, and so far he was making his presence felt even in the formation of his funeral!

But when they arrived in the graveyard and she watched Jack's coffin being lowered into the deep, narrow grave, her newfound peace abandoned her. There was no easy passage through this physical separation, and an overwhelming sense of loss swamped her as Nora and Peter wrapped their arms around her and the three of them clung together. Martha stood blank-faced and remote beside them, while Shiner and Danny wept quietly side by side. Finally the grave was covered, and on the piled earth his old schoolfriends, Agnes and Sarah, laid little bunches of wild flowers.

The flowers brought a sense of completion to the burial, and then the neighbours and friends lined up to sympathise. Kate had sometimes questioned the value of this exercise, but when old friends of Jack's or her own appeared in front of her, she found it comforting. Then the crowds ebbed away and only the family and close friends were left.

"Isn't it great that Dada's grave is just beside Jack's?" Nora whispered, her teeth chattering with the cold.

"I always thought that too," Kate told her, "but now it means far more with Jack here beside them all."

"There is only Jack and his mother in that grave," Peter said, trying to steady his voice and get a grip on himself with normal conversation. "Where's Jack's father buried?"

"He is with his own people," Sarah cut in. "That happened when a husband or wife died young and there was a possibility that the one left might marry again."

"We'd better all get out of this cold or there'll be a few more of us joining the crowd here already," Martha told them impatiently, heading for the gate. They trooped after her in pairs and little groups, with the older people stopping along the way to pray at other graves.

Back at the house, Ellen Shine had the fire lighting in the parlour, and rounds of tea and chat began again. *The prospect of yet another cup of tea is too much for me*, Kate thought, and just then Martha shepherded a few of them out into the back kitchen where she had a row of steaming bowls of soup lined up.

"Thank God," Kate breathed as the warm creamy soup slid down her throat. "I'm burnt up from tea."

"Mom, how did you get round to it?" Nora said gratefully.

"Ellen had it ready, and she slipped it out here before the masses would descend on her," Martha told them.

"I'm so cold," Nora shivered.

"Graveyards are cold places," Kate told her gently, "and death chills you from inside out as well."

"Will we ever get over this?" Nora asked her piteously. "I can't imagine Mossgrove without Jack."

"We'll have to, Norry," Peter broke in determinedly. "If Jack taught us anything, it was that you had to keep going. Jack never gave up. I remember the day after Dad's funeral when we were all in a desperate state, he said to me, 'Come on, Peter lad, down to the river and we'll do a bit of fencing, because there is healing in doing.' And he was right, because we were better to be out in the fields than huddled up in here."

"All I remember of those days was the blur of pain and feeling that my world had come unstuck," Nora said quietly, "and Jack was the only solid rock in the middle of the terror. Now there is no rock." As she started to cry, Kate put her arms around her and ran her fingers soothingly through her long, soft hair.

"It's not going to be easy," Kate said, "but Jack would have kept the flag flying, as he used to say. In many ways I suppose we have much to be grateful for because he gave us so much of himself, and maybe now we should be able to go it alone."

"I don't want to go it alone," Nora sobbed.

Her crying set them all off, and Martha, coming into the back kitchen, looked at them in disapproval.

"Will you for God's sake pull yourselves together and look after the people out there with Ellen and Sarah?" She marched back into the kitchen with a full teapot.

"I suppose she's right," Kate sighed. "We'd better help."

"She's not," Peter raged, heading for the back door. "She's all about law and order. I don't give a damn about that kind of thing."

"Let him off," Kate advised when Shiner made an attempt to follow him. "He needs time by himself. Some of us need to grieve alone and more of us need people. We all learn the best way for us."

"Well, I have learnt nothing," Nora said quietly.

"Come on, Norry," Shiner said gently, holding out his hand to her, "and we'll walk down along the fields. It will clear your head to get out."

"I can't go down to Clover Meadow where it all happened," she protested.

"No, no," he assured her. "We'll go up along the glen."

"All right," she agreed doubtfully, trailing him out the door.

When they were gone, only a white-faced Danny and Kate remained.

"I'm glad that you were under Jack's coffin," she told him quietly.

"I couldn't believe it when Peter asked me," he said tremulously. "It meant the world to me, as if I was being invited in from the cold. I feel kind of responsible for Jack's death, because when he got that turn over in my place, I should have insisted on coming over with him."

"I feel guilty too, Danny," she confessed, "because I knew that Jack had a dodgy heart, as he called it. I should have insisted on his looking after it. But he did not want to go down that road, and I felt that it was his right to do it his way."

"I can understand how you feel," Danny told her.

"The strange thing about death, Danny," she continued, "it's full of guilt. So over the next few weeks when you feel bad about Jack, just remember that it is part of the aftermath of death. But you have probably discovered that yourself."

"I thought that it was only me on account of how my father died. His death haunts me at times," he confessed.

"As time goes on the guilt will fade, and your perspective on the whole thing will balance out," she assured him. "Jack knew and understood how the whole thing happened."

"Did he tell you?" he asked in surprise.

"No, Danny," she assured him. "Jack would never betray a confidence."

"I have always felt since the night my grandmother died that you knew more about us than we do ourselves," he said ruefully.

"Well, I suppose if you are with families in childbirth and death, you come very close to their inner core," she told him, "but the strange thing is that your grandmother made me feel that she knew more about the Phelans than we did ourselves. But remember one thing, Danny, that it was Jack's dearest wish that you would restore your grandmother's homeplace, because he felt that he owed that to my grandfather."

"Thanks, Kate," he said gratefully. "I might need that thought to keep me going, that and money."

"Sometimes, Danny, solutions come from the most unexpected corners," she encouraged him, though privately she wondered where on earth the money could come from to restore Furze Hill and to pay off Rory, "but for now why don't you follow Nora and Shiner up the glen?"

All afternoon she moved between neighbours and old friends, discussing Jack and his sudden death until eventually she felt that she had talked herself to a standstill. She saw Mark and Nora cuddled up close together in the window seat of the parlour, and she slipped gratefully in beside them.

"How do you keep going, Aunty Kate?" Nora wanted to know.

"Auto pilot," Kate assured her, "but now I need the sustenance of you two."

"Are you bleeding inside?" Nora asked.

"That's as good a way as any to describe it," Kate told her.

"But how can you behave so normally then?" Nora demanded.

"Maybe because it helps her cope," Mark interjected thoughtfully, his long sensitive face full of concern.

He was such a contrast to everyone else in Kilmeen, with his long hair and blonde beard and clothes that always looked, as Peter had once put it, as if he was wearing the kitchen curtains. But all the disarray covered an artistic mind that turned out pictures of startling originality. Now Rodney Jackson marketed them all over America. Until Rodney became involved they had more or less considered Mark locally as a bit of an oddity. But nothing converts the public mind like the ability to earn large amounts of money, and now Mark was viewed with awe in Kilmeen. But either way it had never bothered Mark, who had little interest in the human and viewed the natural world as a wonder for his canvas. That he was Martha's brother was a puzzle that Kate had never been able to solve, because Martha was the most practical person you could imagine and Mark did not have a practical bone in his body. But Jack had an explanation.

"He's a throwback," he told Kate. When she had repeated questioningly, "a throwback?" he continued, "Every few generations a family can turn up 'a throwback' who somehow embodies the bloodline of someone long gone. The chances are that back along that family line there was a talent that might not necessarily have been developed, and then down the line it breaks out in a descendent and everyone is amazed. But sometimes the explanation is not lost in the mists of time, as is the case of Danny Conway, who embodies all the bloodline of his grandmother."

She smiled at the memory of Jack's words, and Nora demanded in surprise, "Aunty Kate, what are you smiling at?"

Kate gave them a detailed explanation. When she was finished, Mark chuckled in amusement, "So that explains me; I'm a throwback!"

"And you're a lovely throwback, Uncle Mark," Nora assured him, "and because there is a family connection between you and Rodney Jackson, it probably makes him very proud of his bloodline too."

"Well, he believed in it anyway, that's for sure," Mark said.

"Did you hear from him lately?" Kate asked, curious to know if Mark knew anything more than she did.

"He was supposed to come for Easter as you know, but now he'll be coming in a few weeks' time, probably the end of the month," Mark told her. "He has some big plan up his sleeve that he is quite excited about."

"Like what?" Nora demanded.

"Well, for a hotel in Kilmeen," Mark told them.

"Where?" Nora persisted.

"I think it's the school, because he wants to take all those paintings down, and I'm to prepare new ones for the hotel," Mark told them.

"And where is the school supposed to disappear to?" Nora demanded.

"I've no idea," Mark told her.

"But, Uncle Mark, whose idea was it that we needed a hotel?" Nora wanted to know.

"Your mother's, I think," Mark said mildly.

"My God," Nora gasped. "Peter was right."

"Why?" Kate asked.

"Well, he said that it was Mom's idea. That while she had no notion of marrying Rodney Jackson, she would still use him."

"Dear, dear, but Peter has no false illusions about his mother," Mark said quietly, and then added thoughtfully, "but then I suppose he inherited that trait from her."

"Surely Rodney Jackson would not throw Uncle David out of his school?" Nora protested in dismay.

"I doubt it," Mark said.

"But you're not sure," Nora persisted.

"Well, no, I suppose I'm not," Mark admitted.

"Let's change the subject," Kate intervened. "Today is enough to handle without burdening ourselves with the future."

"Aunty Kate, you sound just like Jack," Nora said sadly.

Kate waited until all the neighbours were gone home and then walked up to Jack's cottage. Toby was waiting at the gate and went ecstatic with delight to see her. She gathered him into her arms and hugged him.

"Darling Toby," she asked him, burying her face in his bristly neck, "what are we going to do with you at all at all? We can't take you away from here after all your years, and anyway you'd find your way back, so you'll have to stay, but we can't leave you here alone."

The sight of the little dog looking at her with such absolute devotion brought a lump to her throat, and suddenly her tears were running down his coat.

"We all depended on Jack," she told Toby as he furiously licked her face and then jumped out of her arms and ran to the door ahead of her. She dreaded opening the door into the silent cold cottage, but to her surprise the fire was lighting. She almost expected to see Jack sitting beside it.

God bless you, Sarah, she thought. *You knew that I'd call.*

She sat by the fire for a long time, thinking of all the times that Jack and herself had shared these evening hours, and gradually a quiet peace came to her. Toby slept contentedly at her feet. Then she became aware of a subtle difference in the sounds of the cottage. The clock over her head was not ticking, and she wondered if Sarah had stopped it, or did it need winding? She got up to wind it and put her hand down into the base of the old clock to find the key. Her fingers touched a roll of paper, and she brought it out with the key. She was holding a little bundle of letters tied with a faded blue ribbon. It was the last thing that she would have expected to find in Jack's clock, and she slipped them back hurriedly, feeling guilty for having taken them out in the first place.

She walked around the cottage. The place without Jack filled her with pain, but still the sense of his past presence comforted her in another way. She opened the door of his bedroom and the smell of his pipe reached out to her. His brand of tobacco gave the room a sweet aromatic whiff. She went over to the window and looked out over his little haggard. All locked up for the night. Sarah had been at work here as well. How Jack loved this room, and when the lads had taken down the dividing wall last year, he was so pleased with his extra eastern-facing window to catch the morning sun. He loved the sky in the early morning and always said that it set the tone for his day. She drifted into his little parlour. He was so proud of this cosy corner where he lit the fire at Christmas. This was his treasure store for all his mother's beautiful cloths. When she opened the tall press beside the fireplace, a lavender scent floated out to her. All the cloths were neatly folded with little bags of his garden lavender hanging off the edges of the shelves. *How well he looked after them*, she thought as she gently slipped her hand along the top of the folded rows. Her hand touched a small flat box, and she drew it out and opened it. It contained more of the same letters tied up with the same blue ribbon, and this time she recognised the handwriting. She put the box back carefully and left the cottage, closing the door quietly behind her.

KEN BRUEN

THE GUARDS

IT'S ALMOST IMPOSSIBLE to be thrown out of the Garda Síochána.
You have to really put your mind to it. Unless you become a
public disgrace, they'll tolerate most anything.

I'd been to the wire. Numerous

> Cautions
> Warnings
> Last chances
> Reprieves

And still I didn't shape up.

Or rather sober up. Don't get me wrong. The gardaí and drink
have a long, almost loving relationship. Indeed, a tee-total garda is
viewed with suspicion, if not downright derision, inside and outside the force.

My supervisor at the training barracks said,

"We all like a pint."

Nods and grunts from trainees.

"And the public likes us to like a pint."

Better and better.

"What they don't like is a blackguard."

He paused to let us taste the pun. He pronounced it, in the
Louth fashion, "blaggard".

Ten years later I was on my third warning. Called before a
supervisor, it was suggested I get help.

"Times have changed, sonny. Nowadays there's treatment pro-grammes, twelve-step centres, all kinds of help. A spell in John O' God's is no shame any more. You'll rub shoulders with the clergy and politicians."

I wanted to say,

"That's supposed to be an incentive!"

But I went. On release, I stayed dry for a while, but gradually, I drank again.

It's rare for a garda to get a home posting, but it was felt my home town would be a benefit.

An assignment on a bitter cold February evening. Dark as bejaysus. Operating a speed trap on the outskirts of the city. The duty sergeant had stipulated,

"I want results, no exceptions."

My partner was a Roscommon man named Clancy. He'd an easygoing manner and appeared to ignore my drinking. I had a thermos of coffee, near bulletproof with brandy. It was going down easy.

Too easy.

We were having a slow duty. Word was out on our location. Drivers were suspiciously within the limit. Clancy sighed, said,

"They're on to us."

"Sure are."

Then a Mercedes blasted by. The clock hit thermo. Clancy shouted,

"Jaysus!"

I had the car in gear and we were off. Clancy, in the passenger seat, said,

"Jack, slow down, I think we might forget this one."

"What?"

"The plate . . . see the plate?"

"Yeah, so what."

"It's government."

"It's a bloody scandal."

I had the siren wailing, but it was a good ten minutes before the Merc pulled over. As I opened my door, Clancy grabbed my arm, said,

"Bit o' discretion, Jack."

"Yeah, right."

I rapped on the driver's window. Took his time letting it down. The driver, a smirk in place, asked,

"Where's the fire?"

"Get out."

Before he could respond, a man leaned over from the back, said,

"What's going on?"

I recognised him. A high-profile TD. I said,

"Your driver was behaving like a lunatic."

He asked,

"Have you any idea who you're talking to?"

"Yeah, the gobshite who screwed the nurses."

Clancy tried to run block, whispered,

"Jeez, Jack, back off."

The TD was outa the car, coming at me. Indignation writ huge, he was shouting,

"Yah brazen pup, I'll have your job. Do you have any idea of what's going to happen?"

I said,

"I know exactly what's going to happen."

And punched him in the mouth.

PAUL CHARLES

DUST OF DEATH

I T HAD EVERYTHING to do with light, which itself has everything
to do with darkness.

As Garda Inspector Starrett wandered around the space, he
couldn't help but think that this crime wouldn't have been half as
effective on a dark winter's morning as it was on the first Friday of
summer.

No, he thought, for this crime to enjoy the utmost impact, it
needed the power of the early-morning summer sunlight that was
shining through the stained-glass window. The coloured light gave
it the illusion of being itself a biblical scene cut in a stained-glass
window.

In his twelve-year career as a member of Ireland's national
police service, An Garda Síochána, the inspector had found that if
he focused on this kind of thinking he could pick his way better
through the minefield of the crime scenes he came across. One
slight trip and he might stumble into the area of "How could
humans possibly do this to each other?" and he would be of
absolutely no use to the poor unfortunates before him. Not that
catching the perpetrator, or perpetrators, was ever going to be of
any real use to the deceased. It could, however, act as some kind
of closure for the relatives and loved ones left behind.

Starrett walked slowly towards the remains of what had once
been a human body.

The body would have been visible to any man, woman or child who might have entered the Second Federation Church on Church Street in Ramelton, County Donegal, that morning. Geographically speaking, Donegal is in northern Ireland, although politically it's part of the Republic of Ireland, or, as it is now popularly known, southern Ireland. The church had been started in Dallas, Texas, in 1908 by a Donegal man, William O'Donnell, and the premises the gardaí were cautiously starting to search was their only church outside of the USA.

"My God, my God, why hast thou forsaken me?" Starrett murmured. When Jesus called out that verse from Psalm 22, was he pointing the finger of accusation at his father, or merely accepting his fate? Starrett's mind wandered down through the rest of the psalm to, "My throat is dried up like baked clay; and my tongue cleaveth to my jaws; and thou hast brought me into the dust of death."

Starrett wondered what the last words of the victim before him might have been. Who did this poor unfortunate in front of him accuse in *his* final moments? Because, just like Jesus, the victim had been pinned to a cross. But unlike Jesus, he had been crucified inside a house of worship.

Two

"Our boyo hasn't just been nailed to the cross," Starrett said, as much to himself as to Garda Sergeant Garvey, who, as usual, was by Starrett's side. "No, Packie, he looks like he's suffered the indignity of a copy of the full crucifixion."

Inspector Starrett, a forty-five-year-old local, spoke in a slow, considered drawl, punctuated with many pauses, which sometimes gave the impression that he was voicing thoughts that had just occurred to him.

Sergeant Garvey, thirty years old, from Galway and a hurling champion, tended to let his superior do most of the talking—and most of the thinking. However, Packie, as he was known on and off the field, wasn't scared of rolling up his sleeves and getting stuck in to less cerebral police work. It wasn't exactly that he didn't need directing (on or off the field); he positively thrived on it.

Starrett and Garvey considered the victim in silence.

The victim was male, Caucasian and probably in his early forties. He was roughly five feet ten inches tall and approximately 140 pounds in weight. Aside from a chamois loincloth, he was naked. What must have been dark brown hair was severely matted and almost black from the blood which had wept from the lesions his barbed-wire crown of thorns had caused. His head hung slightly to the left and at about a ninety-degree angle to his chest.

A stainless-steel nail had been driven through each wrist, fixing one to each end of the horizontal beam of the cross. The right foot was placed over the left, and another six-inch stainless-steel nail pinned them both to the lower part of the stipes of the cross. There was an inch-wide stab wound six or so inches beneath the heart.

His lifeblood had dripped from his many wounds, and the red and blue patterned floor was distorted with what looked like the outline of a great red-black landmass, similar in shape to North America—with Australia grafted on to the east coast for good measure.

"Who discovered the body?" Starrett asked.

"The caretaker, Thomas Black," Packie replied, not for a single moment taking his eyes off the cross. "He came in here as usual at about 8.40 this morning to clean up after yesterday's service."

"How many services do they have?" Starrett enquired.

"Every weekday at 7 p.m., and then there's three services on Sunday: eight o'clock in the morning, noon and seven in the evening," Packie replied. "They work on accommodating the farmers: eight in the morning's just after milking time; noon's just before lunch time; and seven comes after second milking."

"Was the church locked up?"

"No. It's the Second Federation Church's policy to leave its doors open at all times as a safe haven for those in need. Apparently in America, at least according to Thomas Black, they leave bread and water as well."

"If they tried to do that around here, people would start using the church as a café," Starrett said, walking towards the body, carefully skirting the blood.

The rough, weathered pine cross had been attached crudely by rope to the front of the high pulpit, into which Starrett cautiously climbed. From his new vantage point, he could see—just—that the victim's upper torso around the shoulders and on the sides was a crazy maze of congealed bloody welts.

As Starrett turned to descend the nine steps, he noticed that local Garda Francis Casey and Bean Gharda Nuala Gibson had entered the church and were standing by the door, four eyes transfixed by the cross.

"Make sure no one else comes in here," Starrett ordered before continuing his journey around the congealed blood shape. But once again the elegantly carved antique oak pulpit obscured his full view of both the victim's back and the front of the cross.

Starrett turned towards Packie. "Did Thomas Black say whether or not he generally had a lot of cleaning up to do after their services?"

Starrett could see that the blood had drained from the usually rosy-cheeked sergeant's face. Years had been added to the deceptively youthful looks of his sergeant; neither he nor new arrivals, Gibson and Casey, could drag their eyes away from the horrific scene.

Starrett clapped his hands three times, the sound echoing around the church loudly, snapping them out of their trances.

"OK?" Starrett said loudly. "Let's get stuck into our work here, please."

"Sorry," Packie replied. "Ahm, yes, the caretaker said that it was mostly sweetie papers and tissues."

"And was there any such mess this morning?" Starrett interrupted.

"Well, Thomas Black did say that when he first arrived he didn't immediately notice the addition to the altar, and he worked his way through the pews cleaning up. It wasn't until he'd made it up as far as the elders' front pew that he registered our friend here."

"You're joking!" Starrett said.

"I know, I know. I said the same thing to him, and he said he was so preoccupied by his own thoughts. He said that when he did see it though—when he'd reached the front pews—the shock was so powerful it literally took the legs out from under him. More so because he'd been in the victim's presence for so long without realising it."

"And the sweepings?" Starrett pushed.

"Still beside the front pew."

Starrett heard a slight commotion at the door and turned towards it.

"Sorry, sir, you can't come in just now," Gibson was saying, stepping into the path of a stout, five-foot-five ball of energy.

"Whatdoya mean, trying to deny me entry to my father's house?" came the reply from a fine oratorical voice, one you would never have placed inside its owner's body.

There was a little pantomime scuffle as both Gibson and Casey tried to restrain the intruder, who, when he saw the cross and the body nailed to it, dropped to his knees, clasped his hands in front of the most southern of his chins and recited: "My God, my God, why hast thou forsaken me?"

"Hello, Ivan," Starrett said as he made his way back towards the entrance. "I've been expecting you."

"First Minister, please," the wee man said as he awkwardly rose from his knees, using Gibson and Casey as human crutches. "What exactly is this travesty, Inspector?"

Starrett offered his hand in friendship. It was ignored. "Sorry, First Minister Morrison, pray forgive me. It's just that I'm not used to seeing you without your cassock. Let's you and me leave the professionals here to examine the scene, though I'm not sure how much good it will do. I've always thought that if a murderer is stupid enough to leave any incriminating evidence, he might as well leave us a note, and most murderers in my experience are anything but stupid. My sergeant here, on the other hand, believes in getting out the proverbial fine-toothcomb. Tell me, First Minister, have you ever seen a fine-toothcomb?"

Moving his ignored hand to Morrison's back, Starrett applied a gentle force to turn the First Minister of Ramelton's Second Federation Church back in the direction of the early-morning light.

THREE

INSPECTOR STARRETT AND First Minster Morrison stood on the steps of the church. Starrett, his hands buried deep in the pockets of his black polished trousers, swayed backwards and forwards on to the toes of his well-polished, black leather shoes. The pink collar and cuffs of his shirt stuck out from under his blue woollen jumper, and his protection against the legendary and lethal Donegal winds and frequent showers was a black, American-style, zip-up windcheater.

Morrison was dressed straight off the peg in a yellow and black patterned three-piece suit and a mismatched light blue paisley shirt. The sandals without socks and the uneven buttoning of his shirt were further testimony that he'd dressed in a hurry.

"Look at that, would you?" Starrett said, nodding in the general direction of Rathmullan. They could see in the distance—over the rooftops of Ramelton—Lough Swilly and beyond Buncrana to Slieve Main, Slieve Snaght and the other mountain ranges of the Inishowen Peninsula in all their majestic and colourful glory. "I can never figure out, when we have all this incredible natural beauty on our doorstep, how anyone could ever be inspired to create a man-made scene of such darkness as the one we've just witnessed inside."

"It appears that we humans find more inspiration looking within ourselves than we do looking outwards," Morrison replied smugly.

"Too deep for me, First Minister," Starrett said, and they both fell into silence. The inspector continued to be captivated by the views while Morrison turned around to gawk at the several crows on the roof of the church playing a precarious game of leapfrog on the ridge of the Bangor Blue slated roof of the church.

"Have you figured out yet who played the part of Pontius Pilate in our indoor drama?" asked Morrison

"Bugger Pontius Pilate; I still haven't figured out the identity of the boyo pinned to the cross," Starrett admitted.

"Oh, that part's easy. That's James Moore; he's a local carpenter."

"One of your flock?" Starrett asked, thinking that the great thing about clergy, no matter their denomination, was that you just needed to give them a wee push and they were off. Wind and push.

"No, no, we're not divine enough for the likes of him," Morrison admitted, looking as if he were trying to act uncharacteristically chummy. "Some people really do need to see that you're able to walk on water before they'll join your flock these days. Now, at the Second Federation, we do believe that there is a practical explanation for the majority of miracles."

"And that particular one?" Starrett asked.

"Well, when you take into consideration that Jesus' father was in fact a carpenter, it's easy. What we'd say was that he built a platform half an inch beneath the water level and, *voilà!*"

"Ah now, come on, First Minister Morrison, you're kidding."

"I'm not kidding. I never kid," Morrison snapped indignantly. "In this world, and in today's society, more than any other, all religions boil down to is a simple ability for mankind to coexist. The rest is all window dressing. So, you give people an odd trick or two, let them see that there is something more to life than just themselves; a man walking on water is really just a political spin: 'Hey, vote for Jesus of Nazareth. He can walk on water; he can come back from the dead; he can feed thousands with five loaves and two fishes.' And they follow in their droves. Why, do you think, are congregations called flocks? It's because they act like sheep."

"Well, I'd thank you to keep your voice down a bit. The majority of my team are members of somebody's flock, and I'll tell you that after today's job they're certainly going to need something they can look up to."

"I agree," Morrison replied, dropping to a conspiratorial whisper. "I've certainly never knocked any other religion or denomination. Our view at the Second Federation Church is that men by themselves are weak, but men bonded together by a shared goal or ideal are strong. They can become a very potent force, in fact."

Starrett was half tempted to inquire why, if the Second Federation Church was such a potent force, it had only one church in the whole of Ireland.

"What can you tell me about James Moore?" he asked instead.

"Not a lot really," Morrison replied, turning to face Starrett and attempting to ape the Inspector's hands-in-pockets stance. Either the First Minister's short arms or else his large stomach made such a gesture impossible, so he chose to rub his hands together instead.

"At this stage in the investigation, a few choice crumbs will suffice," Starrett offered in encouragement.

"Well, I know him only because we had to replace all the bookshelves in the library at the Manse a few months ago," Morrison said, a shower of spittle ejecting from his mouth as he spoke. "We couldn't find a master craftsman amongst our own flock, so my wife, Mrs Morrison, sourced James."

"Do you know how she found him?"

"I do, as it happens. Mr Moore had done some similar work for her best friend," the First Minister replied.

"OK, so where does our Mr James Moore live?"

"A cottage over in Downings."

"Do you know exactly where?" Starrett asked, beginning to grow impatient at having to drag every morsel of information from Morrison.

"Oh, up on the hill somewhere. Mrs Morrison will have his exact address. She took care of all the business end of the transaction."

"And how long did the job take?"

"Around four months. You know what tradesmen are like," Morrison said.

"So when exactly was this?" asked Starrett.

The reply was interrupted by the arrival of the forensic team, including the local pathologist, Samantha Aljoe. Starrett was surprised that Morrison hardly acknowledged her presence, even when he went to the trouble of introducing the beautiful young lady.

Fuss over, Starrett and Morrison resumed their conversation.

"I already told you that James Moore did the work a few months ago. Why ask the same question twice?" Morrison responded defensively.

"Well," Starrett said, his ice-blue eyes bearing down on the First Minister, "as you'd told me he worked for you for four months, I just wanted to pin you down to when he completed his work for you."

"Oh right, I see," Morrison replied, with all the innocence of a child. "He concluded the work two months ago. He started work on the project in January and completed it for us on the last day of April."

"And were you pleased with the standard of Mr Moore's work?"

"Well, the shelves are still standing," Morrison offered, less charitably than one would expect from a member of the clergy, particularly when the person under discussion was pinned to a cross not more than thirty yards from where they stood. "Mrs Morrison seemed extremely happy with his work, so much so that she recommended Mr Moore to another of her friends, who was in need of some cabinets for her kitchen."

"Could I trouble you for the names of both of her friends, please?"

"Yes, let me see, now . . . Mrs Eileen McLaughlin and Mrs Betsy Bell."

"And in that order?" Starrett continued.

"No, actually it was the other way round."

"OK," Starrett continued, raising his right hand to his face. His index finger was permanently bent in a less than acute V, which fitted perfectly around his chin. Starrett was always joking that his forefinger was so shaped for giving directions around the hilly winding roads of Donegal.

"What?" Morrison said impatiently.

"Sorry, I was just thinking. When James Moore was working for you, did you ever spend any time chatting to him?"

Morrison looked at Starrett as if he'd just asked him if he ever stepped in cow clap in his bare feet whilst walking in the nearby hilly fields.

"I may have passed the time of day with him on a couple of occasions, and I wrote the cheques," Morrison replied.

"So, you can't tell me anything else about him?"

"I'm afraid not."

"When did you first see him this morning?" Starrett asked, hoping to pull a rabbit and not a turkey from his invisible magic hat.

"Why, just now . . ." Morrison started slightly flustered.

"I don't think so, Ivan."

"I'll thank you not to use that tone of familiarity with me, please, Inspector."

"OK, First Minister, I'll apologise, if you will."

"Sorry?"

"Well, I'd respectfully suggest that when you entered the church a few minutes ago and fell to your knees in prayer, you were too far away to recognise exactly who the victim was, particularly with his head bowed and his features obscured by his hair."

"Look, Inspector," Morrison tutted, "do you really think that my caretaker was going to report this to the gardaí before he reported it to me? Guardians of the Peace you may be, but at the end of the day, I pay his wages."

"At the very end of the day, First Minister, the church pays both your wages," Starrett replied quickly, "and I'm sure it doesn't pay those wages just so you can waste my time. So, what I'd really like to know is, why did you go through that whole charade, pretending you hadn't seen James Moore's body crucified on that cross before?"

"Shock," Morrison offered quickly, without any apparent degree of remorse. "I'm afraid I can put it down to nothing more than shock."

"Ahm," Starrett said, stretching the word until he could find what he wanted to say, "I can't see how it would have advantaged you to behave in that way."

"Exactly, Inspector," Morrison replied, looking slightly relieved but still transmitting an air of superiority. "Trouble yourself no further, as I can assure you there was no advantage. And I'm afraid I can't swear to that on a Bible. We don't have a Bible in the Second Federation Church, although we do work to a version of the Ten Commandments, only we have twelve and they are infinitely more practical."

"If you haven't succumbed to the Bible, how come you dropped to your knees in prayer and quoted from it when you first entered the church?"

"I didn't claim I was perfect, and in times of stress, I find myself reverting to my childhood instructions and beliefs. What you were witnessing was purely a knee-jerk reaction."

"Right then," Starrett said. "Is Mrs Morrison in the Manse at the moment? I'd just like to ask her a few questions about James Moore."

"Ach, no . . . Mrs Morrison is not currently in residence," Morrison replied, looking somewhat uncomfortable.

"Oh, and when do you expect her back?"

"That's the problem," Morrison said, refusing to meet Starrett's stare. "I'm afraid I have to report that I know not where she is, nor do I know when she will return."

SAM MILLAR

THE DARKNESS OF BONES

"You may house their bodies, but not their souls . . ."
Kahlil Gibran, *The Prophet*

"**A**NY MORE ON those two bodies, Shaw?" asked Benson impatiently, sounding slightly irritated. Jack's remarks on the phone mystified him. He kept going over the short conversation, again and again, until he drew a blank. Perhaps all the strain of Adrian's disappearance was beginning to take its toll. It couldn't be easy, especially after Linda's death.

Guilt was gnawing at Benson. He should have called on Jack more often, gone fishing like they use to do. But instead he had deserted him—just like the rest of his so-called friends.

Shaw was leaning over a table, his eyes firmly embedded in a microscope. He appeared deaf to Benson's question.

Ignorant old bastard, thought Benson, standing at least six feet away from the cadavers stretched out on trolleys. To his nostrils, the distance felt like six inches. The stench was insufferable and the enclosed quarters only strengthened the smell. It was difficult to tell whether the bodies were adults or teenagers. The clothes were no help. They looked like painted-on tar, meshed with muck and rotted leaves.

Creatures had feasted joyously on the faces of the two bodies, the harsh winter granting the animals a wondrous appetite. Benson shuddered involuntarily, as if a million insects had just crawled over his body. The cadavers' horrendous condition reminded him of his own mortality. Despite all his macho bluster, Harry Benson dreaded death, the thought that one day that grumpy old bastard, Shaw, would be poking around his hairy hole, slicing and dicing like a chef preparing a banquet for Hell.

Boldly removing a cigarette from its packet, Benson placed it in his mouth. He fumbled in his pockets for his untrustworthy lighter. "How the hell can you stand the stench in here? Give me a good open-air killing any day." The unlit cigarette jerked in his mouth. He couldn't find the lighter, and was becoming more desperate in his searching.

If Shaw heard, he did not respond—not immediately. A few seconds later, he glanced up from the microscope and squinted his eyes, as if sunlight had touched them.

"Why are you always so hungry for conversation?" asked Shaw dismissively. "As soon as I find something relevant, you will be the first to know—oh, and don't even attempt to light that thing. This is a no-smoking area."

"Are you serious?" asked Benson, reluctantly returning the cigarette to its home. He knew he shouldn't have come down here, into Shaw's domain, to be spoken to like that, but something in Jack's voice had bothered him—the entire conversation had bothered him—and if it meant humbling himself in front of Shaw for a lead, then so be it.

Shaw's eyes returned to the microscope, much to Benson's annoyance.

"Can't you pull yourself away from that thing for one minute, you nasty old fuck?" said Benson. "I spoke to Jack on the phone, less than ten minutes ago. It just didn't sound right. He didn't make sense. He was incoherent. Kept calling me John."

"That must have been nice for you," replied Shaw, finally easing away from the microscope, rubbing his tired eyes.

"Have you checked dental records?" Benson cleared his throat with a loud, deliberate cough. "Do . . . do you think one of the bodies . . . do you think one of them could be Adrian?"

When Shaw didn't answer, it put Benson on a war footing. "It's okay, you hiding away down here, not having to trek through all the shit out there, in the real world. The rest of us are doing our best to locate Jack's son. What the fuck are you doing, Shaw? Playing the mad scientist?"

Sighing, Shaw stood, and then walked a couple of feet to the trolleys. A few seconds later, he gently removed the covering sheets, exposing fully the bodies beneath. It was a tender, delicate movement and Benson understood immediately that no matter how much death or how many bodies this grumpy old bastard had witnessed, he still retained a modicum of respect for the dead.

"Come closer," said Shaw. "They won't bite. I promise."

"I'm fine, where I am," said Benson.

"You'll not be able to see anything from that distance. I want to show you something, up close and personal."

Reluctantly, Benson moved his feet in front of each other, until he stood perilously close to the two bodies. For one horrible, heart-stopping moment, he had a vision, a vision that the bodies were his and Jack's, sprawled out in some godforsaken landfill, a banquet for rats and insects. Finally, able to summon a few words, he asked, "Well? What is it?"

Shaw stared directly into Benson's eyes. "Post mortems are a slow process owing to the necessity for thoroughness. One mistake by me and the killer's mistake will never be discovered. Would you prefer the killer to escape justice because of your lack of patience? You think I don't care about Jack's son? Of course I damn well do. But unlike you, I can't afford the luxury of being so irritatingly transparent."

"I . . . well," mumbled Benson, caught off-guard by Shaw's outburst.

"For your information, both bodies were dumped, semi-buried within close proximity of each other—though at different times. The condition of this particular body"—Shaw pointed at the smaller of the two, with his index finger—"tells me that this was the first to be buried. Most of the skin is gone—caused by the elements and forest dwellers. Once the warmer weather arrived, the ice began to melt, pushing the bodies closer to the main stretch of water, allowing the fish to nibble and feast."

"Fish? The ones in Alexander Lake?"

"Where else?"

Benson felt his stomach heave. Just a few weeks ago, he had done some late-night ice fishing, catching at least ten well-fed fish. The subsequent days saw him devour all ten. It made him wonder if more than fish had entered his mouth.

"Fish can be quite carnivorous when the occasion arises," stated Shaw.

"Can we stop talking about fish?" asked Benson, believing he saw a ghost of a smile appear on Shaw's lips.

"Very well, but let me show you something before you throw up all over my floor."

Skilfully, Shaw dropped an object into a cleaning cloth. Little twists of his wrists and he appeared happy with the results, removing most of the darkened layer from the item.

"What is it?" asked Benson, slightly weary.

"Hold out your hand," commanded Shaw, a teacher about to administer the cane to a naughty pupil.

Obediently but reluctantly, Benson complied, stretching out his massive hand while Shaw deposited something in it. The item felt strangely cold, yet warm and bizarrely disconcerting.

"What the hell is—?" Before he could say the last word, Benson knew exactly what is was; believed beyond a doubt the identity of its owner stretched out before him. His stomach did a little flip-flap and suddenly all of Jack's words were coming back to him, clear as crystal, making him feel foolish and angry that he hadn't known their relevance until it was too late. Far too late, he feared.

I shouldn't be long, John . . . Long John . . .

Like a charging rhino, Benson ran through the doors, and up the first two flights of stairs, leaving a bewildered Shaw staring at the flapping doors.

Benson had never been fit, and over the last few years had piled on pounds of extra fat, lying to himself that, once retirement came, he would have plenty of time to get into shape.

He reached the third flight of stairs, out of breath, feeling dizzy, sweating like cheese. His heart was pounding mercilessly in his chest, sending tiny bolts of electricity up his left arm. He rested his back against a wall, desperately trying to obtain an intake of air, managing only to slither down the wall, unceremoniously, on to his large arse, as he felt his face redden and swell like a red balloon being given too much air.

Get up, you fat waste of space. Do something right for a change. Stop fucking moaning . . .

Sucking in beautiful air, Benson willed himself to stand and crash through the barrier of pain like a whale surfacing from the sea. Within seconds, he had slammed through the doors of Wilson's office, startling the superintendent.

"What the hell! What do you think you're doing, barging in like this, Benson?" asked Wilson, quickly regaining his composure, shuffling papers at the desk.

"It's Jack, Superintendent. He's in danger." Benson sucked in the stale, smoky air. "I believe he's gone to the Grazier place. He thinks . . . he thinks his son is there, held by Jeremiah Grazier and Joe Harris, our main suspects in the—"

"I warned Calvert to keep his nose out of police work. I also warned *you* about getting involved with him."

"Yes, yes, I know, you do a lot of warning. Right now, Superintendent, I couldn't give a monkey's tit about your warnings. I need permission to get a chopper into the air immediately."

Momentarily taken aback, Wilson simply stared at Benson.

"I would be very careful of how you speak to me, Detective Benson. Your retirement is coming very—"

"The chopper. *Now.*"

Wilson fluffed himself up like a peacock.

"There will be no chopper. Not now; not *ever.* Calvert can stew in his own mess. Now, I advise you to turn—"

Leaning over the desk, Benson forced his face in towards Wilson's. "If anything should happen to Jack Calvert, I will hold you personally responsible, you desk-eating piece of cowardly shit. I'm going to make sure every newspaper in the country knows that you had a vendetta against him because you were envious of his courage, while you for the last twenty years hid behind a desk, brown-nosing your way up the fucking ladder. Now, do I get that chopper or not?"

"Get out! You're finished here, just like your friend! I'll make sure that both you and—"

Benson slammed the door, shaking wood and glass, before making his way towards the front exit.

"Sir?" a young voice called after Benson, trailing behind him.

Benson ignored it until its owner caught up with him, tapping his back.

"*What?*" snarled Benson.

"I'm . . . I'm Johnson, sir. You saved me from being dismissed from the force, last week."

"Johnson? Oh, Starsky. Where's your shadow, Hutch?"

"Taylor, sir. He's been given traffic duty for two months."

"Rightly so. Next time, neither of you will be so fucking lucky. Anyway, nice chatting. Now, if you don't fucking mind, I'm in a hurry."

"I couldn't help overhearing the . . . conversation you had with Superintendent Wilson, sir."

"Couldn't you? Worth the watching, aren't you? Well?"

"I think . . . I think I can be of assistance to you, sir."

"What? You be of assistance to me? What are you mumbling about? Spit it out, lad."

"Fly, sir. I know how to fly."

For the first time in days—weeks, possibly—Harry Benson smiled. It was a fatherly smile.

"I always said you young cops could teach us old dogs a few tricks. Let's go, lad."

Less than ten minutes later, Benson and Johnson were airborne, though the older cop was wondering what he had walked into, feeling the chopper jerk a few times in midair.

"Are you sure you know how to fly this thing, Johnson?"

"Yes, sir. I've been taking flying lessons, in a light aircraft."

"A light . . . for fuck's sake . . . just keep your eyes on the road—or whatever it is you're supposed to keep them on up here."

The chopper narrowly avoided hitting the roof of a nearby factory, before panning away from the city entirely. A few minutes later, it eventually steadied—as did Benson.

"You know, you're going to be in the shit with Superintendent Wilson, taking me to the air, lad, going against his orders?"

"No, sir. I didn't hear Superintendent Wilson's orders. I was just obeying *yours*."

Benson smiled. "Crafty sort of bastard, aren't you?"

"Yes, sir."

BIOGRAPHIES

Gerry Adams is the President of Sinn Féin. His most recent book is *An Irish Eye* (2007). His first book, *Falls Memories*, was published in 1982, and his other books include *Cage Eleven* (1990), *The Politics of Irish Freedom* (1986), *The New Ireland* (2005), *An Irish Voice* (1997) and *An Irish Journal* (2001); his autobiographical books, *Before the Dawn* (1996) and *Hope and History* (2003) were international bestsellers. His story is from *The Street and other stories* (1992), of which the *Times Literary Supplement* wrote that "*The Street* demonstrates that Adams can write well." The *Sunday Times* wrote that "He brings a wry humour and a detailed observation to small events... If there is a unifying strand, it is compassion for people in difficult situations."

Ken Bruen won the Shamus Award for the Best Novel of 2003 for *The Guards*, the book that introduced Jack Taylor; the 2005 Macavity Award for Best Novel for *The Killing of the Tinkers*; the 2006 Novelpol Best Noir award in Spain for *The Magdalen Martyrs* and Brigada 21 for Best Novel for *The Guards*. He received the best series award in February 2007 for the Jack Taylor novels from The Crime Writers Association of America. *The Dramatist* was nominated in March 2007 for a Gumshoe Award for the Best European Crime Novel. In France in 2007 he won the Best Noir award for *The McDead* and in the same year in the USA won the Crimespree Award for *American Skin* and the David Godis Award for "Body of Work". He was born in Galway in 1951, where he now lives. After turning down a place at RADA and completing an MA in English he spent twenty-five years as an English teacher in Africa, Japan, S.E. Asia and South America. *The Guards*, Ken's first Jack Taylor novel, was published to glowing reviews in 2001 and has become an international bestseller. It was followed by *The Killing of the Tinkers, The Magdalen Martyrs, The Dramatist, Priest* and *Cross*. He is also the author of the Brant novels, a London-based crime series.

Mary Rose Callaghan is the author of several novels, including *Mothers* (1982), *Confessions of a Prodigal Daughter* (1985), *The Awkward Girl,* (1990), *Has Anyone Seen Heather?* (1990), *Emigrant Dreams,* (1996), *The Last Summer,* (1997), *The Visitors' Book* (2001). As well as writing extensively for periodicals, she is also author of a biography, *Kitty O'Shea, A life of Katharine Parnell,* (1989) and a play, *A House for Fools,* (1983). She has been assistant editor of, and wrote thirty articles for *The Dictionary of Irish Literature*, edited by Robert Hogan, and she has broadcast several stories on BBC radio. She was runner-up in the first Maxwell House Prize in 1979. Her most recent novel, *Billy, Come Home* (2007) was described in the *Examiner* as "a compelling tale of lives lived on the margin, of the increasing problem of homelessness and the ever-increasing coldness at the heart of our society."

Paul Charles was born and raised in Magherafelt in the north of Ireland and is one of Europe's best-known music promoters and agents. His most recent book is *The Dust of Death* (2007), which introduces a new series of novels featuring Inspector Starrett. He is the author of eight critically acclaimed Inspector Christy Kennedy novels, the most recent of which, *Sweetwater* (2006), was described in the *Guardian* as "An exemplary case for the quiet sleuth of British crime fiction." The other Kennedy novels are *I Love the Sound of Breaking Glass, Last Boat to Camden Town, Fountain of Sorrow, The Ballad of Sean and Wilko, The Hissing of the Silent Lonely Room, I've Heard the Banshee Sing* and *The Justice Factory.* He is also the author of *First of the True Believers* and *Playing Live.*

Evelyn Conlon was born in Co. Monaghan and is the author of three collections of short stories: *My Head is Opening* (1987), *Taking Scarlet as a Real Colour* (1993) and *Telling* (2000), and three novels: *Stars in the Daytime* (1989), *A Glassful of Letters* (1998) and *Skin of Dreams* (2003). Her stories have been widely anthologised and translated. *Skin of Dreams*—"A courageous, intensely imagined and tightly focused book that asks powerful questions of authority" (Joseph O'Connor)—was shortlisted for Irish Novel of the Year, 2004. She has been described as "one of Ireland's major, truly creative writers" (*Books Ireland*).

PJ Curtis has been a professional broadcaster, record producer, author, lecturer and music historian. He has worked in Nashville, Memphis and Phoenix, Arizona, but has returned to his native Burren, Co. Clare and to his memories of meeting as a ten-year-old the remarkable Mariah. He has won many awards for his radio programmes and other work, including the 2005 Bram Stoker Gothic Short Story Award. He is the author of four books and is a recent recipient of an Hon MA from NUIG for his work over the last three decades. His most recent book, *The Lightning Tree* (2006), was described in the *Sunday Telegraph* as "an elegiac and moving portrait of Irish rural culture." Nuala O'Faolain has written that "Mariah's voice comes from an Ireland in which there was time and space to attend to the delicate detail of both the natural and the supernatural worlds. In PJ Curtis's hands, her story becomes a poignant elegy for that more beautiful Ireland."

David Foster is an award-winning Australian writer who has been described as "Our most original and important living novelist" (*Independent Monthly*), "The most original and daring of novelists writing in Australia today" (Geoffrey Dutton), and "A master storyteller" (*US Newsday*). He was born in the Blue Mountains of New South Wales in 1944. He is the author of twelve novels, some radio drama, short fiction, non-fiction and poetry. *The Land Where Stories End* (2003) was described as "imaginative and fantastic... truly amazing" (*Books Ireland*) and "A post-modern fable set in the dark ages of Ireland... [A] beautifully written humorous myth that is entirely original" (*Irish World*).

Drago Jančar, born in Maribor in 1948, is a Slovenian novelist, short story writer, essayist and playwright. His works have been translated into many European languages, and his plays have enjoyed a number of foreign productions. In 1974 he was taken into custody over alleged propaganda, and he was active in the democratisation of his native country as President of the Slovenian PEN Centre between 1987 and 1991. In 1993 he received the highest Slovenian literary award for his lifetime achievement, and in 1994 he won the European Short Story Award. He lives in Ljubljana. His short story collection, *Joyce's Pupil*, was exceptionally well reviewed on its publication in 2006. The *Times Literary Supplement* wrote that "Jančar writes powerful, complex stories with an unostentatious assurance, and has a gravity which makes the tricks of more self-consciously modern writers look cheap." *Time Out* described the stories as "ambitious, enjoyable and page turning fictions"; the *Financial Times* as "elegant, elliptical stories"; the *Sunday Telegraph* as "powerful and arresting narratives".

John B. Keane (1928–2002) was one of Ireland's best-loved and most prolific writers, who achieved success not only as a playwright but also as a novelist, poet, essayist, music composer and journalist. Among his many awards were the *Sunday Tribune* Arts Award for Literature (1986), the *Sunday Independent*/Irish Life Arts Award (1986), the American Irish Fund Literary Award (1988), People of the Year Award (1990), Irish PEN Literary Award (1999). His plays include *Sive, Sharon's Grave, The Man from Clare, The Year of the Hiker, The Field, Many Young Men of Twenty,* and *Big Maggie.* His novels are *The Bodhrán Makers, Durango, The Contractors* and *A High Meadow.* He also published many books of humourous essays and letters. Of *The Bodhrán Makers*, his first and finest novel, the *Irish Press* wrote: "This powerful and poignant novel provides John B. Keane with a passport to the highest levels of Irish literature."

Walter Macken, novelist, short story writer, playwright and actor, was born in Galway in 1915 and died in 1967. While a theatre manager in the 1940s he began to write both in Irish and English. By 1946 his first play in English, *Mungo's Mansion*, had been successfully staged at the Abbey Theatre in Dublin and his first novel, *Quench the Moon*, had been accepted for publication in England and the United States. In 1948 he joined the Abbey, and his second novel, *I Am Alone*, was published. His third novel, *Rain on the Wind* (1950), brought him international recognition. In all, he produced ten novels, seven plays, three books of short stories and two children's books. His posthumous collection of stories, *City of the Tribes* was published in 1997; the *Irish Post* wrote of it that it "does for Galway what the writings of Frank O'Connor did for Cork."

Bryan MacMahon, an author of novels, short stories, pageants, radio features, plays and television scripts, was born in Listowel, Co. Kerry in 1909. His plays include *The Bugle in the Blood, The*

Song of the Anvil, The Honey Spike and *The Master*. His novels include *Children of the Rainbow* and *The Honey Spike*; his short story collections include *The Red Petticoat, The Tallystick, The Sound of Hooves* and *A Final Fling*. His other work includes his autobiography *The Master*, and *The Storyman*. A teacher all his life, he also wrote stories for children. Amongst his awards are LL.D (hon. causa) National University of Ireland (1972). He was President of Irish PEN and a committee member of the Academy of Irish Letters. A member of Aosdána, he died in 1998. His last novel, *Hero Town*, was published posthumously in 2005. Professor Bernard O'Donohue wrote of it that "*Hero Town* is the perfect retrospective: here the town is the hero, a character of epic and comic proportions… It may come to be recognized as MacMahon's masterpiece"; fellow Kerry writer Gabriel Fitzmaurice wrote that "*Hero Town* is a *Ulysses* for Listowel and it is more than a novel; it is a work of philosophy, the philosophy of a 'wild, old man', to quote Yeats."

John Maher is a winner of the Francis McManus Award, the P.J. O'Connor Radio Play Award, the Lar Cassidy Memorial Award, a Marianne Palotti Fellowship, an Arts Council Writer's Bursary, and other awards and fellowships. Born in Dublin in 1954, he lives in Dublin, working as a writer and researcher; he has three children. His highly praised collection of short stories, *The Coast of Malabar*, was published in 1988. Under the pen name Jack Barry he is author of a crime novel, *Miss Katie Regrets* (2006). His first novel under his own name, *The Luck Penny*, was greeted with exceptional acclaim on its publication in 2007: "An expertly crafted, tender tale of grief, language and land… A richly rewarding read." (*Metro*); "Maher writes with wonderful sympathy and insight… *The Luck Penny* is the work of a dedicated and gifted writer who has plenty to say." (*Sunday Business Post*); "John Maher confirms

himself as one of Irish writing's bright stars…. [A] superbly executed story about bereavement told through characters that intrigue
from the first." (*Sunday Tribune*).

Douglas A. Martin was born in Virginia in 1973 and raised in
Georgia. A novelist and poet, his first novel, *Outline of My Lover*,
was named an International Book of the Year in the *Times Literary Supplement*. He is also the author of a collection of stories,
They Change the Subject. He has taught writing at the New School
for Social Research since 2001. *The Irish Times* wrote of *Branwell*
that "Martin has evocatively captured the sad parameters of
Branwell's world, revealing the pattern of his self-destructive path
through life in a way that is painful but also memorable." *Publishers Weekly* described it as "a tender, tragic portrayal of a
doomed artist" and praised "Martin's marvelous free and direct
telling".

Emer Martin is a Dubliner who was awarded the Guggenheim
Fellowship in 2000 to work on *Baby Zero*, her third novel, and
who was recently awarded a major two-year bursary by the Irish
Arts Council. Her first novel, *Breakfast in Babylon*, won Book of
the Year 1996 at Listowel Writers' Week. She won the 1996 Audre
Lorde Prize, and the 1996 Miriam Weinberg Richter Award, for
work on her second novel *More Bread or I'll Appear*. She is also
author of a novella, *Teeth Shall Be Provided*, and her short stories
have appeared in *Shenanigans* and *Fortune Hotel*. *Baby Zero*, published in 2007, was received with rave reviews: "If there is any justice in the world, her latest novel, *Baby Zero* (Brandon), will see
her break through to the major league of literary writers and
cement her reputation as one of the most exciting voices to emerge
from this country in the last decade." (*Books Ireland*); "A riveting
page-turner… A compelling satire on the clash of civilisations."

(*Sunday Tribune*); "[Martin's] portrait of a world defined by the collapse of all notions of community contains lasting strength and beauty." (*Metro*); "Martin's gaze is undaunted and courageous— and her artistic and moral integrity are to be applauded." (*Irish Independent*); "*Baby Zero* is a literary unit so flush, confident and unique that it should win a big fat prize... It's as sharp and sore and dizzying as a bullet wound, and will probably stay with you for just as long." (*Verbal*).

Kate McCafferty was born in the United States and has taught English in colleges all over the world; she has published essays, poems and short fiction in a number of publications. Her novel, *Testimony of an Irish Slave Girl*, was published in the US in 2002 and in Britain and Ireland in 2003. "Thousands of Irish men, women and children were sold into slavery to work in the sugar-cane fields of Barbados in the 17th century... McCafferty has researched her theme well and, through Cot, shows us the terrible indignities and suffering endured." (*Irish Independent*). "McCafferty's haunting novel chronicles an overlooked chapter in the annals of human slavery... A meticulously researched piece of historical fiction that will keep readers both horrified and mesmerized." (*Booklist*)

Sam Millar's writing has been praised for its "fluency and courage of language" by Jennifer Johnston, and he has been hailed by best-selling American author Anne-Marie Duquette as "a powerful writer". He is a winner of the Martin Healy Short Story Award, the Brian Moore Award for Short Stories, the Cork *Literary Review* Competition, and the Aisling Award for Art and Culture. Born in Belfast, where he still lives, he is married and has three children. In 2005 and 2006 Brandon published his first crime novels, *The Redemption Factory* and *The Darkness of Bones*. Of the first,

Publishers Weekly wrote: "Twisty, dark, and fetid as a maze of back alleys, this vivid ramble about the fate of a man caught up in the family drama at a slaughterhouse packs a powerful punch." And the *Irish News* wrote: "His latest novel, *The Darkness of Bones*, takes us into the very heart of darkness with a gruesome yet compelling story of murder and revenge…" *Daily Ireland* wrote: "His talent for writing a riveting, dark and purging tale of unspeakable horror—namely the Kincora scandal—and fashioning it into a fascinating crime drama is nothing short of genius." He is also the author of a bestselling memoir, *On the Brinks*, and one previous novel, *Dark Souls*. In 2008 Brandon will publish his third crime novel, *Bloodstorm*.

J. M. O'Neill was born in Limerick, where his father was the city's postmaster, and educated at the Augustinian College, Dungarvan, Co. Waterford. His plays include *Now You See Him, Now You Don't, Diehards,* and *God Is Dead on the Ball's Pond Road*. His first novels, *Open Cut* (1986) and *Duffy Is Dead* (1987), were hailed as truly original works, earning him the accolade of being "the laureate of the London Irish". These first two novels were followed by *Canon Bang Bang* (1989) and *Commissar Connell* (1992). He moved to live in Kilkee, Co. Clare, where he completed his two last novels, *Bennett & Company* (1998) and *Rellighan, Undertaker* (1999). He received Irish Community Awards in 1979—as founder of the Sugawn Theatre—and in 1987—as author of his first two novels. *Bennett & Company* was awarded the Irish Book of the Year award at Writers' Week in Listowel. The *Times Literary Supplement* wrote of it that "O'Neill's is a strictly modern and undeluded vision of the past. The writing is shockingly credible."

Tom Phelan was born and raised on a farm in Mountmellick, Co. Laois. He is the author of the novels *In the Season of the Daisies*,

Iscariot, Derrycloney and *The Canal Bridge*. His novel *The Nailer*, the story of a serial killer set against the backdrop of Ireland's industrial school system, is forthcoming. Phelan has also written for *Newsday* and for the *Recorder*, the journal of the American Irish Historical Society. His first novel, *In the Season of the Daisies*, was selected by Barnes and Noble for its Discover Great New Writers Series and was a finalist for the Discover award. In 2007 Tom Phelan was awarded a writer's residency at the Heinrich Böll Cottage in Achill Island. *Iscariot* was first published in 1995 and was described in *The Irish Times* as "Universal in its dark, intense exploration of the underside of a parish and the life of its priest."

Chet Raymo is an award-winning author of both fiction and non-fiction; a former professor of physics and astronomy at Stonehill College, Massachusetts, he has been a teacher, writer, novelist, illustrator and naturalist, exploring the relationships between science, nature and the humanities. In addition to *Valentine* (2005), he is the author of two other novels, *In the Falcon's Claw* (1995) and *The Dork of Cork* (1993), which have been widely published in translation. His non-fiction includes *Climbing Brandon, Skeptics and True Believers, The Soul of the Night, Honey from Stone,* and *The Path: A one-mile walk through the universe*. The *Irish Independent* described *Valentine* as "This atmospheric, lyrical and sensual tale of epic proportions... Though Valentine's end is achingly poignant, there is a nice uplifting twist... Raymo's interpretation may be controversial, but he is a gifted storyteller and philosopher."

Judita Šalgo (1941–96) lived in Novi Sad, Vojvodina, Serbia. She published several collections of poems: *Along the Shore, Sixty-Seven Minutes, Out Loud,* and *Life on a Table*. She also published the novels *Skid Marks* and *Does Life Exist* as well as a collection of short stories. As director of the Youth Tribune, an alternative cultural and artistic space in Novi Sad, Šalgo was persecuted during the civil war in the former Yugoslavia. Her short story, "The Story of the Man who Sold Sauerkraut and Had a Lioness-Daughter" was published in *The Third Shore: Women's Fiction from East Central Europe* (2007), which was edited by Agata Schwarz and Luise von Flotow. This collection was described by the *Sunday Business Post* as "a treasure trove of quirky, funny, touching and insightful work by 25 women writers from 18 countries in the former communist bloc. Flipped open to any page, it offers a window into unique worlds—some political, all intensely imaginative and often unexpectedly funny... Reading the stories was an eye-opening, refreshing experience, offering a rare feeling of discovering worlds that are entirely new but at the same time deeply familiar. That rare feeling is made more evident by the surpassing quality of each tale, and made more exhilarating by the maturity, variety and humour to be found in them."

Alice Taylor was born in 1938 on a farm near Newmarket in Co. Cork. Her first memoir, *To School Through the Fields,* was published in 1988 and was an immediate and unprecedented success, becoming the biggest selling book ever published in Ireland, and her sequels, *Quench the Lamp, The Village, Country Days* and *The Night Before Christmas*, were also outstandingly successful. Since their initial publication these books of memoirs have also been translated and sold internationally.

In 1997 her first novel, *The Woman of the House,* was an immediate bestseller in Ireland, topping the paperback fiction lists for many weeks. It was followed by her second novel, *Across the River* in 2000, and by her third, *House of Memories* in 2005. Of her most recent book, the *Irish Independent* wrote that it "shows her in her prime as a novelist." The *Irish Book Review* wrote that "It is Alice Taylor's strength to make the natural everyday world come alive in clear fresh prose. In this book, as in her memoirs, she does so beautifully."

Peter Tremayne is the pseudonym of Peter Berresford Ellis (born 10 March 1943), a historian, literary biographer and novelist who has published over eighty books to date under both names. As Peter Tremayne he is best known for his Sister Fidelma Mysteries, set in seventh-century Ireland, which have appeared in sixteen languages and are international bestsellers. *Aisling and other Irish Tales of Terror* was first published in 1992. The *Times Literary Supplement* considered that it was "Deliberately calculated to give nightmares to anyone whose veins contain one drop of Irish blood", while *Time Out* said that "The telling of each eerie legend is surefooted and convincing, with Tremayne clearly enjoying his role as a curator of arcane knowledge."

John Trolan, born in a Dublin tenement in 1960, lived for fifteen years in the high-rise flats of Ballymun. His powerful first novel, *Slow Punctures* (1999), was described as "a brilliant debut novel" (*The Irish Times*); "its mix of social realism, irony and humour, reads like a cross between Roddy Doyle and Irvine Welsh" (*Sunday Independent*). His second novel, *Any Other Time* (2000), was described as "wonderfully written, and confirms Trolan's talent" (*Books Ireland*). Since the publication of his second novel he has completed his Masters in Mental Health Studies at King's College, London, and has devoted most of his time to working as part of a team developing the treatment programme for people with drug and alcohol problems at Nelson Trust. As Programme Director he is invited to speak at national and international conferences and writes numerous articles. His most recent published work of fiction was as part of *The Quiet Quarter Anthology of New Irish Writing* (2004). He is currently working on another novel.

Nenad Veličković was born in Sarajevo in 1962. He is the author of novels, short stories, essays, TV and radio scripts and plays. He has received many awards for his writing and he teaches Literature at the University of Sarajevo. He served for four years in the BiH Army and in the early 1990s was Secretary of the Institute for Literature in Sarajevo. *Lodgers* (Brandon 2006) was first published under the title *Konačari* in Sarajevo in 1995. A best seller in the Balkans and widely translated in Europe, it is an uncompromising novel about a modern tragedy yet it is also hilarious. In *Metro* it was described as "a beautifully constructed account of the ridiculous nature of the Balkans conflict, and war in general, which even in moments of pure gallows humour retains a heartwarming affection for the individuals trying to survive in such horrific circumstances."

William Wall is a full-time writer from Cork who in 2005 was longlisted for the Man Booker Prize for his novel *This Is the Country*, shortlisted for the Hughes & Hughes National Book Award and The Young Mind Prize; in 2004 he won the Sean O'Faolain Award and in 2003 was shortlisted for the Raymond Carver Prize. His novels to date include *The Map of Tenderness*, *Minding Children* and *Alice Falling*; he is also a poet and author of a children's book. His collection of short stories, *No Paradiso*, was published in 2006 to outstanding reviews: "a fine collection from an underestimated writer." (*Observer*); "The reader cannot fail to be mesmerised by the quality of the prose and the poet's gift for the perfectly chosen word." (*Sunday Tribune*); "The stories of *No Paradiso* engage, challenge and reward the committed reader." (*The Irish Times*).